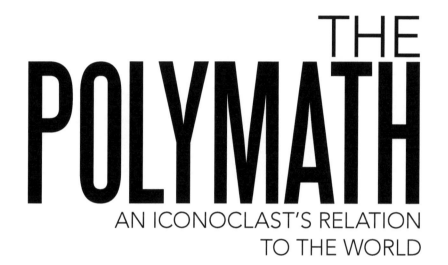

THE
POLYMATH

AN ICONOCLAST'S RELATION
TO THE WORLD

BREO GORST

ISBN: 978-1-7165-8244-8 (sc)
ISBN: 978-1-7165-8243-1 (e)

Library of Congress Control Number: 2020915484

Lulu Publishing Services rev. date: 11/04/2020

Praise and comment for The Polymath

All aboard for a lively romp through multiple personalities and
lives, sometimes futuristic, sometimes retrospective, but always
energetic. If you disembark slightly breathless and with
wobbly knees, you will have had the full experience
intended when you bought the ticket!

Jean Ellis *— Australia, Writer*

I really enjoyed this book! Impressed by Breo Gorst's narrative
skills, poetic mind, and convincing dialogue. I also enjoyed the
humour, particularly in the wedding speeches. The ironic
humour reminded me a little of Anthony Powell.

Memorable sayings include:

- Sartre might have said "Hell is an arid heart," but he didn't. I did.
- God was a mushy peas uncertainty for me as yet.
- Amber Rudd's stiff gin with her DVD of Brief Encounter lest she shed
  tears in public.

I loved Elliott's description of the ghastly prep school, his precocious
questioning of the Virgin Birth, his frank description of sexual awakening,
the awkwardness of speaking with a dying father, his astute comment
on education: learning more and more about less and less.

Canon Richard Truss *— retired C of E Clergyman*

Breo Gorst writes in an accessible way, and intrigues us with a story so ambitious, that it appears to be perhaps three-books-in-one, even though contained in some 250 pages; travelling over the entire life of Elliott Self, the Polymath, 1940-2025. An entertaining read.

Stella Charman – *Hampshire UK, Booklover.*

I was very taken by Breo Gorst's usual energy, enthusiasm and imagination. I can only begin to imagine the fun he must have had blocking out the story line and the time changes – I liked those by the way, I enjoyed the breaks from one era to another and adjusting to them. I was constantly on the watch for autobiographical details..!

I'm very envious, I would have loved to find the motivation to take on something so exciting and life-changing, and I very much hope that he has enjoyed it all as much as he appears to have done from the telling of the tale.

Clare Codd – *Retired Lawyer and cousin to Breo Gorst*

The Polymath, Elliott Self, takes us on an odyssey through his life from earliest years, a childhood of rural delight; a freedom only darkened by the prospect of a school away from home he doesn't relish.

Darkness of a different stamp is hinted at in the opening chapter, when we meet the mature Elliott after he has experienced a dystopian Britain, but which, when it becomes clear, is far from what we have assumed.

It is during his secondary education that he forms friendships with a handful of people who become his sheet-anchor through life.

James Gilmour — *Manchester, Retired Teacher*

It is a truth universally acknowledged that we all believe we have a novel somewhere within us. I suspect Breo Gorst, has several. My theory is that he has failed to establish exactly what type of novel he wishes to write and, therefore, has combined a myriad of genres and themes in an attempt to be all things to all men.

That is not to say that the piece is not entertaining...

Tim Guilding — *Hampshire UK, Retired Teacher*

The theme of friendship running throughout is heart-warming and supportive. The speculation about a post-Brexit Britain is very interesting, plausible and appropriate to the thinking of such a wide-ranging Polymath. I was touched by the account of physical and mental decline and how warmth and friendship shine through.

It's certainly exuberant and easy to read and moves fast.

Ruth Garwood – *Oxfordshire, Thinker*

"...Why am I now so engaged, so aware, so willing to live these precious seconds as if they were my last? Such tiny instances do have meaning, coming unasked right into the very centre of my chaotic existence..."

And so the Polymath's tale begins, as he seeks to unravel the events, relationships and meaning of his life with sporadic shafts of insight.

Breo Gorst has chosen to write from the perspective of a man very conscious of his place in the elite. It is a skilful weaving together of the personal and political, the real and the fanciful, even the politically prescient.

The last part of the book one can only hope is pure fantasy!
A dystopian and disturbing fantasy... All in all this book offers a thought provoking account of the world of the elite as it perhaps is.

Kitty Lloyd Lawrence – *an intrigued bystander, artist, political agnostic, cross-sector community builder.*

Acknowledgements

*To the many people — too numerous to name but all are important nevertheless — of **Lulu Publishing**, for taking this, my first novel, and turning it into the splendid book that you now hold in your hands: a beautiful book!*

*To the **few people who read my book** — off computer screens, with all the difficulties that that entails — who have given of their time to criticise, and indeed to praise, The Polymath. Their comments are listed in the opening pages; these comments are so, so much appreciated; it indeed matches their considerable surprise when, finding out that I, an old friend, had achieved the considerable task of writing a full-length novel! Thanks indeed!*

*To **Michael, Alan, Jean, James** and **Patricia**, all Proof-Readers, whether self-appointed or commissioned, I am immensely grateful. I think I get it right, but I don't, quite. I just need you, my friends and colleagues...*

*To **Kitty Lloyd Lawrence** for being my conscience throughout the book. Her ability to nail exactly what I was thinking has been a real blessing.*

*To **Colum Hayward, CEO of Polair Publishing,** for his invaluable advice, his practical assistance, and overall, his friendship throughout the process of getting **The Polymath** off the ground and into print — and into your hands — I am unreservedly grateful.*

The Polymath is dedicated
to my loves:

Winkie Northcott

Clive Harrison

Ruth Hazeldine

Contents

Book 3: Fact and Fantasy

Foreword
by Magnus Self
Autumn 2026

I'm Magnus Self. I'm writing to introduce this extraordinary work by and about my father, Elliott Self. A man who grew, via doctoring and consultancy, to be close to the very essence of England's Government, its Banking, its Inventions, its Industry; and most sensitively of all, its Arts and Culture. Never a Minister, never a Knight, his work was ever for the good of our country; yet his life and his heart were so essentially those of a frail and failing human being. He left my mother, my sister and I when Lil and I were very, very young – in an unforgivable display of egotism; and yet, and yet, I loved and love him and his memory deeply, and I forgive him, as does, I'm permitted to say, my wonderful sister.

Sometimes you'll find this a hard read – not indeed because of its complexity, but more to do with motive: you'll find Elliott writes as if he's an insensitive and insincere man, calculating the best financial and appropriate profile results in many of his arrangements and deals. Then you will find him capable of astounding acts of generosity and prodigious commitment to work to obtain even-handed good results. He's certainly a mixture, and the family and our advisors can't be quite sure how deeply into his cheek his tongue sometimes stretched. Had he lived, would he have revised some of these pieces? This question we can never now resolve...

The family has agreed that I act as his literary executor – no, he didn't ask me to do this, as he made no arrangements for us in his simple will, nor did he agree Power of Attorney should his abilities fail to the point where he couldn't help himself. His death was, as we all know, very sudden. We have to accept that he was forever young in his own mind, and had no intention of dying before his century at least. Such was not to be.

How he intended this account to end – to be ended – we don't know – perhaps he thought he could somehow write its ending from beyond the grave; although his occasional insights into a spiritual or other life would have left another man little urgency to take such a risk. Try to keep your reading to his twisted sense of un-order; it's how he wanted it. Please try to read this brave account without excessive blame; we, his family, feel sure that through all his life, he was intent upon doing good.

Magnus Self
Shropshire

Book One
Setting Out

Chapter One: Summer 2023

Gaudi and Enchantment

I first saw her yesterday in the Park Guell, Gaudi's garden-park – a large, rangey place, bestrewn with trees and tourists and unusual buildings and gazers and – one likes to think – DIY philosophers wondering at the great architect's ideas of a more communal life. But it was *unmistakably* there. That rare but wonderful, almost instantaneous glance of one person to another – most often I have to admit with a woman – that tells a million stories in its nano-second half-smile, which speaks of not-being-alone, of humour, of "you, like me, don't take all this completely seriously," of eternity, of kindness, of... love. It may be human communion at its highest level: so uncommitted, unknowing, unflinching; yet so giving, willing, communicating...

We pass. The moment is over. Lost and gone forever? Maybe... No! Else why am I now so engaged, so aware, so willing to live these precious seconds as if they were my last? These tiny instances do have meaning, coming unasked right into the very centre of my chaotic existence.

But that was yesterday. Today I'm at the Casa Batlo, the Gaudi street-house, with a structure that alone invites the dull-in-all-of-us to participate anew, the flagging will to burst open with joy, the cynic to find a moment's happiness. Visitors are few, thankfully, so I can see the details better. I'm in a reverie about how Gaudi seems to have come out of a vacuum – no one preceded him to give him much guidance, and certainly – except for high-wage-earning copyist sculptors repeating his motifs still now nearly 100 years after Gaudi's death – no one has taken his work forward in new, developing ways. An unkind cut, to be so famous, but acquire no plagiarists...

All at once her presence is here. She's stooping forward to examine the "folded concrete" window surround. I pause and gaze at the one who, just yesterday – and at my age – had sent such a bolt of electricity through me when our glances met. And now, oblivious of my presence (I guess), I have a chance to view her at my leisure. Raven dark hair, maybe she's in her late-fifties, slightly-built but tall for her frame – 5'4" maybe. My glance has become a stare. I try to look more casually but still in her general direction.

As must happen, eventually she turns. Seeing me, she gives an infinitesimal little start, and this time beams a smile of recognition in my direction. I'm only six feet away and, smiling, I say these stupid things "Still on the Gaudi trail then? This man sets me such challenges. Here for long? Do you love Barcelona like I do.......?"

She's better at this sort of thing than me. Probably meets a lot of people... "Well, I just love Gaudi, I think he must have been so truly inspired... yes, I love Barcelona and have been here a few times now. Yes, Yes. Would you like coffee?" So, within minutes, we're talking Gaudi and sipping Cappuccino and looking into each other's faces. Francesca's cheek bones are high, her eyes like a small doe's, and she has a generous mouth which has spent a lot of time smiling and laughing. She seems to have the kindest of natures and she listens really well. She's into Arts and Culture, but also Economics and Banking. There must be blind spots, but I haven't seen them yet. She's much nicer than me...

"You seem so very English – yet at the background to your voice I hear some North American origins, yes?"

She replies: "I'm from Oregon. When I was very young and rather too impressionable, I married an Englishman for a few years. Then, when that came unstitched – as seems par for the course nowadays – well, I simply forgot to go home. I just love the English humour, I'm fascinated by your play with and use of words – and I really love your temperate weather – which surprises everyone, I know. In America the weather is far too extreme, too hot in summer, too too cold in winter."

"And you're staying even after 2020 And All That – lots of residents from oversees are fleeing since The Trouble."

"The White Flight? Huh! Depends what you like, where your real, felt base is. I like the place too much. My home is in Wales, and it's unaffected, and all my friends are English people now. Anyway, the population's falling now, so – although there are economic issues – life will, probably, be good."

I notice this "probably" and approve...

"Anyway, Elliott, tell me of you and your life. Has it been good so far?"

"Grmmh... Rich, anyway. And probably in both senses. Read my first volume of auto – it's sort of accurate."

"Oh, come on, you bastard!" – big wide smile, dancing eyes – "we're *talking-talking*, not doing each other's CVs." I love that voice. "Are you an actor? Is that an unmistakable charisma I see there, all about you? My, you must 'belong' to so, so many people. I guess you're much loved."

"Not an actor, no. I'm well known in some tight circles. The arts, design, intelligence, music. But less so than I was. I'm out here in Barcelona to be on my own – oh, I can instantly change all that!" I laugh, then turn serious "I suppose I'm grieving for the place we both seem to call home."

"Me too, probably for quite different reasons. Let's unravel slowly, shall we?" She shifts emphasis, from the deeply friendly to the urgently concerned: "I mean – have you *time*? Aren't you *too important*? I couldn't bear to try to get to know you, slowly and wonderfully, moods and means and motives all unfolding as you talk and be, only to have some mobile go off and you smile wistfully, wave goodbye and step back on that plane."

"No chance of that – no one knows where I am... At least no one who's going to be a nuisance – my housekeeper Nan can find out if necessary, but her contact would be very discrete." I adjust my sitting position, I've got something to say I always find difficult – maybe as a fully-paid-up male of the species, feelings cost me dear, and I always feel I do it wrong. Nevertheless, Francesca's waiting, a bemused smile: "I was very – err – touched just now when you said you'd like to get to know me slowly and well. When I first saw you yesterday at the Gaudi Gardens Park, I had *just* that feeling of wanting to get to know you, also. It would be a pleasure. Please..."

"Come off it, Elliott, you've gone all formal on me! Lovely! Although yesterday sounds a bit early – we hadn't even spoken! Just one of those Instant Decision Guys then? Lonely, over here, on your own, evenings spare, enjoy company while enjoying Gaudi?" All this said with a full wide smile, more to set me at ease than mock me as the words seem to tell. Her left hand is alternately squeezing and playing the drum on my right. "I think we'll be good companions around this city. What are you doing tomorrow?"

"I haven't given it a moment's thought."

"Well, on a Monday, everything's closed, nothing opens, but nothing. Dead city. So I'm taking the circular rides atop open topped busses. I guess it'll be a new experience for you, yes?"

"No, not really, I do travel by bus. Just not often. You're on. Just so long as I can take you out to dinner tonight?"

"Well... the rules say 'Go Dutch for a while, till you really get to know him', but I've lived a bit and you feel like just the man I'd like to dine with tonight; and I bet you know your wines!"

*   *   *

Francesca

The waiters withdraw leaving us to our conversation and the remains of the wine.

We're quiet for four or five minutes... I really love that. A woman I've scarcely met and we can already *enjoy* significant silences! Then she breathes: "The view up here insinuates the present forever – no, that's an awkward way of saying it! I mean that I don't ever want to move and I feel exactly right here. I do kind-of know in the penumbra of my consciousness that there *is* a future and I will be leaving this high rise penthouse perfection one day, one year..." a long pause "you?"

"I just adore the way you put it, or is it the way you're saying it – or is it just you? Once, Sir Michael Redgrave read, on stage, with his mellifluous tones, straight from a stock telephone directory...name after name after name...it was delicious..."

"So!" she responds with fire and teasing in her eyes "You don't care what I say, your new friend tonight could be telling you about shaving her legs or a visit to the hairdresser, or all those stories pimpy-boys give you!"

"Have another brandy? Pimpy boys? Is this a little business you run – *in Wales!* – or just your pictorial language, hey?"

"Just the language, darling! You're getting me a little boozy. Was just fine till this latest brandy... Is it cognac?"

"Yes; very mature, very good... I've got an idea – why don't you tell me what, when you aren't out dining with unknown men, you tend to get up to?"

"Mmm... – love to. Not much to say. I'm fascinated by installation arts, but in my corner of Wales the nearest thing you get to such things is either trying to imagine the old mining derricks are works of moving art – or roll down to a gallery in Cardiff, 100 miles. But I do draw; mostly just pencil and for the enormous relaxation and also fixation on my subject. I enjoy it without being particularly good at it. I'm hours out there, with the sea and the sky and a bit more subject than that."

"Ever exhibited? Ever sold drawings? Or do you put them up? Around your house? And have them take you back to the subject again and again? Or just throw them away, see them as therapy for that hour, then over?"

"My," she exclaimed, coming slightly out of her reverie "You want to know a lot, yup? I enjoy the drawing, so it's therapy at that point, but then it's a whole other thing. I get grouchy here for a moment," long pause followed by a sigh, "You see I have a *doctorate* in hoarding – *with honours!* So now you'll think I'm not so perfect. And NO ONE has ever got that from me *so quickly* before – you're some kind of magic?"

"Francesca –do you like to be called by your full name? Yes? I love it! I just love hearing your voice and whatever you have to say. You're wonderful! Now I want to offer this for us both.."

"Don't go formal on me Elliott, please!"

"No – I won't" I try to soften my reply "but I wanted to say that we are both from England/Wales, and we must both be carrying such a burden of depression, dismay, regret, general unhappiness after what England went though in '20/'21/'22 and I just wanted to say with you I can be happy again! End. Nice and simple. Agree?"

"Yeeerrsss. Yes, love, it was hell, wasn't it? I remember those days so – regrettably – clearly. I try to forget, but... you know how it is, comes back, comes back." There were tears in her eyes. "It's all so emotional – isn't it?"

"Tomorrow, on the sightseeing bus, I'm not going to mention it; but it will be there. That's the trouble with memory. Never goes away." My memories have also flooded back and I feel for the whole past as it were in the present.

She said, brightening up a touch: "Let's, in a minute, just walk by that window, and make our way down, and walk a little bit... yes?"

She let me pay without fuss. We left our penthouse restaurant after a long lasting final view over the oddly-named roads – Las Ramblas – and the harbour, we descended in this mini-lift. At street level we walked for a while, arm in arm, feeling comfort one from the other; and went for a late nightcap in an open-all hours-hours bar. We're in Old Town, but with occasional high rises. We've already got to know each other well enough to enjoy some medium silences. Coming out of her reverie, Francesca speaks, quietly:

"So, my dear Elliott, what happens now? Where do we go from here?"

"What does your book say? Does it even allow for night-time proclivities? And do we obey it – or, as before with dinner, do we not?"

"Oh, the book! It's dreadfully old-fashioned! It says "Say a polite goodbye, a kiss on the cheek might be permitted, and let a few more of these dinners go by before...getting...any...closer...!"

"And what does your heart say?"

"Oh my heart! It's bounding ahead! It says sleep with him tonight – to keep off the sexy sirens at breakfast! But my heart is really out of place. No suggestion of the night, or sex, or sleeping with, has been mentioned by The Other Party...?"

"The Other Party says: you'll be most welcome; do come home with me! You've realised I'm no longer young, but 'where there's a will'..."

"'There's a way' ", the lady cries, invitingly. "Give me 20 minutes to grab my toothbrush. Just don't move. That's an order!"

Chapter Two: 01.07.1961

Elliott 21 on the Brink

"Life-affirming moments, my son. In the midst of learning to be a doctor, it's necessary to take a short time off. Enjoy! Send the bills to me. Just this once, mind! Your mother and I will arrive at about 8. With your godfather, Dennis, who's always cared about you. 21 years old! My!" a quick, but characteristic, change of tone: "Asked those odd friends of yours have you? Surprised after three years you're still together.... Thought we'd brought you up to be more discerning?" With these words, old-worlder Jack Self, Consultant Urologist Doctor at Peterborough, resident of Wisbech – Capital of the Fens – felt he was giving his only son Elliott – that's me! – a real send-off into life; but as ever, I thought better and fought back:

"Dad, your monstrous words about my friends are deeply wounding and not what I expect of you, consultant Old Man's Wee-Wee Doctor – please in future keep your opinions about my really fantastic friends to yourself. Next time I will *not* be saying please... and remember – as if I haven't told you a thousand times – I met Lesley, Derek and Shirley at that expensive and privileged school you both *insisted* on sending me to. *Bedales!*" I got as much energy into that exclamatory-word as I could and it didn't miss its mark. Now with a great effort: "But, dad, I would like to thank you for this dinner, set in your flatlands of tulips on the banks of the Nene, looking up at these historic house facades lining the river. Brinkmanship! It's a particularly fine show, how you managed to bribe everyone to hold it just here is not a story I'm after, but just please accept: Thank you!"

"Thank your mother, not me. It's *she* who has the *real* money, I have to earn my little stipend." Gales of laughter from me, then Jack, as we are now back to father-son ribaldry of old. Quick back-slapping – then over, we're both assertive men on our ways to hospital and hospitality. Oh, how I love my old-crony father! Jack's wicked abuse of everything PC – and the rest - was his hallmark.

*　　*　　*

A Fenland Station

March is a railway station of huge importance, quite paralleling Clapham Junction and Crewe for number of lines against moderate obscurity. Of course, March, serving those deep Fenland flatlands, with the lowest population in the UK – of course March *is* much smaller than Clapham and Crewe. But it qualifies as do its big brothers for the station where one is most likely to miss a connection or 'lose your way' – in the whole of East Anglia.

I have commandeered what the parents on our estate liked to call a Shooting Brake – but just an enormous Estate Car to you and me. On the station platform now, my red scarf blowing like an excited signal in the ever-present Fenland wind. The ancient steam train, with 7 sub-compartments per carriage, approaches the station and I see with growing excitement, other scarves blowing out of just one carriage window.

"Hi, darlings, all of you!" I utter.

Lesley descends from the carriage – all flowing 60s robes – and plants an enormous kiss on my mouth: "Rotten journey, sweetie, where did they ever find all this flat country? We thought we were falling off the edge of that old square map they used to believe in!" Dark and interesting, her presence seems to fill the station.

"Well my old bugger, how are you? Happy bloody birthday of course. We've clubbed together to buy you a new pair of braces – to keep your morale up in these bewilderingly un-English parts." Derek, blonde, tall and tousled, looks about him in amazement, his duffle bag a-shoulder on his duffle coat.

"That coat you won't need, Del-boy, it's the first of July! Blink, and summer's gone. Hi Honey, how! The birthday boy? Had sex yet today?" Shirley is the wildest, the long mane of untethered red hair leaping about like an ad for a breeze.

I riposte: "Twice, or was it three times? And it's only 12noon-ish. Come, we're off to the local for lunch. We can fetch the others around five. Are you all fit for the limo?"

The four Edinburgh medic undergraduates raise the roof with song and speech as we trundle along the unnecessarily winding lanes in the slightly hay-bestrewn Shooting Brake, probably last used to take a few sheep to market. The empty gun-rack down the centre of the car speaks of other of this prehistoric ute's many jobs. Then the pub: Shirley: "Oh God! It's the Cock Inn! To celebrate – is it your 16th? Not 21st, surely? Is this all you can do for us, sophisticated young would-be doctors ready for Tomorrow's World? Come on, sonny, look lively and get us somewhere suave..."

"Shirley, this is the best the countryside around here can offer you, as I'm keeping The Capital of The Fens as a special treat for this afternoon. So, look lively! Let's see the menu. Ahh – well, not much choice, and if you don't like dumplings, it looks like we're all having lamb cutlets."

Shirley: "Where's that fake-real-shammy Champagne you promised us....!"

Del: "...and the smoked salmon, the caviar, the rest?"

I reply: "Hold your horses, boys and girls, that's all for to*night*, when Dad's paying. Right now I'll pay alright, but it's off my allowance..."

Lesley: "You and your cosy little allowance, Elliott! Born with not only a silver spoon, but also a silver voice!"

Shirley: "Yeah and they say the rest of you is golden, yes, Elliott? Lesley?"

"Don't ask me, darling, I never look at the poker when he stokes my fire."

If the Fenland Daff and Poppy area fare is not as sophisticated as they pretend to be, our three visitor-undergrads have replete stomachs and a happy outlook as they drive through the late poppies to Wisbech, the Brink and the historic houses – and find, after a somewhat yawn-laden trip around this Holland-like territory, they are billeted around the town with families also asked to the Party.

*   *   *

Brinkmanship

Part under canvas, mostly in the open air, the Great Party that evening was at least thunderous, and whether it was a success or no depended on whether you were a guest or an uninvited neighbour. Jack and Peggy Self thought they were the nearest thing to Landed Gentry and that everyone would understand their only son having a knees-up in public. My sister Camille was perhaps pretending to be the beautiful hostess – flowing blonde hair met an off-the shoulder pink-pink dress that did – well, *everything* – to help you know she had, besides a beautiful face, also a ravishing body. She introduced madly, my Edinburgh friends to the local Fenland types, to the extended family of cousins, to Jack and Peggy's friends (asked without asking me, it's just how they did things then...)

Toby Elgood, younger son of the local Elgood Ales brewery family of Wisbech, was standing no nonsense. "Elliott, you've got a lot of posh coves – and strange uni friends – here tonight, and the Wisbech folk look a bit alarmed. Even these posh Brink-livers are easily out-argued. They're used to the Soil, and Things Not Answering Back. I'll look after them, Elliott. I guess we two understand where we're coming from. We weren't good friends as kids for nothing, eh?"

"Thanks a mill, Toby, as you can imagine it wasn't my idea to create this radical cross-culture mix – and there's something definitely odd about a pack of my cousins here on – obviously – mother's side. More inbreeding than their birth certificates indicate." They smile, knowingly as they part. Good old Toby.

"What will you *do* with your life, Elliott, my dear?" screamed Lady Monica Mangold, a towering lady of the Wisbech elite (*definitely* with a house on the Brink), "I mean, just be a doctor like Daddy? I think you have the makings of greatness in you! Now, young man, don't waste it! I have a particular interest in you. Starting out in life with all the assets my – err – husband had, and he fluffed it. But *completely*..."

"Oh Monica, I'm sure Sir Ralph has done very well for the country – just look at the handle..."

"Inherited, darling, and never ever had the courage of his own ideas. We Mangolds have little to say for ourselves beyond a fine house on the Brink here, and some adequate kids. But you! You'll get a first, you know. And then adventure!" Don't just vegetate! Use your ideas! Travel! Invent things! Get in the way a bit – you know, you might make PM if you play your cards right."

"With my little knowledge of the world at merely 21, I guess I can't both be the independent thinker and play my cards right. An oxymoron, yes?"

"Look, darling, you play it your way, I'm not going to be marking your essays – but BE OUTSTANDING!"

Attempting an answer, I was dragged away by Lesley and Shirley to see fair play between some Wisbech young and a few haughty cousins, who'd started an argument. I summed up the situation in a second: "Look, Giles, could you please take your hands off Will, whatever he said to you. This is a party of goodwill and I want you *all* to enjoy it." Not before time, Giles released his grip on the Wisbechian, as they were on the very Brink and might both have fallen into the muddy waters below. "Over here, Toby!" I called.

Lesley said to me: "Good marks, good man. Sometimes I wonder why I've made you my friend and then I remember what a spectacular guy you are. Enough charisma to spread across ten US presidents and see them all well endowed!"

Derek and Shirley, blonde and red heads, both with hair as askew and wild as ever, draw up and the foursome have a quick exchange. Derek: "you two getting married one day?"

Elliott: "Err, no, we've decide not."

Shirley: "You two *not* going to marry then? Thought you were rutting for England!"

Lesley: "Yes maybe, but marriage – never! Shirl and Del, we've an announcement to make, which might as well be now, oiled as we are with Jack's champers."

Derek: "Oh yes? Now make it good and we can tell everyone," and he makes to silence the crowd.

I interrupt fast: "Please don't. It's nice and odd, but it's for your ears *only*. So we hope you can keep a secret?"

Derek: "A secret may be kept between three people OK, but only if the other two are dead."

Lesley: "Shut up, Del. Here it is: Elliott and I will never ever marry, even if he becomes Prime Minister, never..."

"Oh, why not?" Del and Shirley speak as one.

Lesley: "Cos, although we love the tits off each other and probably always will, we actually can't stand the actual living-together bit. It's ghastly!"

To which I reply: "So, if either of us gets married, the other has a very special duty."

Shirley: "Ooh, I bet this bit is kinky..."

Lesley: "If Elliott marries, I will be his best man in a dark suit and make a speech and organise his stag do, all that."

Derek: "Gosh! Do ask us, please. Anyway, what's Elliott promised?"

I confess: "If Lesley gets married, I will be her chief bridesmaid and wear a pink dress."

A roar of laughter went up from our foursome, and suddenly Peggy and Jack were there with us all. Peggy: "Hello, hello all of you. Still in that same grotty house are you? I'm sure Edinburgh can do better. I'll come up and help look."

I respond fast: "You'll do no such thing, mother dear, and I mean that."

Peggy: "What was all that guffawing about? Good enough joke to share?" This woman is deeply argumentative, and it's best to keep controversial subjects to a private hour or two; another time...

I say: "No, mother! Now let me introduce you to some other friends from Edinburgh – now here's Pru – she's probably going on to be a Psychiatrist."

"Trick Cyclist! My father always used to call them! I wish you well, Pru, but all that sitting down – try not to fall asleep and do take exercise."

Pru: "Thank you, Peggy, the most valuable advice I've had yet. I find the transference keeps me well awake."

"Err, yes, what was that, dear?" But mother is now well behind us as I continue around this over-large party with just too many factions to integrate well. A bit like a double wedding. So many families and ways of doing things. Tonight the Wisbech people are making out badly in their home match, not being quite equal to all the multiple groups of visitors' nuances and ironies flying about.

Chapter Three: 1947

Boyhood home on the Brink.
Prep School looms

A wide and ready smile, a wide and tousled fringe, always wore short trousers held up by a snake belt. As a young lad in Wisbech, this was me. Sleep soon over – pointless stuff except in the late evenings – I was out and about before most everybody, except paper and milk deliveries, vans driving through, just those going a distance. Down by the river, catching sticklebacks, avoiding – but only just – the antediluvian mud that attempted to wall-in the sluggish waters with its silent cry of 'come, try your boot here, I am soft and exciting'. Crossing fields, ditches, rough ground, along the back streets, along the fine front, the Brink, always with our family spaniel – known, ridiculously as Cocker (Dad always called him Cockerleg – I didn't see the 'joke' until I was about 8, when I saw him write down Cock-A-Leg when I was to feed the little fellow one evening). However, my life was my own. Allowed a freedom seldom seen these days, I and other young lads in Wisbech came to no harm. I didn't think about poetry then, but I guess I had a poetic mind. It was – well, it seemed it was – forever summer – unless there was actual snow on the ground. All those cold, windy, grey, dull, anxious days – they must only be experienced by grown people, as I remember them not.

    Breakfast was at a quarter past eight in the Sitchen. Silly word of mother's to describe a kitchen you can also comfortably sit in. There was only cornflakes. Then – every day, as if we were in a B&B – egg and bacon "To set you up for the day, young man!" and toast and butter and sometimes marmalade.

The mornings at home were unpleasant as Mummy would be grumpy, or depressed – or on a really good day – downright tearful. Daddy was the brusque Scot he ever was, to the point of rudeness. He ate quickly, reading The Daily Telegraph in a gloomy stupor and never, ever spoke to mummy. Camille was a pretty little girl, who could be turned into a red-faced unhappy little mouse-urchin if "things" got too bad. We didn't pray, but if we had done it would have been for a day when mummy was only depressed and daddy was only silent.

How did we spend our days? Ask any child, they don't know. Oh, they can say something. Something like "I had a Box of Minibrix and built things" but that won't have taken all the time we weren't at school... I DID have one fabulous toy building set – Brick Player – where you stick bricks together with Actual Cement (it wasn't, it was flour and water) and build, say, a house. Once, dad and I, in unusually good moods with each other, built a model of our house all entirely out of Brick Player! It was fantabulous! Dad was really great that day...

That was when we were at home. One summer in three, we'd head for Canada, for the lakes North of Toronto. There we would sit and vegetate on the lakeside, amongst clans of Canadian Cousins – who we got to know relatively well, and who we'd entertain in Wisbech when they came over – much more occasionally than we visited their country. It all comes down to Great Great Uncles who'd made good in Toronto and Canada, starting up the Toronto Dominion Bank and other good services, and setting thereby a course of steady money flow into the pockets of my mother and her siblings and cousins; thus we say she was born with a silver spoon in her mouth. If only it had made a difference to her temperament! But no, she remained depressed and forlorn for almost her entire life.

A new school? Apparently I'm going to be sent away from home. When I'm eight, next year. *Why?* The other lads round here aren't going to a Prep School. Oh, maybe Toby Elgood is. Brewery boy. But Will and Bert and Harry and Fred will just go on mucking about here in Wisbech at the local school. Mummy's been telling me all about this. After her 20-minute nap following lunch, she gets almost cheerful. Well, cheerful for her, anyway. It's then that

14

she does things with me and Camille. "Soon, Darling" she says, "we'll be getting you measured up for your new school uniform."

"Why, mummy, why do I have to go to a *boarding* school? And so very far away! The Norfolk coast is miles and miles and miles…"

"It's just 45 miles, and your father will be glad to drive you there in the Rover, and fetch you home. And, for exeat weekends, we can either come and collect you and bring you home, or come and stay nearby and see you. You'd like that, wouldn't you, darling?"

"I just can't imagine it. Why can't I stay on at St Margaret's?"

"Well, St Margaret's is a Convent School, and it's done you very well until now, but it's attached to a convent where the Nuns live and they won't accept boys after you're 8. Anyway, you are – they say – immensely intelligent, and the Mother Superior's view is that you need a different kind of teaching now, different surroundings too. More boys of similar intelligence and the same age you can meet and get to know – you've been rather a King Pin around here, you know. Do you good, and you'll have a more rewarding life, if you join in with all the young lads at this boarding school. Give that temper a chance to cool down, make a fine man of you."

"Mummy – I really do not want to go to this school! I'll be very unhappy there……You wouldn't want that now, would you? I can feel a big bad temper coming on *now*. I *insist* I don't go to this place. I need you all, all of you, at home, here, with me – Camille as well."

For me this was a real cry from the heart. Mummy closed the conversation with a huge sigh, and: "Well, the school's called Bickley Grange, it's well-recommended for boys from 8 to 13, and you've still got a few months to think about it. Now, shall we have some tea? I think Monica's going to join us this afternoon, and I know she's *very* keen on you going to Bickley."

Monica. That's interesting. One of our neighbours who's too big for her boots. Pretends to be very interested in my life, making me her Clever Boy. Takes a real big interest in me and my life. Is that kind, or demanding? Suffocating? Her own kids aren't that bright, so she's trying to make me her silver knight. Huh!

Mention of Monica made me think: daddy had a Private Practice in the house. Patients would come and sit in our hall every Wednesday afternoon and wait for him to call them into our dining room. Camille and I were forbidden – absolutely forbidden – to hang around inside the house or near the front door. Patients needed quietness and privacy, we were told. Daddy's secretary, Fran, sat in the family study, typing, and attended the front door when the bell rang. Daddy was a skilful surgeon, and he specialised on what was described as "Old Men's Waterworks." Something to do with peeing, I think. Anyway, why weren't Old Women having Waterworks Problems? I mean, I know we're different, I've had a good look at Camille, and there's something missing, it seems to me. Poor Camille; poor girls! I've got a willy and she hasn't. What's that got to do with Waterworks and Old Age? Dunno.

But Daddy didn't see women. I'm sure of that as on wet Wednesdays, I kept cavee up the stairs so I could see who came in. It was fun. And that's the funny thing. Regular as clockwork at 5pm, along would come our neighbour, Monica Mangold. Probably a clever woman, held back in this tulip-town when what she needed might have been a good job of work. She would sit, prim as you can get, in our hall-waiting room, and Daddy would – eventually – come out to see her and take her in. Funny thing is he used always to kiss her. He never does that to mummy! And the secretary, Fran was never involved in seeing her in or out, she just worked steadily at her desk, typing away...

But, when I got bored with the house and the town and the countryside and the dog and my mates and my sister – then I read books. Hundreds of them. Couldn't get enough information, I was thirsty for it. I read about science and mechanisms and about plays and artists and friendships and living together ... and then ... I read about ... democracy and government. The nuns at school didn't know the meaning of the words I used. In all this I had absolutely no friends – except for dad in a good mood, and for Monica – in any mood at all, she was so keen! With both these I could begin to stretch my mental legs in understanding *concepts*, not just things. I learnt, most of all, how man had had to conquer language before he could conceive of concepts, language gave him the idiom and the power to argue. I hope I never lose the gift of being a good arguer throughout my life. About anything, everything. The danger is in getting too specialised, learning more-and-more about less-and-less.

* * *

Mr Moondy Elliott Chequers

When I was 4 and 5 I was obsessed with having three quite separate frames or states of mind. Not differing personalities as, from one, I could be aware of, but not become, another frame of mind. Maybe this all revolved around my sometimes very strong temper; which at other times led me to be the most peaceable of beings. Right in the centre of all this was The Norm. And this, at aged four, I quite suitably named Elliott. But the fiend, the unruly, terrible tempered little boy, was always Chequers. And the extra-accommodating, kind, do anything for anyone, really nice little boy was called Mr Moondy. I think when Mum was talking about my going to Bickley Grange, I was very much in touch with the Chequers part of me.

I guess these concepts – Chequers, Elliott, Mr Moondy – never left me across my long life. What I had was coping strategies; and some really wonderful friends who kind of knew without explanations when I needed time to myself.

* * *

The General Specialist – Oxymoron be Damned!

Mummy said, as I sat on her knee – a very occasional intimacy – "what do you reckon you'll do with your life, Elliott?"

Not knowing at the age of 6 quite how to answer this, I played for time: "Well, what do people usually do?"

"Generally, clever people – like you – spend their lives studying one thing or group of things, and eventually call themselves Specialists, and go on through their lives, learning more-and-more about less-and-less. The trouble is, they learn so much on a very narrow subject, that they can't be understood by a wider community."

I must have missed that last line…

"Then" I said, with a finality which has proved my touchstone though life "I want to be a General Specialist…"

Nearing the end of my life as I edit this chapter, I realise that I've inhabited the role of General Specialist all life long.

Chapter Four: 1965

New Guinea: Doctoring Overseas

"Have I got used to this place yet? Do you mean the living conditions, the heat, the diarrhoea, the people generally, the sick people, the typical illnesses, or the ex-pat life?" In 1965, phone lines under the ocean had this sepulchral echo to them, and a long delay before you could reply. So this occasional conversation with my over-argumentative mother, still bright and observant in her late forties, was usually slightly political in that I didn't want to be cornered and lectured, which she could still do even to her brightest child.

"Oh, I don't know, Elliott, just trying to find out how you *are* there. You've no idea how a mother *worries*. How are you, dear boy? Monica was only asking me this morning..."

"Tell Monica I'm remembering just *some* of her advice and living a very full life and – oddly enough – actually enjoying myself. The hours in hospital are killing and I operate on people when I'd prefer to be asleep, but somehow I manage, being young and able."

"Do be careful with your health, darling boy, we read about such lack of care in those regions with antisepsis and so on. And the bilharzia! Are you getting enough to eat? And not drinking too much?"

"Mother! I am a grown man! Look, I've got to go now, I'm picking up a girlfriend, we're driving out to an open air cinema, should be fun."

"Oh darling! Is she one of those *local* girls, do be careful!"

"I'm not going to give you the pleasure of knowing – I've been here three years now, and should know how to look after myself. And now, mother, I'm going, so love and the rest to you and dad. See you at Christmas."

"Hope Camille reaches you safely – do look after your beautiful sister, won't you?"

"I will, mother, I will. Bye now."

*   *   *

Camille

The scant palms around the airstrip – not exactly an airport – waved a touch in the slight afternoon breeze. Waiting for a plane. A solitary plane. How had I got myself into this god-forsaken hole? Doctors Overseas wasn't my first idea. After a year 'off' after uni, a qualified doctor now, I'd been toying with the idea of following Sir Ralph Mangold's reputation and "doing nothing" very busily till it was time for me to die. But here Monica had stepped in and got together with Jack – a relationship I observed was surprisingly comfortable and symbiotic, making me wonder about their pasts – and so Jack was persuaded through his medical contacts to 'try to get the kid overseas to sow his wild oats and learn about the world – and maybe do some good.' I fleetingly wondered if they realised that I'd been sowing my not-so-wild-oats ever since at Bedales I met Caroline when I was 14, and, at 16, Lesley. And, yes, at 15, Lesley was then technically a minor... Yes, I do miss her out here in New Guinea, but I have other friends and a life to live. Lesley and I'll be friends for life; I can catch up with her any time.

Jack and Monica's over-kindly patronising stuff made me angry – and I'm no novice in the anger field – yet I now have to admit that their strategies serve my present purposes rather well: getting through callow youth without being much noticed, and gathering worldly experience along the way. An innocent has to get across the road somehow, has to learn about the traffic. These years are filling me in with such experience.

"Hi, my gorgeous brother, you've taken time off from the hospital to come and meet me!" As Camille and I swing in the air with a huge hug of rekindled kinship and undeniable love, she seems to have brought England, Wisbech - and home here to me - and we're walking along the Brink in Wisbech, the two of us hand in hand just as we were when kids. "Just so much news, about Jonquil's pregnancy and Sam and Ben are now officially An Item, and Janey's left Paul and Paul's now with Suzie, who'd only just herself (I'm not sure she had left him actually) left Saul and – mum's taking cooking lessons at last!"

"OK, OK, love, slow down, I need to take notes... Who is Saul anyway? I remember one in the Old Testament – you won't be meaning him, so..."

"No, NO, you clot! – he was at your Party, that event on the Wisbech Brink we all now call The Brinkmanship – he was sort-of young and lovely and..."

"Oh, SO sorry Camille – he was *your* bloke that night, I do remember now. Any messages from my lot at all?" I ask hopefully.

"Oh yes, of course, you'll want to know that first, you must! Well, let me see" – definitely thinking hard now – "Yes! Shirley – what's her other name? – rang me two nights ago and said "Remember me to the Old Bugger" – she turns up her nose at the description – "you're all *so rude* about each other – I don't do this to *my* friends!"

"Yes, Camille and what did she say, my lovely redhead friend Shirley Shawley?"

"Oh no it can't be *that* name surely? Shawley?" Gales of laughter, but how do I get the message?

After a giggly-fit of explanation, I respond slowly and clearly "So, Shirley's had a spell in hospital sorting out her lymph system and she's OK now, and Derek's now in the London Doctors' Rugby team and they need some more verses for their – err – songs; and Lesley sends me oodles of love and says not to worry about her, she's well and sorted, but there will always be room at her table for me. Note she didn't say bed... Thank you, darling. I'm having to do a bit of translating, though."

We've been through the tiny airport office and have driven some way back to town. A lull falls, which is kind-of welcome. After a couple of minutes, we both speak at once:

She says: "What will I do all day here when you're working?" while I'm saying: "I don't really know what you're going to do..." We both laugh very heartily and feel such a family bond. It won't last, we'll soon be into sibling rivalry, impatience and selfishness – at which we're both champions.

I say: "Well, probably in the next day and a half, which I have off, I can give you a good grounding in what's what and where's where and how to get home without any language; and as decent lavs are something of a rarity, I've made a wee map for you..."

"A *wee* map! Back to the nursery, both of us! We don't take long..."

And so we continued on our trip back to my apartment, stopping at a simple store to get some stuff for a tea break and for breakfast. Then home to relax, have a snack and a bath before donning fresh clothes to go out to dinner. However, it's so hot, the clothes stay fresh for merely seconds. Never mind, I've asked a couple to join us this evening – both doctors – and we hope for a good time. None of us are specialists yet, but we all act as physicians *and* surgeons – moving with the ease of youth from a case of diabetes to an amputation at the high thigh because of gangrene, to the inevitable anti-smallpox injections, to an appendectomy. We hope to send the specialist heart, eye and brain ops elsewhere.

Don and Phil, sort-of married, are my closest friends, and good drinking buddies. We don't go far, just to the over-exaggerated palm restaurant on the next avenue, The Extravaganza. Run for 20 years by Cyril – who doesn't get up till noon – he's got a lazy approach to life and survives on hope, liquor and fresh sunlight. Where he gets his money from, God knows. My radiant, oh-so-blonde, sister is a real fillip to both Don and Phil and also to Cyril, not surprisingly. She keeps her end up in conversation with three doctors who all know each other inside out, and we pass off Cyril's more blatant advances as his "peculiarities" in this heat.

Camille became well known in the vicinity within hours and by the end of her stay was renowned. If people didn't actually motor far to catch a glimpse of her, it appeared that way. By the end of 9 days – flights didn't go every day so we had to make do – she felt she knew the area as well as I did, and indeed, she'd used local buses and transport in ways I'd never conceived. Very resourceful, intuitive and ever radiant, she also knew how to deal with men. Oh, where is the school to which I could direct so many other of my female friends?

Chapter Five: 1948-53

Bickley Grange – Arid Pastures

"Sickly Strange" lived up to its reputation from the beginning – a provincial, unendowed, under-funded, but most of all, unenlightened, prep school for the nearly rich, those faking it perhaps; and for those who honestly believed a boarding mono-sex education can actually teach well. For better or for worse, I was stuck here from age 8 to 13, and there was nothing I could do about this. What were the good points? Well, there was the sea, just a mile away, at Dersingham. The range of subjects and the library didn't feed my avaricious knowledge needs; nor have the staff (nor fellow pupils) done much to provide that one essential, gleaned at my father's knee and Monica's "morning room" – *constructive, listening-both-ways, argument.* Most staff and pupils thought I was just 'argumentative' but this on the whole means quarrelsome and unruly, arguing for its own sake, but – although I was unruly – actually I was starved of the need to test out my theories with other enlightened and knowledgeable people. Sartre might have said 'Hell is an arid heart'. But he didn't. I did.

So Bickley Grange lived up to its soubriquet: 'Sickly Strange'. Do you know, I even missed the company of *girls*? I never realised how much girls and women add to society until I was without them for most of five years of my developing life. And *this* part of my missing had nothing to do with sex, or not physical sex – most of my time at Sickly Strange I was not yet able to produce seed – but women we've only recently given the vote to and our society still doesn't pay or represent women equally with men, are a whole experience of richness, softness, alternative, variety, delight, joy – and of course anger and frustration as well. I identified this lack – my mother (poor dear, in her sadness), darling beautiful sister Camille, arguing-neighbour Monica, and a host of other Wisbech townsfolk – in about my second year at Sickly.

Oh, yes, most of the staff were married (and those who were not, there could be other issues...). And, yes, I saw them from a distance. We had maids – I regret we called them skivvies – who served us our meals, but... And there was Matron. I'm not even going to try to explain why these employees and others simply weren't my confidants, my mates, my intimates. An incident stays in my mind which is not very laudable. One of the maids came down the dining hall with a kipper on each of two plates, at such a pace that, when she suddenly stopped prior to putting them in two boys' places, the kippers carried on, shooting off the plates and whoosh! Under the table, somewhere... This poor redheaded slightly vacant girl had no idea what had happened (she should have studied physics – what chance!) that she asked around several times "Who's got it, where are they?" and actually we didn't know! It was the high point in a very dull day in a dull term in a dull year.

How about my work, then? English, Maths, Geography, History, RE? If I was cooperative and bothering, I was usually top of the form in every subject; I'd studied history beyond the books we had as standard text books, geography I'd got to know with Monica – and, surprisingly, with Mother. Maths at the level taught was obvious, I'd done it at 6 or 7 with Dad. English – the very stuff of our daily communication – how could I not *know* it? RE could be a joke. "Please sir?" "Yes, Self?" (What was it with all these surnames only? Who did that help, exactly?) "Sir, it says in the bible that there were 21 begats between Isaiah and Jesus, but of course the line was broken – at Joseph." "Come on, boy, what do you mean, what are you saying? Be brief!" "Well, sir, religion can't have it both ways. Either there *was* a virgin birth, and Joseph was *not* Jesus' father, or, more likely, that there was *no* virgin birth, that Joseph *was* Jesus' father, in which case the 21 begats from Isaiah *do* work. I think it's *that* way sir, *no* virgin birth, what do *you* think, sir?" Oh I did make them all so cross! My argument was usually impeccable. And they couldn't cope, because their learning was so slight, and their interest minimal. I was the one problem in the class. Clever and cranky.

BICKLEY GRANGE – ARID PASTURES

*   *   *

Sexual Awakening

A very lonely place. An isolated event, but with enormous feelings. So staggering are the feelings, you'd have thought many books of poetry would have been written to try to explain, to take away the surprise, the pain, the oddness, to immortalise this tiny but explosive point of utter change: before it you were a boy, after it a man, however much a mere sapling. But not so, this supremely private moment is not explained, extolled, nor merely recalled by poets, nor by lay people anywhere. Oh, yes, there are some dirty tales, big-guffaw stuff, but I mean serious writing. In 1953 there were no handbooks, Matron was the last person you would want to talk to about this so-very personal event. Yet it happens to all. When a man matures into a sexually able being, there is, there has to be, a manifest change. But we none of us talk about it. Not in 1953, anyway. There at Bickley Grange, you've got maybe 100 boys – yes, all boys, we've been there! – all climbing this same mountain, and all getting there – sometime – alone. But when? How? Where? No one – but no one – has said anything to you about this monumental change. Unless it's a guffaw joke. I guess it's likely to be a very private moment. For most of us, anyway. Else, if it's in public, it could be, in addition to all the other very extreme and mixed feelings, also embarrassing to a greater or lesser degree. But my 'coming of age' was in private. I was 13. Early-average.

This change won't happen to all the boys at Bickley during their stay there. For some, it will occur at their public school – most boys from Bickley went on to Greshams, around the coast a touch. It symbolises the age-point break of prep- and public-schools: 8-13, 13-18. And, historically, perhaps that's why. Oh, not written down in the history books, nothing like that. But this simple division: Boys::Men.

This day, I have the feeling that I want to be alone. Mind you, at Bickley, that was quite a frequent feeling! But today I'm feeling strangely odd, suddenly bad-tempered, suddenly at the mention of a hardship or sadness, I feel I want to cry. I'm Mr Moondy *and* Chequers, both at once, and very little Elliott.

I'm dangerous... It's strange. After lunch, the sports for the afternoon are agreed and I choose the Long Bick. It's a run, it includes the sea, and miles of countryside, and as it's the longest, I guess I'll get away with being the only one. The only one! Sudden rush of joy. I'm over-reacting like I do on these emotional days...

On a long run, although you're not supposed to, one can go off on one's own routes. I suppose if I didn't get back from this 6-miler at about the right time, questions might be asked. I aim for the beach. Dersingham has such sharp gravel, such an odd 'beach', but it's exhilarating, it's exhausting, it's magical in the wind and the surf. I'm not exactly allowed along this beach – supposed to stay inland – but in a maddening mood and I don't, I don't care. Through the spray and the surf, I see my family, my mother, Camille, other girls in the town – all banned from Bickley. I still want to cry. Is this homesickness? Well – I don't want to go home. So it seems unlikely. Suddenly I see images of the boys' genitals (we change and shower communally) and some – some particular boys, about three I think – suddenly feel very, very strokeable. I'm running up now to the coast path at an enormous pace, I seem so strong and fast I could run back to Wisbech in an hour. Suddenly I'm no longer about to cry, I'm exhilarated. And. I've just acquired this enormous erection. I've been getting these annoying, yet lovely, much bigger erections for a while now – well, I've always had them, I suppose, but recently they've been so much more urgent, meaningful, tender, large – and very recently, rather smelly. There seems to be a Boys' Barrage against talking *actually* about these happenings, although the bravado stories of hyperbolic sex range across the dorm at night after lights out.

I clamber over a gate and into a field. "The trouble with Norfolk is it's so fucking flat" I hear myself say to ... me? I don't use that word normally. I'm instinctual now, I'm looking for a dip in the field, there must be one, there must be *one*. There is, but not deep! I race towards it at a hundred miles an hour. I don't look round, I lie down. I scramble to free my aching penis from its constraints and there! Tall as a Hunstanton water tower! But it's under such constraint, so tight, so urgent. It only takes – oh, oh, four movements, maybe and sslllooouuff!

Really painful and watery and smelly and icky and weird and sad and distressing and ... *over*. For a nanosecond I think, 'well that's it, I'll never need to do *that* again!' till I wonder if I didn't, along with all those *other* feelings, really *hugely enjoy* it, pain and all. Yes I'm a man! Well truth to tell, not quite, as the first ejaculation is unlikely to carry sperm, only semen, that magical lubricating fluid that will one day – soon? – see my soon-to-arrive *real* sperms all the way up into the soft, yielding – we'll call it the heart – of a woman. A Woman? Suddenly I'm afraid. Afraid of all the responsibility I carry between my legs. But I'm sober, in my right mind, and back-into Elliott again.

I trot home - well, back to school – bemused. There isn't a soul I can mention this to. What would I say? And so I begin to think: *I'm* the one who believes in friendship and I've made such a balls-up (my language seems to be changing!) of making friends at this wretched school. But why? Couldn't I have used my undoubted charisma and male-bonding abilities to get across to just *some* of the surname-only described boys? Robinson and Giles and Tayor Major and Holman and Kendrew. Damn it, man (oh, I like it!), Kendrew is really oddly also Andrew. Andrew Kendrew. Kind of silly, but Andrew is his *real* handle, the one given to him. Like it's Chris Giles, Tim Robinson, Richard Taylor. Why have I been so blind? I'll go back to BG and *just use* those first names I know in my age-band and see what happens. You never know...

But: another five years at Gresham's looms shortly. A word with Monica, methinks. Never mind if I don't get anywhere, I'll have tried.

As I suspected, no one at BG has any idea that I've been to 4-D cinema in Kodascope with special specs to see things in close-up. Just Monday Muck – baked beans in potato – for all as per usual... The name-changes I'll have to go slowly on, the first took it badly and said "we're men here, you ought to know that by now!" I did, and am, but is he?

*　　*　　*

Moving On

Somehow, in the next few weeks, Bickley, Greshams, Monica, Dad and I worked the most fantastic change in my life so far. It seems that messages had arrived with Dad and Mum from Bickley purporting to say, in a roundabout,

27

mostly polite way, that Bickley thinks I'm appropriate for a different sort of education, something more liberal and open to my kind of enquiring mind; and Greshams, which, being the school I was down for, received a copy of that, replied to say that they would not want to stand in the way of my achieving potentially higher goals in life, and said they would gladly return the deposit already paid on the first year's fees – they were happy to free me for whatever life had in store. Clearly the Norfolk Coast was in cahoots about getting rid of me, a thought that, I regret to recall, made me inordinately proud, and immensely happy.

My dad had softened more than a touch. Perhaps work was no longer so competitive. He seemed almost to enjoy life, perhaps for the first time. Equally so with Camille - she thought perhaps he had never liked children, his own nor any else's, and now we were 11 and 13, we were treatable as young adults. Whatever the reason, the change was most welcome. And to conduct this investigation into my future education, I needed dad in at least an approachable mood.

After a chat, when he let slip that fees would not be likely to be a problem, his father having died after a long illness very recently – no, they didn't inform me at school, I was given no chance to attend the funeral, things in some quarters were still very unenlightened – and so "a little more money is available these days." He then suggested I go and talk to Monica, so I did, immediately.

Monica seemed also more in possession of herself, more ... well, business-like I suppose. She was fully genned-up. After a fulsome reception, tea and cakes, she produced paper and pens and we both set to work. "There are several schools, all very expensive, but your father doesn't mind, that cater for very bright, lateral thinking children. Mill Hill, Summerfields, Flygate Mill – all these have a certain overtly hedonistic feel to them, in some, kids have no curriculum but still do very well. In others there are quite wild members of staff – teaching, for example, Shakespeare in a field, or anywhere that would stand in for the environment portrayed. But this one – Bedales, while being a lot freer in style than conventional schools, actually has a proper timetable and – I think you may like this feature – the pupils are made up of 50% of each sex."

There was a lot more argument and discussion, there was the matter of intake – would they have me? – but, really, it was all plain sailing, and soon my acceptance letter arrived, and I mentally prepared to meet this group of thinkers and Guardian-readers, and longed to get there to see if they wore trademark sandals and beards.

Chapter Six: 2005

Dangerous Zones

My experience had been prodigious across so many fields. But most of the postings or consultancies I was pleased to accept I would never have got from my CV. Why? Well... A standard career is one where the next job follows – relentlessly you might say – the one that went before it. But, of course I had never ever intended to have such a boring sequence in my life. Not just the boredom, on my mother's knee she taught me that the older and more experienced you get in some interesting, maybe scientific field, the more you know about an ever decreasing field; from which one deduces that you learn more and more about less and less.

I started in Medicine and travelled the world with Doctoring Overseas, then Médecins Sans Frontières and indeed became experienced and knowledgeable. I then – with enormous help from my so-nearly ex-father-in-law (one does live on the brink, not just in Wisbech...) and set up a consultancy to advise on – really – anything, so long as I could undertake it and it paid the wads required. I kept up doctoring along the way two days a week for about three years, but found that the introductions to Think Tanks, Government Departments, Arts and Cultural organisations, were welcomed because I brought a more open mind and indeed an independent *frame of* mind. And so – my credo – I've been able to communicate with all souls about nearly anything. I guess I've never got so narrow in a subject that I was learning more and more about less and less, which condition can only produce really bad communicators and upon which, M'lord, I suggest it is the illness, the malaise of society these days, and I thereby rest my case...

I say I know and understand so many facets of life, but there are the odd rough patches, God being one of them, never quite figured him out. All Powerful yet All

Merciful; Ruling yet Loving; Free Will yet no chance for many to demonstrate it; Sin and Forgiveness; Original Sin – what's that when it's at home? – something about Apples, Eve and Adam, I feel sure. The Power of Prayer – ah, that's where we might hold hands again, as I do this and it seems to be good. I'm all for meditation and understanding one's unconscious as one may glimpse it occasionally.

Where was I? Oh yes, introducing this chapter on my association with the Secret Services – MI5, MI6 and GCHQ. When I was that child, this is the very last thing I thought I'd be doing. I wasn't involved at all till my 60s – 2000-plus to you – and certainly not after my 70th birthday (2010) – well, except for a skirmish around the 2020 disasters, but that will come later.

It was my relationship with Jack Straw, and later David Blunkett – who succeeded each other at the Home Office in 2003 – that got me involved with MI5. Jack had said that my work on the logic of parking was something quite other (huh!), and he wanted me to meet people – at the time unknown to me, and unrevealed – who had problems they needed new input, new eyes on. The queries were much to do with the digital age – which had just arrived – and in terms of both our home security and defence (sort-of MI5) and our intelligence gathering – spying – (sort of MI6) there was simply a shortfall of knowledge, and explanations were comparatively simple. And I began to learn about the considerable fear of internet abuse and cyber attack (sort of what GCHQ protects us from). MI6 and GCHQ both answer to the Foreign Office, but I didn't then go via the Foreign Secretary, the men (and women!) at MI5 were tumbling over themselves to introduce me just anyway!

But that led on to associated areas and my having to sign Official Secrets Act forms to say that I would – no, not just for 20 years, not for 30 years – that I would *never* divulge till the grave gave me rest. And I must say this leads me into a spot of bother with the events I want to tell you about now. I could try simile or metaphor or I could invent a whole scenario of parallels. But I think I'd get unstuck with my dear publisher long before I became clapped in irons and marched off to prison by the surveillance authorities.

So – this is your easy chapter. You will hear no more from me about the MI5, the MI6 nor about GCHQ; more's the pity.... There were deliciously good anecdotes from those times... Never mind!

Chapter Seven: 01.07.1940

Self Alone

This is the only chapter I write from hearsay; that is to say it's the only chapter devoted entirely to my birth and supposed first six weeks of life. I presume I'm the child of Jack and Peggy Self, and that I was born on 1.7.40. My parents were married on 3.9.1939, the day WW2 broke out. It was a hastily brought forward wedding so Dad could get back to his hospital duties on 4th September. It seems that it was also a hasty conception, since nine months had only scarcely elapsed since their marriage... Adds a bit of sparkle perhaps?

Incredulity is stretched a little further by the knowledge that I was born abroad. In Canada, to be exact. Father wasn't there to accompany his wife, my mother – no way! He saw to it that his clinical colleague, Dr Monica Smithers, who was engaged in obstetrics and gynaecology at Dad's hospital in Peterborough, was there to assist this Dominion into bringing me to breath and life. Mother was born a Bolsover, so with a silver spoon in her mouth; and this would have assisted in all the expenses. But not the ocean-crossings, which must have been so touch-and-go, with Hitler presuming all liners were troop ships and thus sinking them. As, however, she had much family in Canada to support her, so maybe it was a change from the Home Guard in Wisbech.

Successfully these two ladies brought me home; both were great actors! Much brinkmanship about my arrival as about later sessions of my life. Perhaps it gave me a taste for living on the edge...?

Chapter Eight: 1972

Marriage to Charlotte Whitby

Time passing. After seven years of working unstintingly first for Doctors Overseas and then for Médecins Sans Frontières, I decide to return to England and settle with a conventional job, and even perhaps a conventional wife and maybe 2.4 children. I'm NOT a conventional man and this may have been folly, but it looked like a good idea at the time. In the last year, I've transferred within Médecins Sans Frontières to Kuala Lumpur and made a few trips to Singapore. Strange city, full of rules and free of litter, it's nevertheless maintained by a very rigid police enforcement arm, ridiculing democracy.

But it was here in Singapore – in the most unoriginal and clichéd meeting place in the world, at Raffles Hotel – that I'd met Charlotte, that I'd fallen for Charlotte, and that – men don't get much practice at this – I'd proposed to Charlotte, and – men aren't always prepared for this – been accepted by Charlotte. And all I got back from my lifelong friends in England was "Go for it!" – Shirley; "Wonderful News, I suppose..." – Derek, and: "World's best Shag, take all my Love and Enjoy Hugely, I'm already writing the speech and hiring the suit – just tell me *when!*" – *obviously* Lesley. Even Camille wrote a letter (probably her first ever to me) and said never mind what Jack and Peggy said, the family was dying to meet Charlotte, and Monica was in seventh heaven.

Charlotte's mouse-haired (oddly, in England, I'd mostly known brunettes and blondes to date) but she has the most piercing and loving green eyes, making me feel sumptuously-caressed at twenty feet, as her eyes run over me with love and burgeoning loyalty. Close to, she sets the flesh a-quiver and alert whether she moves or stays – as she often does – statue still. She's an experience beyond time, she is magnificent. I don't so much as love her, I worship her. Perhaps there's a note there for fellow travellers. Perhaps all that stillness is down to all that Yoga. And don't use the word Pilates, it's off limits. Yoga or nothing. And a very special branch of Yoga that "You wouldn't understand, darling, so don't worry your sweet head about it." Very, very thin, you'd suspect anorexia, but see her at victuals! Fairly puts the food away… You could wonder that those alimentary tubes were all wide enough to engulf such portions…

So, after serving out due notice everywhere, I returned to little England and bought a house in Worcester. Why Worcester? My old tutor at Med School, Taffy Temple (a Welsh-Italian mix indeed) had advised me that the best research jobs were going at Worcester hospital and he could put in a good word for me… All this cronyism's going to have to stop, I thought, but for the moment, let's live out its dying throes properly and advantageously.

Charlotte had this statue-like family (so it wasn't just the Yoga?) in Chelsea – yes, quite ordinary people used to live there in the 70s – and she just *had* to get married at HTB. You don't know what that stands for? It's like the AA or SLR – in modest Christian terms, you have to know about Holy Trinity, Brompton. Seems bands of friends had been freed onto the world still with strong links back to the old HTB, links they mutually agree had a lot more to do with the Breakfast than the Communion. [Way back in the 60s, with permission from the Vicar, one Revd Pat Gilliatt, later Prebendary of St Pauls – when they put the family service unnaturally early in the morning, one Sheila Eagleton had started frying sausages and eggs for the famished worshippers].

*   *   *

Marriage 01.07.1972

So the date was set: Saturday 1st July – my actual birthday! – and families and friends had settled into hotels, B&Bs, flats, bedsits and homes throughout Kensington from around the country and across the globe. Jack and Peggy, as co-parents, stayed with Charlotte's parents, Cedric and Florence Whitby, and Monica was somehow staying nearby so she could help Cedric and the Best Man – "a *GIRL* called Lesley Grant, who'd known Elliott since they were 15 and 16 at Bedales – what do you make of *THAT!?"* Don and PhIl had come home from New Guinea on a three-month leave of absence and were tucked away in a borrowed bedsit in Earls Court; as, in a way, were Lesley, Derek and Shirley, who, all with their own partners (remarkably, for the times, all of the opposite sex) had hired a house also in Earls Court and were having a ball across London.

Camille and her new "stud" (I think this one was called Zavier?) were with Robert – Charlotte's handsome brother – and his lovely lady, known everywhere as Minx. No one ever knew her real name. The Wisbech Elgoods were putting in a good presence and again, Toby was keeping an eye on the fenland locals. The Reception was to be at the Hyde Park Hotel, so one could tell from the invite that no expense was being spared to pair this couple off in a magnificent manner. Pale and elegant, Charlotte spent a last evening with me dining at the Dorchester. How we felt that we'd arrived! Little did we see the years ahead… If we were going to marry it's surely good we couldn't see far ahead. We did manage to sleep together that night – or, rather, have sex – but in the face of so many would-be chaperones, a quickie was all we could contrive. Which remains our secret to this day…

*   *   *

The Wedding Service

A stunningly beautiful day, and almost every pew taken (what HTB does these days as a Top Charismatic Church with no pews at all is beyond me…) and my! Already in my life there are a smattering of MPs, financial boffins, and Arts and TV Supremos like Melvin Bragg – all kindly introduced by Cedric and Florence, Cedric being PPS to a cabinet minister, and Florence with a seat on the Arts Council. I and Lesley were suitably early and set a certain stir a-buzz as people faced this awful complexity. In the church, Monica expressed it all to Sir Ralph and about 70 others in a horse stage whisper: "So he's chosen to have as his right hand person a woman he's known for donkey's years, OK so far – but what on this day of telling the world who your beloved is, do you say to the title Best Man – she can't be Best Woman except that she is. Let's see how the Tatler handles this one. Saucily I expect."

Mendelssohn's wedding march at just 2pm – the Yogic Charlotte would never be late, she'd magic the traffic jam out of the way if necessary – and presently, everyone standing, as the intro hymn died away, she shimmered alongside, a very narrow confection in white, a narrow train held by two tiny cousins and Camille, Charlotte's veil not quite concealing those piercing green eyes as she looked right into me and .. and to Lesley who stood in her tailcoat suit beside me with the ring handy. It's a moment in history for me, forever etched out – and now, in my old age, with a sepia glow. To be standing between the two women I loved best in the world (at that time...) and to know that what seemed like final commitment was to be made to one, enabled by the other, in the poshest face of the world I could imagine, before God and People. (God was a mushy-peas uncertainty for me as yet).

And yet I held my stance. The service was a doddle after a good practice and no one feeling nervous nor foolish and with a no-nonsense minster with a truly good, projected, sincere voice; followed up by a bishop, rather off-duty, leading the prayers in a devout and small-church manor. Robert read 'Love is not puffed up'; and Camille read, with extraordinary panache, Ogden Nash's un-forgettable tongue-twister, "I do, I will, I have," ending in these immortal lines:

"So I hope husbands and wives will continue to debate and combat
over everything debatable and combatable,
Because I believe a little incompatibility is the spice of life,
particularly if he has income and she is pattable..."

both with good, loud, assertive voices. Rings on fingers, uplifting hymns over, we soon found we were down the aisle and out on the sunny forecourt, hugging and kissing and shaking hands and just touching as appropriate. We felt well and truly married.

Lesley drew me aside and said quietly and saucily: "Well, you can go and play all those games with *her* now. I am of course slightly hurt, but I'll get over it – and" – she fakes away a mock tear, and smiles widely and then hugs me, and whispers: "Oh I wish you so much joy, my darling man, but don't completely go away from me. I just know I'll need you."

I reply: "I know, my long-life love, this is such sweet sorrow. I'll be with you always," and we separate, people of the world again, to engage with the enormous throng of visitors, admirers and well-wishers.

*   *   *

The Reception

The Reception is something else completely in terms of lavish environment, drinks, canapés, people, conversation. It's all so much about style. "The Tatler will love it" said Shirley, unique for a redhead in her pink dress – to see Shirl in a dress was odd enough... Jack and Peggy seem genuinely impressed by my choice and by the new in-laws; they never thought I'd do it! Oh they of little faith! I've been away for so long they're not used to me in my early 30s yet at all.

But Monica is quite another. How she has the gall on my wedding day I just don't know. She drags me into a side room – that alone is significant as she normally utters her socially-dreadful comments in a loud voice to all around – and spoke this possibly prepared speech very directly: "Elliott, darling of Wisbech's heart and of mine, well done, yes, you have done well; but use these wonderful new contacts to further yourself in society. Above all, do *not* use marriage – this or any other – as a reason why you cannot do things your way at your pace at your place of choosing and with whom you desire to work – or play."

"Monica, I know you've always felt I could in some way live the life you had hoped for you and Sir Ralph, but please accept that Charlotte and I are just so happy and will lead innocent, achieving lives and – hopefully – bear children and have a happy family life – this notion we cherish above all else."

"Can she have children? I mean – she's very very thin. Anorexic I wouldn't wonder..."

"Monica, that's very personal and very rude! Let me put your mind at rest – she eats like a.. a.. well, a pony anyway, and for your information only, she has regular monthly periods, so all looks good for us. Please wish us well."

"Good! Nevertheless, you mark my words, Elliott – continue to think independently, travel, invent, get in the way, be awkward, get your own way, push!"

"OK, Monica, I've heard all this before and I'm a lot older now. Isn't it time for you to stop the lectures and start the Good Neighbour Of My Parents role – thinking of which, should I have said the Ex-Mistress of My Father role? Isn't that what you've been playing at all these years?"

Monica said not another word. She stormed out of the room, leaving me to wonder if I'd said too much. But, intuitively, I knew I was right, and this little fracas has ended in such a way that I thought there wouldn't be more... Oh well, I can't be right all the time. And actually, that's what she's asking of me...

*　　*　　*

Wedding Breakfast Over – The Speeches

250 diners had finished their "Wedding Breakfast" (what an extraordinary name – it wasn't bacon and eggs, I'm sure) and were imbibing brandy or port, perhaps with a remaining cheese biscuit and a touch of best French brie. The elderly men and the kids had been to the loo, and all the women had been absent for a social chat and a spreading of rumours. It had been announced that 'gentlemen may now smoke', and a few cigars, with pungent but pleasant odours, were even now clouding the room. Now all were back in the enormous dining apartment overlooking Hyde Park. The Toastmaster stood on the podium beside the lectern under a spotlight and a hush fell across the room. "My Lords, Ladies and Gentlemen, pray silence as the Father of the Bride, Colonel Cedric Whitby will address you."

Cedric pays homage to everyone, but everyone. He's a good speaker, much practiced, and with a lifetime of observing politicians on their feet. He speaks eloquently of this sudden romance that has "taken fire in the Southern

Hemisphere, in Singapore, I believe, and it seems that the love that Charlotte and Elliott radiate to one another is spilling over to family and friends. No doubt the sun will never go down on such a fitting partnership" – cheers and clapping – "Why these two young people, living merely 100 miles apart in Kensington and – err – is it called Wisbech? – couldn't get together in England is indeed hard to say, but no, they kick over the traces and meet each other half way round the earth.... Exciting, isn't it?"

He performed his functions perfectly, proposing a toast to the happy couple, mentioning us by our surname "Mr and Mrs Self" and was I guess much mollified by the thunderous applause, stamping and whistling.

When the toastmaster introduced me, I was in a flap in my mind about not so much how Lesley was going to cope, as how I was going to receive her "Best Man" words. All my life I have dissembled. I think about something that worries me and then I do what I have to do with suavity and aplomb; as indeed I did today – I did *not* make the kind of gruesome mistakes you hear about callow youth making in the first speech of their lives at their wedding feast. I spoke of the great privilege of joining the Whitby family, and looked forward to engaging with the whole family, and keeping links warm across the hundred mile divide, between Whitbys and the Selfs. I joked about needing the Colonel's advice about London, Politics and the City, wholly as yet unexplored avenues for me, and his wife's about the Arts. I really meant all these, too, as I hope to make my way towards a consultancy which would – in my "General Specialist" endeavour – keep me busy and interested and meeting interesting people. I allowed my mind to wander intoxicatingly over the moment, merely months beforehand, when, across a crowded room at a reception in Singapore, I had first caught sight of Charlotte's vivid green, but very still, eyes... I sighed suitably and told little enchantingly-enhanced stories of our courtship, checked out with her earlier.

My toasts to my med-school friends and my Wisbech lads and lasses went down OK but not a bomb. This was a London affair. Very properly, I finally toasted the bridesmaids, with a very friendly note for my sister Camille – "looking today like a Bride in Waiting;" and to the gorgeous little 5 year old twins, Georgia and Joanna, Robert's children, who had amazed and enchanted us all. After toasting the bridesmaids, my sign-off line was "unusually for a Groom, I'd like to welcome my Best Man and to wish her all the best for the Ordeal of Knightsbridge – taking the part of a man in 1970s London" – and that got me a good, sharp, short, fierce clap, but I bet it was from just some of them – caught Del and Shirl's table almost taking off with shrieks of anticipation and slightly intoxicated joy.

It's interesting to see a Master of Ceremonies stumble a moment as he gets caught out in his words. "My Lords, Ladies and Gentlemen, pray now for silence for the Best Man, Ms Lesley Grant, and he will add... err – she will address you..." Thunderous applause and some out-of-order shouting, not pleasing the top brass Whitbys overmuch.

Bless her! I do love her! Well, as well as my prize today, as well as Charlotte. Lesley isn't tall, but she can command an audience. When she and I made this – with hindsight rather ridiculous – agreement, we had no idea that either of us would actually DO this (to us, then) *absurd* thing of *marrying* someone! So it was all theoretical. Yet even now it added a touch of Breaking the Mould which I rather liked. "Unaccustomed as I am to being best man at my great friend's wedding, I am at least accustomed to speaking aloud to people. So, straight off, this is not a gimmick. It's for real. I think we were – oh I don't know – 17 or 18 – and at those times, young people don't imagine they'll get married; but if we were going to, we wanted to remember what good friends we were when we were younger; still are, and that, Charlotte, is going to continue. Oh! I'll care for him from a distance, I won't get in the way. But, Ladies and Gentlemen" (I guess she left the Lords out on purpose...) "there's another half to the agreement that may keep me away from the altar until I'm an ancient crone!" – everyone is very eager, very quiet – "If and when I get married, Elliott has promised to be my chief bridesmaid" – the raucous laughter from the young and the stunned horror from the old is visceral, eerie, worrying – "and – no, quieten down please, I haven't said it all yet." She pauses so everyone can hear her next line. Silence. "And, when I get married, Elliot will not only be my chief bridesmaid, he'll" – pause for effect – "he'll wear a pink bridesmaid's dress." Fifty years later it would hardly have been a story, but amongst people who think they're the Aristocracy of England, back in '72, the news is like a firebrand. Lesley is very, very good at keeping a straight face as if to say 'this is not a joke, it's for real' and so the howling and stomach clenching and whistling and – on the other side – the horror of sexual identity pranks awakening in the ranks of the noble, they were consumed with indignation. But – and it says something for her – Monica was clearly on youth's side. Sir Ralph behaved as if he hadn't heard...

The top table 'kept their corsets on' as it were and 'let the dear girl finish'. Lesley told Charlotte that Elliott was a man of impulse, did things on the spur of the moment, sometimes without rhyme or reason; but that *that* was her test, that's what she had to put up with and attempt to enjoy – "as his uni friends here – principally the blonde lad Derek and redheaded girl Shirley over there on table **Uni** – the three of us have known Elliott for longer than anyone here except his family and the Wisbech lads and lasses. So we have some home truths for you." Thankfully, she never raised the roof as far again, but she told some slightly saucy stories; and brought her 'word' to an end by responding to the toast to the bridesmaids "something I'm better equipped to do than any Best Man before me!" That was her final, much enjoyed, flourish. What a success! Well, I think so. Monica will be pleased but that's definitely not the point.

Chapter Nine: 1953-8

Bedales – Freedom – Caroline

When, three years ago, I first arrived as a pupil at Bedales, I was – probably just within myself and unnoticed – fumbling and confused; yet, within a month, I knew I had 'come home', that this place was *OK* for me to express my ideas about... well, about *anything*. But that didn't mean we had anarchy and hedonism from dawn to dusk; rather we had a tolerant society where there was time for work, for play, for relaxation – and for argument. And there wasn't much sport, and what there was was distinctly uncompetitive, which suited me very well. I had-*never* had such freedom to stretch my mind, and I took my opportunity with both hands. If I had done this selfishly, taking the stage with every debate, I'm sure I would have been shown the door – but that was the *real* delight, so many of us boys and girls, all with ideas, all with a determination to try them out in argument and carry our concepts through in some way.

The secret, or so it seemed to me, may have been in the work culture. Conventional schools apply rods of iron to classes, prep and frequent exam-like tests. At Bedales, we were encouraged to do our research work on projects on our own, with little push from staff. This led to good vibes and much more interest in our subjects. (And for some – a very few – who couldn't take the freedom, an early exit door). Liaisons and relationships with staff were entirely different here; and an indication of this lies in the fact that there was no 'Sir' nor 'Miss' here; all staff – as with all boys and girls – were called by their first names. This gave a collegiate, everyone's-here-to-help, kind of ethos. I can't remember it being taken advantage of at all. The experience of living alongside both boys and girls in equal proportions, a condition laid down by the founder a century before, proved – for me anyway – that the male-only preserve up on the Norfolk coast had been unnatural and restricting to our normal ability to enjoy life alongside all of our fellow human beings. I'd advocate mixed-sex monasteries! What an oxymoron!

So when it came to an *actual* girl with whom to break my sexual duck, when I was fourteen, a tall and lean redheaded beauty sidled up beside me on one of our frequent walking trips to Peef – our name for local town Petersfield – and told me she was called Caroline, and did I like that name? I was a little flattered by her attention, and on the third time we so met, she said lots of the girls think I'm one day going to be Prime Minister, so – if it wouldn't be too much bother! – she'd like to chalk me up on her private totem pole as a one-night-stand lover; said without a blush and in deadly earnest.

For a very short while I prevaricated (thinking, come on, Elliott, this is supposed to be hard work and take ages and frequently fails – what kind of trap might you be falling into here?) and then I made much of the laid-down terms: it was the one-night stand lover that caught me on the hop. Surely, if I was wanted at all, I was worth a short relationship at least. But Caroline, who otherwise was made of sugar and spice, explained that, at our age, experience is the big thing, and if you are seen to bed down with just one person for a while, you lose social availability, which she didn't recommend for either of us!

I wasn't, in those days, used to losing an argument, and, seeing as this matter-of-the-heart was being negotiated via words – which I hadn't expected at all – I pressed my suit for three such encounters. Why, she asked? Well, I said, inexperience and being overwhelmed might almost obliterate the memory of the first, let alone simple failure, and – I think this was my winning stroke – to be propositioned by the most beautiful girl in our year, yet have my tenancy cut so short that I might as well have been a bee, would mean that I got no time to truly enjoy her... Now, all these words were true, but I could see 'you're an exception' creeping across her delighted face. So, three-times it was to be.

There's a farmers' barn on a hillside within a mile – I gather much used for early liaisons – and here one bright Saturday afternoon, we met, apparently casually, as we each came by a different route. A few minutes talk lying on the straw; then we enjoyed each others' bodies to the full, she only adding one more coherent thing: "You were right about three times, why didn't you go for more? You'll never make a good PM if you don't argue for your country's full needs," and on the word 'full' she described a circle so large as to encircle the heavens.

I don't suppose it was the greatest love-making of the era, fumbling somewhat with the hidden niceties of our bodies; but I had a very good guide via her hands and gestures. Such elixir I never thought to experience! I was truly transported. There need now be no heaven, it's right here, between this woman's thighs...

She left long before I did, prancing across the strewn hay as if it were a ballet stage, her tall, slight figure somehow showing off curves I'd scarcely noticed before. She made a wonderful display of anatomy – and now, with my very recent memory, physiognomy too. Our next two dalliances were similar but better. She never once breathed a word about my clearly having been a virgin; she certainly was not. For a rite of passage, I reckoned I'd done well. And I didn't promise 'to leave no boulder unturned en-route to being Prime Minister!'

*   *   *

The Mass Debating Society

Caroline was a couple of years back, serving as a searing memory for any lonely moment. But such loneliness was really unusual, as Bedales was nothing if not a social place. My 'O' levels loomed, all 11 of them. My career advisers were struggling with my assertion that I wanted to be a General Specialist, and pencilled me in for PPE at Oxford. So, for A Levels, maybe English, History, and a language? However, 'A'-levels were two years away, and Uni would be say three. The stuff of life was people, society, drama, and debate. As the old one had declined, I put up a notice inviting everyone to come and join the new Mass Debating Society, and its – when you speak it out loud – double meaning escaped no one, so nearly all the school turned up for the inaugural!

Normally such things would happen in the library or one of the smaller rooms, but rumour had it that all these places would be overwhelmed and so it would be best to use the Quad, which is what one would think a quad should be – a square space surrounded by buildings – but it's roofed-over and used for drama productions and concerts. These more formal affairs are announced long beforehand, but my debating society was a casual arrangement. However, staff allowed me to go ahead, and never mind that the upper floor windows lead onto the boys' dorms, we could do it. I planned hard to make this a success, and persuaded a popular teacher, Al Landross, to chair the event. I then made up teams of debaters – entirely and I suppose selfishly – of my new friends, Lesley, Derek and Shirley. Would they be the best protagonists? Lesley, yes, Derek and Shirley – well, no, but it would show the floor what could happen amongst a group meeting to debate.

231 Bedalians, including a smattering of staff, who I hoped had come for a laugh, were seated by 7.30. Upper and Middle Schools only numbered 275 in total in 1956. I must have over-cooked this one! Never does everyone at Bedales do the same thing at the same time! Until now? I did the intro, at Al's insistence. Included were phrases such as: "Dunno how you all heard about this – apparently auspicious – start to Bedales' renewed debating life..." – a community laugh, in which you could make out the dirty guffaws – "... well, yes, I hope it will be partly humorous, partly informative, and partly entertaining. Sorry if I've cast this first debate with my friends and I taking part – I don't know many of you to choose as debaters yet. I hope, at the end, you'll take those papers – they're on your chairs – and tell us if you'd like to actively debate; what subjects you'd like to present – for or against; or would you like to chair; or would you prefer to be audience and social – looser members of the group. Thank you to Al for chairing this one, thank you all." Cheers and general mayhem.

Al introduces the first subject: "We believe that the old story of the boys' prep school headmaster when he advised his leaving pupils: 'You have two wonderful organs in your body – your brain and your penis. However, you'll soon learn that you can only use one at a time' is in fact true" – screams of amusement – "and to propose this motion I have on my left Ms Lesley Grant, and the seconder is Mr Derek Widmer. Opposing the motion on my right, no less than your catalyst today, Mr Elliott Self, and his seconder, Ms – err - Shirley – Shawley" Her name alone did it, as most of the time here we don't use surnames – and it had clearly been new on Al as, reading it out, he paused for a nanosecond. "I'm told this is a quick opener and should soon – err – be over" Insinuations had been apparent to all the audience and often unintended double entendres were taken with wild glee and quite un-debate-like comedic response.

But when Lesley got to her feet and told us all that the limited quantity of blood in the male body was such as to need to serve the most pressing need at the time, clearly, while that fat great penis was engorged with blood to give it that penetrating erectile quality, there would indeed be almost nothing left to more than superficially service the brain, hence the Hooray Henrys who have permanently engorged penises and are as daft as Donald Duck; and with little more embellishment, said she rested her case. How that was funny I don't know, but it apparently was.

I opposed the motion via this tactic: "At the height of sexual fervour, penetration, etc, men are liable to re-remember where their mother had said, should she suddenly die, she had hidden her jewellery. This proves that a man's brain is on super-top-form during penile engorgement, and that indeed he has enough blood to turn ten flaccid penises virile should the occasion demand it. This secret is normally for men alone to know, it's not for general consumption across the sexes, as women take a poor view of their man's mother coming into mental view at this precise point, so we don't tell our girls this stuff. However, the need in this debate for a worthwhile response led me to divulge..." Well, this was better than any amusement arcade, helter-skelter ride, or prime fillet of beef. And I love to get to people through their brain cells... Tickling the grey matter... I added little more to my silly argument, leaving the seconders and the audience to contribute.

Derek seconded by a quite nimble bit of acting and very few words. Hanging on to Lesley in a provocative way, he appeared to have lost his wits, his normally quite slow but nevertheless ever-present reasoning had gone. Lesley was tolerant to a degree as Del just, falteringly got these few words out with many gaps: "Les...ley..... .love....... .like, too........nice....... ooooh....... forever...... .mmmmh....... and I rest my weary baton...." Shrieks all round.

Shirley, as always, wearing something pink to really oppose that mane of red luxuriant curls, seconded my opposition with: "Well, some people seem short on words today. Not me. In my extensive psychic research, I in truth really know I have to meditate on such subjects. Nothing can give you a truer answer than meditation. It's not an argument, it's an intrinsic truth. Men love love. They love it for itself. They don't even need a woman there to help them. And it happens all the time, probably every day. Usually while reading quantum mathematics or higher physics or – and I warm to this rather more – an artistic book of beautiful nudes. And do they stop their glance while – is the word intumescent? – sounds like something Greek to me – No! They do not! So – their brain is active and at top form throughout the – err – session. I rest my book of nudes." The floor had a smattering of mostly very rude responses.

Soon over, how had we done? Al took shows of hands, and then converted to percentages. Before the debate the percentaged figures were: For 68%, Against 32%, Abstentions 0. Afterwards: For 61%, Against 27%, Abstentions 12%. And that's really odd. Normally, abstentions go down after debate; and the lack of a clear winner against prior thought was interesting. Most important, people were galvanised by the event. Two more, slightly more serious debates followed, after which the group was definitely an ongoing concern and took up too much of my time...

*   *   *

1956 Friendship Lesley Quad

I suppose when I was about sixteen, I began to feel that friendship was one of the cornerstones of life. From observation, admittedly with a teenager's possibly warped view, I was, frankly unimpressed by many of the marriages I was privy to observing; well, after ten years or so. My parents were one couple, but their misery was reflected across so many of their generation's marriages. Some were good, and some were excellent, a real joy to experience. But in so many marriages, at least one party had this beleaguered, sad, lonely – trapped – look. Were they really only staying together because of the children?

Or were they economically only viable as a couple? Was the social frost out there in singles-land so deep that they couldn't jump to freedom? Or weren't they interested? Did they view the singles they knew with a shudder and say 'anything but that' and go on ironing the husband's shirts?

I kind of knew I would get married one day, but, curiously, held out no better hopes for myself. Marry, star-spangled sky, dress, bride, house, and an enormous amount of just plain stuff, procreate (which alone must be fun) 2.4 children in 4.5 years and spend 20 regretting it? So – were there some lessons to be learned NOW? How to set the pathway to marriage? Oh, rather ghastly thoughts!

But yes, what one could do is to decide on and really nurture a group of friends – really good friends one can laugh and cry and go on expeditions and go to exhibitions and sit for a quiet evening with, all that for all of this group. MUST be possible. Sounds like you need to advertise: 'Hearty bloke wants – really – friendship only, must have a sense of humour, our differing selfishnesses must fit together like a jigsaw puzzle'. Oh, perish the thought, how contrived can you get? Well – who then? And when and how many and, and, and, and.....

Why, while I'm feeling this way, why not now? Why not with the very people I've just done this debating think with? Lesley has recently become my lover (we feel very very well suited but we'll never marry) Derek and Shirley. I will propose something much more arrogant than a one-night-stand, I'll ask for all their hands in friendship for the remainder of our lives. Whatever we do, wherever we are, we'll contact one another, we'll be a shoulder to cry on, a friend to rejoice with, a person to be with. We'll know each other so intimately, but we'll probably never marry. After all, *ours is for life* – a happy life. And marriage? Where exactly is *that* going? Don't answer, it's rhetorical.

"Lesley, hi, I've got this great idea. With Derek and Shirley."

"Elliott I'm not doing a foursome with Del and Shirl!"

"No, but you do love them don't you?"

"Mmmm – not like I love you." And we had a long hug as I explained into her adjacent ear just what I meant. She kept on holding on till the end. She eased up a bit and said: "Elliott, it sounds marvellous and I *will* say yes, but just suppose we've taken on too much? We may be sexually mature, but we're immature in the ways of the world. What harm could we be doing?"

"Maybe holding on to a good idea and finding someone wants to rat on it. That won't matter so long as the three that remain are mentally stable beings."

"Yup. I guess I buy it."

We both met Del and Shirl together, a sort of appointment in the world's terms. We said we didn't like the look of life ahead, of marriage and stability, honesty, love in marriage contracts. And we wanted all to agree to be lifelong friends, to support, care for and indulge one another. Well, they were immediately taken with the idea, but said – this is Doubting Del's way, really – he wanted three weeks to turn it over in his head.

Three weeks later, we took cider and pies on a long country walk, and after our picnic, settled to some serious words each to the others, everyone being so enchanted by the idea, until Lesley said:

"We need a name. We started the other day debating in the Bedales Quad. There are four of us. Let's call ourselves QUAD."

And so we did. And so, through all our long lives we go together, friends with each other and if necessary against the world.

* * *

Edinburgh, here we come!

The immediate future turned out to be interesting: Lesley was set upon becoming a doctor, and she was hoping for a place at Edinburgh University and medical school. I changed my 'A' levels to Chemistry, Physics and Biology and joined her on the list for Edinburgh. Shirl had thought of a job to do with the stage – stage managing and the rest – but her family counselled that something more lucrative might be good. So she also switched 'A' levels to suit, and joined us. Then there was tall Derek, 6'2", who said he'd always wanted to be a doctor, but his father, a businessman with a factory, wanted him to follow in his footsteps. Well, six months later, he joined the three of us en route to Edinburgh. All together, then…

Chapter Ten: 1996

Quad's Children

Long in the planning, at last we're having the Summer Get Together of all of Quad's Children – and a few more besides. Held at Taynton in the Cotswolds in July 1996, exactly forty years after we made this compact with our good friends, brunette Lesley, blonde tall Derek and redhead Shirley, to be all and everything to one another over these many years.

The world has happened to all of us – I was married and am now divorced, but have a son and a daughter, Magnus, 23 and Lillibet, 21; Lesley is happily living with Garth with twin girls of 20 – Jonquil and Jessica; Derek at last got it together with Sonya and they have two boys both with rather experimental names – Quentin, 20 and Adolf!, 18; and Shirley, having spent a glorious four years with Josephine in lesbian love, has now settled with her Jerd Carnt and their four children: Harebell, Sorrell, Delilah and Xavier, from 19 down to 16.

Expected to be a pure summer get-together – barbeque, fun-tennis, country walks – with no pious dreams about the perfection of friendship, this is to test whether our 10 offspring can or would like to abide each other's company on this or other occasions.

Just to add to the fray, we've added in my sister, Camille, and her three little girls, Hermione, Rosanna and Clarissa, aged 15 down to 11, as they happen to be in this country (they live in Montreal); and also the kids of Derek and Sonya's closest neighbour: Belinda and Jude's brood are Mat, Mark, Lucy and Joanna, aged from 20 down to 10.

So – 17 offspring from so few of us, really. Some are arriving right now – it's the lot from North London, with Shirley at the wheel, and – her – well I never – it's Josephine back with us all again! and of course Harebell, Sorrell, Delilah and Zavier pouring out of the open-topped car...

These four know Quentin and Adolf – Derek and Sonya's kids – of old as, when Shirley jets off to see her bosom pal Josephine overseas, they come and stay at Taynton; maybe Jerd can't be trusted to look after them, and Derek and Sonya kind-of enjoy having another 4 mouths to feed, for three weeks at a time...!

My ex-lover, Lesley, turns up with her twins, 20 year-old Jonquil and Jessica – each fighting for the rite to drive Lesley's elderly Ford Capri, so Lesley's driving; and the fight is now over who has the front seat next to mum... Apparently, at their separate Unis, all is sweetness and light, and they write loving letters to one another...

My offspring, Magnus and Lillibet, turn up next, in Magnus's Mini; he's just qualified from a business school and is probably going to be a banker. So – it won't be a mini for long, methinks... Lillibet is unsure, and is making her way through Uni at present.

Before any other arrivals can happen, Jonquil and Jessica both aim for Magnus, with his considerable presence. One on each side of him, they're as charming as can be – now! – and would seem to be making up for lost time in the flirting stakes:

"Magnus, that's a grand name, so you're going to be a great man, are you?" beams Jonquil.

"I can see you're _already_ great – magnificent man!" retorts Jessica.

"You two are going to be wonderful hostesses in life!" exclaims Magnus. "With beautiful voices and faces you simply can't lose!"

"No swimming pool here, so we're likely _not_ to see your rippling pecks..." says Jonquil.

"...That's something we really _can_ arrange" says Jessica.

And so they continue, flirting with one another, till Jonquil says:

"I suppose you know that your dad and our mum were – err – once lovers, don't you?"

And Jessica retorts: "And your father's splendid Hyde Park Corner wedding was attended by our mother as your BEST MAN!"

"Well – it shows in what high regard he held her" says Magnus, defensively.

*   *   *

High Noon

A party's High Noon can be said to occur when everyone has arrived, when sufficient alcohol has been drunk to keep an un-shy kind of continuous conversation flowing, and for the "staff" – Quad and the older Taynton residents – are so taken up with duties that they're enjoying it too.

The event started at 12 noon, to a sticky start – apart from the Jonquil-Magnus-Jessica interplay – and didn't reach its High Noon till about 2.30pm, everyone having arrived, and not yet a drunken word, nor a drunken fall. It's at such moments that PARTIES seem to have a point.

Magnus has moved on to Harebell, Mat, Delilah and Quentin; Jonquil to Lillibet, Mark, Hermione and Adolf; Jessica to Sorrell, Xavier and Rosanna, leaving merely young Clarissa, 11, Lucy, 12 and Joanna, 10, to muddle along on their ownsomes. Eating barbecued chicken, and taking sips of this fruit cup we've provided, all is sunny and light.

Magnus has a huge voice, even when not projecting himself. He speaks: "Holy shit, Derek and Sonya, have all you nine families co-existed here really over the past 22 years? Quentin tells us this. That's amazing – it's like a life sentence, being here...!"

"No, but it's lovely living here, you don't understand" says Sonya

"I wish I could live here" says a Canadian voice, Rosanna "We don't have places like this near to Montreal."

"Yes _we_ do!" says Camille "and our extended family live in one! We must go and see it one day, it's north of Toronto – on a lake."

"My, you're lucky" says Jonquil, mimicking Rosanna's accent.

"Sure are!" says Jessica, keeping up the mimicry.

Quentin says: "It's great living here, isn't it Adolf, Mat, Mark, Lucy and Joanna?"

They all agreed it was, leaving Magnus in some mix-up about the conversation he'd started: "Oh, I didn't mean to create confusion over your enjoying life here – I was noting that, if nine families can last for 22 years, it sounds like it's difficult to leave."

"Not a bit of it" says Sonya "Everyone's free to leave whenever they put their house on the market."

"Are we ever going to do that, Ma?" says Adolf "I wouldn't like us to move – where would we go?"

"No," says Quentin "we're not moving. We need to be here to provide a place for you all to come in 10 years time, for the next link-up!"

The little girls don't really know what's going on. They're muttering as they draw drink up the straws they're equipped with "Why does it matter how long a time you stay in your house?" says Clarissa.

"Yes, why?" say Lucy and Joanna together.

Derek starts: "It's all a matter of how much you love your home and if you love it a lot… well there's a good reason to stay there; and if you have so many friends where you live… well, there's another good reason to stay there…"

Shirley continues: "We're all getting very muddled up here, Derek, don't you think? Amidst all the other factors that most people regard as normal, like mortgages, numbers of bedrooms, and closeness to work, there is also the friendship angle. But I think this is all very heavy chat for an afternoon's summer party, don't you?"

A big round of applause for this common sense answer. People drifted back into their previous groupings, or changed these slightly, and chatted on. And on and on… For hours…

*   *   *

Another Party? Like This One?

Quad foregathers at the end of the party. It seems there is the thought of doing this again sometime – or sometimes. A year? No, no! Two, three, or four? Not really. Not under five. Anyway, what's to stop them arranging things for themselves? The young ones, that is. OK, OK. For now it will be five and we'll see...

Some young hear all this going on and say "We'll be scattered across the globe in five year's time." "Leave it up to us." "We can arrange anything we want to." "Anyway, a few of us have agreed to meet up in London soon, so there!"

So there, indeed. Success? We'll see in the future what happens...

Chapter Eleven: 1982

The Thick of It – Sloane

People ask why I have three telephone lines. I ask them why they have two Jaguars – can't possibly drive more than one at a time. Anyway, in this Ground Floor and (euphemistically) Lower Ground Floor (more properly Basement) apartment in very central London, I live out a solo but lively life as an advisor to just so many different Ministers and Quangos and Charities I rarely can list them all at once. Each one – including the needy charities – pays me some sort of retainer, and a few pay massive fees, and I never feel responsible for the advice I so advantageously hand out. Is this irresponsible? Hard to say. They need the answers from somewhere, and in these decades before Google and World Access to All Info, someone has to do it by a bit of graft. And I do also *give* generously, if rather publicly, to the charities I serve. It's hard to say how I got here, exactly. But there is some Monica behind it. And some Whitby. Yes, Cedric and Florence, who bore Charlotte, my ex wife, still get on famously with me, and still frequently pop round to have a G&T and a chat. I don't think I'm anything like the man Monica hoped I'd be, but I certainly do have a facility with people – and, as ever, although I deal with men much more, I guess it's the women I get on with best.

Actually, Margaret Thatcher *doesn't* pop round. No. I always have to go and see her. We're told she's an Unclubbable Woman, but I don't know... Anyway, it's her emissary who does the popping, and arranges appointments. Sometimes No 10, sometimes a private house in the centre of London, occasionally Chequers. Best I've managed so far has been a whole weekend at Chequers. People like to talk amongst their own, and I observe sometimes that she seems closer to me than to Howe, Heard and Lawson. There's a reason for this: I tend to give the answer I intuit my enquirer wishes to hear, but not before I've done a great deal of work (or apparently so) to support my answer. Every question, at its simplest, has two answers. And it's my belief that both can usually be right. Take last weekend. Margaret has taken upon her shoulders – and her shoulders alone – to save the Falkland Islands from being over-run by the Argentines. On the face of it, to operate a minor war at 12,000 miles distance with all the exigencies of no allies nearby, refuelling midair, no base to work from, it's patently nonsense. I'd let it go and learn a lesson re Malta, Gibraltar and the rest – and of course immediately set about heavy diplomatic argument with the Argies for the next fifty years to get the Falklands back again. But my client is Margaret Thatcher and she is – we're told – the Iron Lady. Her will will not be broken; she *will* send a massive fleet to the Falklands in very short order. From this realisation onwards, I know that the only way to stay in her good books – to be able to advise on Matters of State for the next few years of this her albeit temporary reign, is to not only say YES let's go, but also to find fantastic arguments to convince Pym and Carrington and Nott and other would-be Foreign Secretaries and Minsters of Defence that going to the Falklands is a good plan. So I do. I must say my heart was in my mouth over this – absurd! – decision far more than in most cases I have to respond to. Whether the National Trust should remain private, the Post Office be sold off, the railways be ordered to run on time, or patents to be unscrambled into a simple matter of preserving the trading rights of invention for a short period – these are all lesser beer, and they don't upset my sleep at all.

"Apart from your distinguished report, Elliott, you really feel *in your bones* that this Falklands action is the right course of action for Britain? Yes you – *really – feel –* that, don't you?"

"Margaret, I'm sure. Ask no more. Go to war." Well – I can convince, and maybe that's important. But is there a fundamental RIGHT in these cases? Or are we actually dealing with the comparative wills of very strong-minded eccentrically egotistical people? We might as well have asked for a psychologist's report on the relative will power of the Right Honourable

Margaret Thatcher, MP, PM, as against that of President Leopoldo Galtieri. I suppose I kind-of did that in the margins of my process.

Recently, things have become much more serious. I've been asked to become a board member of the BBC Governors, under its incoming Chairman George Howard. Actually "Gorgeous George" asked me himself, as he feels some wide, non-specialist, clearly excellent brains could find a good niche on the Board. Trips to Castle Howard might even be, if not in the package, arranged on the side. I'm drawn to this, but have to think. My strategy is not to expose myself too much... If I also took this Arts Council post – under Sir William Rees-Mogg, yes he of sometime The Times editorship, I might be able to have my say about the current arguments over regionalism.

Despite my saying I do this all on my own, I do have some outworkers, and I'd never have managed all this without Sloane. Oh, she had a proper name like Jill Smith, but I can't remember it now, and anyway she was introduced to me as merely Sloane, worked for seven years with me as just Sloane, used to be under Sloane in the phone book, and I hope, if she's still alive, she'll come to my 80th (which I'm beginning to plan) as Sloane. She was discrete, knowledgeable, very intelligent, worked very well on her own, was one of the oh-so-few-people I asked advice from: her intuition was on High Alert from dawn to dusk. And beyond, but that is indeed another story...

*　　*　　*

The Thick of It

"Sloane, I've 20 for coffee and a chat – you OK for that?"

"Sure, Elliott, right now while it's on your mind." We sit in our grand but tiny reception area in the Charles Eames chairs, the best coffee percolating quietly. I tell her about the requests from the BBC and the Arts Council. "I don't know if you deserve it, but if you want these posts, go for them. You won't get a second chance. With anyone else, I'd say 'define your purpose, narrow your aim, identify your goals, stick to that path', but this is invariably bad advice for you, as you insist on being the General Specialist throughout your life and that kind-of means go for everything that gets you known amongst the Intelligentsia: Cultural, Political, Environmental – as they all warm to you for your embracing personality and your great width of experience. You and I know it's not experience at all, it's a flair for – so far – always being right about what happens next; don't slip up and become a city councillor or some other trumped-up but humdrum role, where one is always wrong – yes, and you would be too! Nine years I've known you not put a foot wrong. Keep crisp and clear. But – how will you take on the extra work and the essential reading that will accompany these jobs?"

"Sleep even less, work even harder, enjoy what I'm doing – that's the essential!"

I move subject: "Ought we to review my readiness to appear in any one of several specialist programme on TV or radio, on the basis that I AM that specialist? It's all very well advising the PM about a war, but that's very private – those papers won't be out till.... Oh well.... for 1982 they go public in 2012, and we'll hear about them and John Nott and all, but – you see? Never me. That's the final clever bit. Having all the charms of being famous without being famous at all. My intention precisely.

"Are you going to go on accepting invitations onto Newsnight and Today and the like? It may be your undoing, going out to these enormous – and these listening, intelligent, participatory – audiences who remember and write criticisms in Sunday papers."

"Mmmm – well, I gave Paxman – and now Humphreys – a run for their money, just by sticking to my same answer, as they do the same question, expatiating the while, of course, to fill the slot."

"Yes, you were very good. In some sub-arrogant way you seemed to be interviewing them! You were so 'Mine Host' you may nearly have thrown them both. Anyway, I assured you really good arguments." Her tallish lean body bends forward a touch, pencil in hand, and I know the pause is to give me time to thank her properly. She's looking, for a lady not less than 48 at this time, quietly lovely without being overly glam – as she can, when the job rather than the person, warrants it. I know I just love having her around. Nothing physical. Oh, yes it is! Anyway, I remind her that I've seen St Peter and he's arranging for her canonisation within her own lifetime, a privilege not yet earned by any of the saints. To be fair, I've said this one before, but each time I add a little bit about the problems of the holy administration that's yet to be processed, and we spin it out a little every time. It's like a little sacrament, weekly tended, and then over and both of us happy.

Moving on now, Sloane says: "You said 20 minutes, but I have a light morning, and we can do an extended review now if you wish. I'll perk some more coff." She knows my diary and is aware that I'm free too, so she takes charge of the agenda. Freshly roasted coffee is the thing.

"It's the things you probably *aren't* thinking of giving up that concern me. Do you have a stake in this business of Derek's? I'm glad at last he's changed its name from – err – 'Cackhanded' – was it? – to 'New Laid Ideas' – although that's suspect too. Remind me – you knew him at Bedales, Uni, Med School – and ever since – whatever took him away from good old doctoring with a comfortable if not brilliant salary attached to it."

"I think he must have been over-pushed by his father to go into the field of medicine. His grandfather had been a doctor in Leicester. His father probably felt the family hadn't the same credentials in trade as they had had in a profession. Anyway, whatever the background reason, Del tried General Practice as a junior but never actually made partner. Then his father suffered that stroke you'll recall and, after nine months intensive rehab, was able to handle his business sitting at a desk with two phones and a lot of help, but couldn't drive, go to sites, negotiate contracts away from base, nothing really. So Del was probably emotionally bribed to give up doctoring – after all those years of training – and join the business. There were strong economic reasons to do with the family's money being tied up in the business, which at that point in time, couldn't be released."

"So Derek just put his head down and worked his butt off to make the sort of profits that hadn't been seen in years. And why did you get involved? I know he's a good mate, but was this really part of your Plan for a Curious Life With the Decision Makers but Without their Responsibilities? And how on earth did you acquire apparently consummate skills in design, invention, market research, intellectual property, marketing and finance? I know we've glanced off this from time to time, but you do seem very set on committing time to Derek's outfit; so, for your biog, I ought to try and understand better; and as your – self-imposed" – a wicked, half gleeful, smile and glance straight at me here " 'Time and Motion Study Officer', it's probably my duty to tell you where you are concentrating, or spending too much time, on the wrong things. Most especially when you now intend to rush to the aid of the BBC and the Arts Council. So?"

"Sloane, you've been closer to me than my own shadow for years now – you must have gleaned most of the answers here! OK, an overview: I've no formal training in any of those narrow specialisms. But I do know – instinctively, but it can be observed at a distance too – that you can't understand one without the other, the several; or, put it another way, you have to do the lot to be a self-respected person involved in introducing new concepts to the market" I glance at my watch "shall we book a table at 'Le Petit Montmartre' so we can talk on? We need reflective moments and indeed we are at a point of considering relative workload."

Sloane picks up the phone, presses just two buttons, is through in no time and, in immaculate French, orders lunch for two. "Good! Thanks."

After a pause, I continue: "Del and I would talk long into the evenings over brandy and cigars about how to restructure their business to help him, his father and their firm, and so therefore their employees; and, if possible, a new generation. We looked at his design and production side, and found a cheerful, able, but low-incentive, low-achieving bunch of lads and the odd lass – joiners, metal workers, assemblers, painters – all craftsmen to a point. But the money the firm was turning over produced a gross profit sufficient to pay to service the mortgage and loans, and to pay the directors really rather moderate salaries...." The phone rang, quietly, could have been left to join the queue on the ansaphone, or... and I chose to look at the incoming caller's identity, and, muttering "talk of the devil," lifted the receiver and kind-of yelled "Del! Just the lad! Come and meet us – can you join us for lunch, Chelsea office, 'Le Petit Monmartre', 1pm?"

Del, on the amplifier so Sloane could hear: "Elliott! I thought you'd said not to ring during the day, always busy, keep our pranks to evenings and weekends.

She Who Must Be Obeyed hasn't got me on her 'Elliott Objectives' – so I was about to apologise, but this one simply wouldn't wait."

"Well, will it wait till lunch? And are your ears burning? No? They ought to be.... Del and Tricks is Subject Number One on Sloane and my agenda this very morning! How really apposite! Love to see you – Sloane too." We ended our call.

Sloane has been making those efficient-people glances toward Heaven; the bubble emanating from her heard may have said 'Bugger! I thought I could tie him down for once, but here we go again! Time lost...' and what she now sweetly said was "Great! Will be good to catch up with Derek" even if a lie-detector tape recorder might have analysed out: 'Voice: cool, detached. Not quite accepting new situation. Yet'.

*　　*　　*

Derek

I say: "So, Sloane, we've got half an hour before Del arrives. This is what you also need to know, speaking in shorthand: Firm had little possibility to lose loans etc because would have to sell company and thereby lose control. Firm working mainly on design-and-build of specials or short runs of goods in mainly wood, metal and some plastics, for the laboratory, university, museum, and (extraordinarily) several theme parks, and others. Basically fully reputable clients who will always pay, but market expansion very limited owing to its special nature. Del called me in. Well, frankly, we had a bloody good weekend together in the (he's in High Wycombe) nearby Cotswolds. I suggested a sleek and low-cost product design initiative to run alongside and out of his offices, with a few carefully chosen people.

"What on earth for? – he asked. Well, I said, if we can identify ideas or problems or challenges that need solving with new products, we design and test solutions, then the profit leverage you can use when the right _other_ manufacturer/sales firm is identified, is so much greater than you, Del, can make, making items yourselves. This way you'll have a parallel consultancy for nearly nix turning out potentially high profit based products and, under patent protection, you can go on profiting from those ideas for maybe around 20 years. Del said that this sounded a bit beyond him to bring it to fruition, so would I, Elliott, please help and steer it."

"I begin to understand where your mouth takes you sometimes! That day you committed yourself to saving his firm. Mmmoh."

"It's been the most extraordinary fun, Sloane! We called it 'Needs Must' and – yes! – I've spent quite a few Friday evenings/Saturdays down there with The Team. How did we collect The Team together? We had a quiet but inspired meeting with all the staff – I appeared as a quasi-consultant! – and we told them just about exactly where the firm stood, financially and how the future looked. Then we gave everyone lunch. I do believe in lining stomachs before asking people to commit their know-how and loads of time to kind-of ensure the future.

"Well, after lunch, we did exactly that. I remember saying something like: 'Some of you won't be up for this, and that's really OK. YOU have to put YOUR backs behind the base company, and keep *that* as efficient as possible. But for others of you – and there will be quite a few who offer themselves, I imagine – and we'll have to consider all comers; some of you'll be given a chance to take four hours – only – off the main production a week! You'll also be asked to add another three hours of your free time – for free to start off with – and in that 7-hour-day a week, to respond to the enquiries for inventions for new products on the market place; and for this commitment, the company hopes after eighteen months to award you slightly and appropriately.'"

"We'd better go, to catch Derek when he arrives; talk more on the way."

While walking, I continued in shorthand: "11 courageous people came forward. We needed four. We chose Keith, a natural manager-type with a very 3-D brain, we took Cliff, a metalworker, who understood maths and mechanisms, Chris, a wood craftsman with a lateral mind, and Marina, a Girl-Friday, used to a spot of painting, presenting, and a real dab hand on the drawing board. Oh, and Derek and me. My first contribution was to say that a firm that works as Dell's did has a certain culture. And that culture usually excludes being able to see things anew. So, once a week, we took another, public, place – a sports pavilion, a library, a small hotel, a motorway service station – wherever we didn't have to pay more than a few shekels – and the team worked there. Still does. Today's the usual day for design development together. Perhaps that's why Derek's coming over."

As the cottagey-door in the middle of the upmarket Chelsea eatery opened, there just inside the entrance was a sort-of-huge man with a mop of blonde hair. "Del!" "Derek" we both said, and slipped inside.

Chapter Twelve: 1974

Marriage Blues

Set up completely to Live the Life. I'm driving home. OK, so I work in medical research in Gloucester, and we live in Birdlip, the village at the bottom of that massive hill you all come down when you leave the Costwolds and head for Wales. First child about to arrive, and Charlotte ready in every way we can think of. Nursery ready, the layette (god, what's that? I had thought) almost out awaiting the infant's arrival. Two cars so Charlotte's independent. And a local regime of efficient and conscientious health people to cope with any malady. I'd prefer a boy, but whichever. Pity you can't tell which beforehand. *There's an idea for someone to invent...!*

Two years back, almost, that fabulous wedding behind us (I can still hear the echo of Lesley's speech – and her prodigious applause at the 'Red Dress for Elliott if I Wed' bit) – wedding behind us, we were off to South America in pursuit of the Inca civilization. Some honeymoon, that! Some climbing! Neither of us will EVER forget it... Bit ambitious and active, though – for a honeymoon. Since then we've been living in a social whirl, getting the house straight and 'getting pregnant' – not as demanding for me, and I realise I'm not the one that gets to feel sick all those months.

Charlotte has set herself up down here with half a dozen yoga classes, four of these are in schools in Gloucester, and the other two – which she truly prefers – are in a War Memorial Village Hall nearby. Apparently the vibes are altogether better in this little hall. No wonder! At these Gloucester schools, she's let down left, right and centre, the rooms are left either dirty or unheated and are, in winter, very draughty. They are school gyms or assembly halls and can suddenly be the base for an exhibition of – for a peaceful yoga session – quite inappropriate, rather ugly, daubs. Add to all that for these evening sessions, occasionally the caretaker's gone home and therefore the place is locked up for the night, with absolutely no notice. And the get-out! The group likes, I gather, to have a candle burning at the end, while they all concentrate their minds and meditate and then, standing, hold hands in a communion circle to express their joy at being together. BUT dead on 9pm – the contractual end-time – instead of allowing a few minutes to quietly roll up their yoga mats and take the kit away, the caretaker will have burst in and created privacy mayhem.

Anyway, to cope now in her late pregnancy and over the time of birth and – well I call it "swaddling" – when a mother can't really do much else, she's breast feeding, changing nappies, playing with and trying to quieten baby down from his or her natural inclination to bawl; anyway, to cope for six months or so, we have her friend Beth taking the classes. But Beth has no car, and can, on foot, get to the local venue, but the town venues will have to rely upon clients picking her up as buses don't run that late. I suspect, in emergency, I'll be doing the Beth trips to help out...

We've fitted in to the local society well, and as a couple, we're moderately popular. We invite people in and we get invited back, which I guess is the normal commerce of semi-country life for middle class people. Am I happy here? With my work, certainly, very exciting – not for ever, mind, I'll need to branch out soon. With my home life? Mmm – well, time and this baby will perhaps tell.

Now I paint a glowing picture. Always been good at that. But in a mo you're going to re-meet Charlotte, and she has a different take on nearly everything. Makes out I'm a selfish bastard, which, after only two years of marriage, isn't a good record. Maybe after twenty years, a wife of mine might reasonably take up this point, but NOW? On the brink of the first birth?

"Hello, darling, good day? Did you remember the dry cleaning from that High Street place? The bills are on the kitchen table for you to attend to this evening. And it seems you never got back to that plumber, right? The leak's now worse... And that Shirley's been on the phone a couple of times – please get back to her – no idea what, no. And you were going to pick up a curry for us both tonight. Bring it in, I'll put it in the oven for a bit later. Do hurry, *please* darling."

So much for a couple of 'darlings'! I've done none of these things I've so-called *promised* to do. I work my butt off with my research colleagues in the hospital. And I come home to this, nightly. If I get my time-travel binoculars out, I see myself as a bent old man at 55, still saying sorry – and *still* trying to get all the things that She Who Must Be Obeyed has asked for, pronto. All this, writ large, might make a discussion paper on Arthritis in the Elderly, especially Married Men." But I jest. My research at least is serious.

I could do without all this. I've done just *so* much for her – well, for us, together. Maybe those oh-so-still green eyes across that crowded room in Singapore, were only just so much come-on, and the stillness was just that – idle. Every couple has to work out their own subtle game of weights and balances so we can all actually live selfish lives, doing what we want to, but trying to please others as well. It's a wonder marriages work out as well as most do – the odds must be stacked so heavily against. It's not like say *friendship*, it's not like our *quad*, where all four of us meet from time to time - and we *truly* love one another and are *really* supportive. Friendship is *key*. Marriage is a convenience – some say a contrivance – to many to ease their loneliness and to vex couples into bringing up kids for fifteen or twenty years.

*   *   *

A Chelsea Christmas

It's Christmas and we're in Chelsea with Charlotte's family – somehow they can afford to keep an enormous house in the very centre of Town that can absorb us – that's now Charlotte, me and three-month old Magnus, all smiles and gurgles and pee and poo – but divine; Charlotte's brother Robert with his wife Minx and their twin daughters Georgia & Joanna, who both so charmed us at our wedding in their bridesmaids dresses; as well as younger son of the family, Dirk, who is unattached; and at least two – I lose count – single or widowed, anyway aging, siblings of Florence and Cedric. A real FAMILY Christmas.

Cedric and Florence and I get on inordinately well. The letter's come from Downing Street offering Florence a Dame-hood for her outstanding work in the arts world. It's hard for a political conservative to turn down stuff like this, as they're all born to *expect* it. So, protestations about others more worthy, and such a surprise, will, I predict, over Christmas and by the New Year, have settled into a responsible YES.

Although, until his death, I never knew Cedric's age, he has about him those characteristics of alertness, sharpness, wit and alacrity and, that makes one metaphorically hang about his neck the soubriquet: 'Young-for-his-Age'. I delighted in their company as two mature people who each enjoyed and – it seemed to me – gained by indulging in honourable argument. If for one moment one doubted Charlotte's parentage – or for that matter, Robert's – one would have crossed a taboo line in the stair carpet that might then bar you from their door and their hospitality for life. And that's odd, bearing in mind the open-argument lien of the couple.

Of course, this not-mention-parentage notion was my personal take on the situation; people are pretty good at emanating through body language and parallel phraseology those areas that are no-go, taboo.

With good intention, we had arrived on 22nd December, quite early for Christmas. It gave – as I didn't explain to their daughter – several long brandy-and-cigar-featured late evenings in which to talk, after Charlotte would most likely have gone to bed, and before Robert, Minx and Dirk had joined the house party. Florence would leave all the clearing up to a maid who came in in the evenings for events and this Christmas period. So the three of us would sit, beside the entirely unnecessary roaring log fire, deep in almost club chairs, brandy goblets warmed by our hands, Jamaican cigars emanating their strong-soft odour to the night; actually, Florence smoked those little cigarillos and drank port. One day, I thought, all this smoking will be banned. But not yet.

I listen to their concerns about politics and the arts. Cedric has to have his say about PM Harold Wilson, "Ghastly little man! Whenever he sticks that horrid pipe in his mouth and says, striking up, 'I want to be perfectly frank 'frunk' with you...' you know he's about to come out with a really big whopper! – look at the pound in your pocket speech!"

"Yes, dear," says Florence, "but he did get Britain Working Again after your darling Mr Edward Heath nearly closed England down. He's won three elections to date, and may yet win more, so the Man on Top of the Clapham Omnibus thinks he's sort-of OK. I don't take to him any more than you do, but his argument is usually seamless and his time will pass, no one stays forever. I think we can put up with him for a while. He's an economist and who better to see us out of the present shenanigans?"

"I regret it's our Mr Heath that's the problem. His kind of opposition is simply not seemingly coming from the common man. Where are you on all this, Elliott?"

I reply, thoughtfully: "If only I could see good men and women leading the Liberal party, I really would want to back it. Jo Grimmond's decade of office should have been our identifying moment – a fine leader, a moral, upstanding, distinguished man; but it didn't happen. When we took upon ourselves to promote to leader the one showman the party possesses, we knew little of his history, we were reaching out in hope. But, now, it reaches my ears that Jeremy Thorpe has a more 3-D, Technicolor private life than us members knew at the time, so we're destined to more unfortunate years on the sidelines. I regret."

"Yes, Elliott," says Cedric, "I have some sympathy, if not with your political view, then with the position that the Liberals find themselves in. Moving on to you personally, do you ever think of entering Politics? You'd be very good!"

"Yes, dear," supports Florence, "I think our Elliott would make a fine future leader of the Liberals!"

"Well" ripostes Cedric "I didn't say that – I thought that, when you get to be 40 plus, you'll *naturally* become a conservative, like sloughing off the skin of childhood!" Laughter all round. A sip of Cognac, pre-warmed in the palm. A pause to reflect: the Big One, asked at the hearth of my most ardent well-wishers – well, since Monica anyway – who have it between them to advance my life...

After a lapse I speak: "I feel a move coming, in my bones, and, yes, in a slight way, I hope politics will be a part of it. I can't tell you how frustrating it feels to be like a prophet – well, someone with far-sight – trapped in a human body with colleagues who expect only the humdrum of me as of themselves. More than others, I probably have the tools of logic, analysis, argument and an ultimate urgent concern for the peaceful survival of our human race, and its animal kingdom too; more so than others I currently meet. I cannot from my present position as a medical researcher, a position in which I shall, if I continue, do just what Mother and Monica said –learn more and more about less and less – till I can no longer communicate with those of other narrow specialisms."

"Hear, hear" Florence adds with almost applause.

"Yes, using these tools I seriously need to communicate with people in power." I'm warming to my subject, now: "I don't need a 'constituency' of people, I need private access. I suppose all this sounds incredibly pompous, but with you two, Cedric and Florence, I feel I can have my head and explain properly where I'm coming from. I have this ghastly ability to see every side of every argument – makes me quite contrasuggestible in everyday life – and I need, constantly, to find ways to express the – shall we say? – talents I have, in a useful way for the world. Yes, bugger the country, it's the world. And, pardon me or not, bugger 5-year parliaments, we need long distance thinking. Does Harold Wilson have a department responsible for really much longer-term thinking? So that today's decisions can be taken in the light of further goals? No!" – (I'm almost tub-thumping!) – "he believes that 'A week is a long time in politics'. So – and here's the sixty four thousand dollar question – how do I keep a wife and growing family in the manner etc etc, when what I want to do is advise and consult with the high and the mighty over weighty questions such as climate change, power generation, deforestation, the over-use of meat, the ozone layer, mass population problems, food supply for all these people from a static-size one-off planet, Earth....." I stop, I'm over-doing it. A glass of water, I catch my breath. I'm asking for the impossible. Maybe I'll outstay my welcome here if I'm not careful...

After a pause, when Cedric glanced at his wife a moment, he said, more quietly than before: "Now, Elliott, we've heard you, we believe in you, and, yes, we are probably the most influential people you know at this time." A pause. "And yes, Flo and I will talk this over together, and I guess we're going to have more chats this very week while you're here, and I welcome it all. I cannot promise you very much, and we have no red carpet to lead you to No 10, MI5, GCHQ, the Foreign office, the Tate, the South Bank complex, the Arts Council" – a glance here at his wife, a current member – "the BBC, News Editors, Think Tanks – in fact all the institutions across the land. But we take your point, and will see what we may be able, through introduction and persuasion, to do for you. You'll have to undertake to co-operate and actually go and see these people – even if your appraisal of them isn't a wholly good one. Now I suggest, for tonight anyway, I'd like to enjoy your company in other ways. Young Magnus, have you opened a savings account for him yet? We'd like to make a contribution – and we'll keep a careful record so we can give similar moneys to any further children you may together have. And Robert, of course – More cognac? Port, Florence?"

Book Two
Settling In

Chapter Thirteen: 1959

Edinburgh University Medical School

Waverley Station. How often we would arrive and depart from this iconic railway transit place over these years of learning and living! Waverley Station has a sense of straddling the old and the new cities, somehow hoisted slightly above the valley where the river runs, well beneath the ancient castle, with a taxi-way rising up to this fine road slung across the valley. Well, in our penniless student ways, more of a walkway *beside* the taxis!

Our little group of four permanent friends – now called Quad, after we had entertained nearly all of Bedales in the Quad with our spoof debate, had discussed where to live in Edinburgh. Over the vacation (oh, yes – we all went to Venice together) whether to take a house for the four of us, or intentionally split up so as to 'spread ourselves more thinly' at this university and medical school, or – last resort this – live in university Halls of Residence; or, the most interesting prospect and the one we finally went for, to get a house for about eight or less people, we being the ongoing resident four, others to join us as and when. Lesley and I already being an Item, it meant that Derek or Shirley could have a Special Friend to stay, short or long term, and we could take 'lodgers' – not that we anyway weren't lodgers... So we had (by pre-term reconnoitre) found a house for the right number and money just off the Peffermill Road, where it's quieter, only a short walk from most uni buildings.

Just a two mile bus ride or walk to the sea at Leith, with quintessential Edinburgh right there – The Royal Mile, Holyrood Palace, the Castle, Grassmarket, Lawnmarket, Cowgate, and so much more, all, as pedestrians, on our doorstep! What a truly grand studentship we seemed to have set up for ourselves. Within weeks, to augment our meagre grants, we had all got little part-time jobs – Shirley, as we might have expected, was an Extra at the Pleasance Theatre, covering in other's absence box-office, props room, or assistant Stage Manager's role – anything, really; Lesley was helping in both the Official and the Fringe Festival Offices in innumerable ways; Derek was attached to the Edinburgh Tourist Office and would become massively important in the summer when they mount the Military Tattoo (his height, 6'2" may have got him this one) – and I was by now a regular leader of historic, night and dungeon walks around the old city.

We'd all settled down into the timetable of uni and medical school lectures, tutorials and – frankly – bloody hard work. This becoming a doctor is no breeze. But it's got to be done, and we're doing it. My tutor is an ex-doctor herself, and she clearly prefers uni tutoring to the workload of either general practice or hospital specialism. None of us has yet decided what we want to do in final doctoring; this will come after the years show up our interests and predilections. We've all been assigned a portion of a dead torso, rich-to-the-nose in preserving formaldehyde. I share a man in his sixties with three other students, the body well preserved. I get his upper right hand side. In dissection practice, I'm supposed to share the work with a Chinese girl called Ling, who's been given the dead man's lower right hand side. And for heart and other organs that happen on one side only, I share with an Irish lass called Sinead. Our fourth is Pru, so one man and three women. I wonder how our relationships will develop as we tackle this grim task, the total dissection over the next two years of this body. We've had the group courage to give him a name, which seemed to humanise his lab number a touch. Yes, I hear you asking, it was my idea to name him! He's now called Isaiah. Well – no one minded and it seemed faintly aspirational and other-worldly.

*　　*　　*

February 1960 Winter Distempers

Christmas has gone – spent with families all down south – and here we are in a freezing February, trying to get on with the simple matter of living. Never mind work and studies, we've got a cold house, with at least head colds all round – some of us very flu-ey and others much iller; there's snow and ice outside and our bills are mounting. Lesley does the bills for us all, but, having someone efficient doesn't keep the costs down. We need coal and logs and electricity and gas and we can't really afford any. We've two 'lodgers' in addition to the Quad four at the moment – Pru, who dissects with me, and Gladys, an acting/ stage management extra friend of Shirley's. None of us has heard of anyone in our generation called Gladys – so she's exciting for that alone.

We try to cook communally each evening – which saves money and enhances relationship, fun and story-telling. We're down to our favourite simple plonky red for Fridays and Saturdays only. We're trying to *like* water more... Our main trouble is obvious but a bit unsolvable. We're too generous. Lots of people come round, and 'seem to stay' for supper – and it's a really good thing that we have this one big room with a coal stove and *enormous* table and we squeeze up to 20 in here when we have to. But getting anything like the value of a meal out of the visitors is like getting blood out of a cadaver. Yes, we love their company, their stories, their entertainment and they *do* give good value. And, usually – we being a base number of six, we sit down to dinner with perhaps nine or eleven of us. Over a week, Lesley worked out, we 'do' an average of nearly 30 *extra* meals.

But I love the company and the ambience, so what to do? Tonight, Shirley comes home with two young men from the Pleasance – actors, who will be on contract to be at the Pleasance for maybe seven or more weeks. And they've nowhere to live. We've not met them before, and so we feel short of the kind of engagement we like, which is to know people through and through before inviting them to stay or live here. But Luke and Mark (maybe Matthew and John will follow soon...?) – homosexual, indeed – will only need one room; but they're asking for the last room (very small as well) to do their daytime rehearsing and line-learning in. We suspect that they'll use a lot of fuel during the day while they are alone in the house. And – they usually won't be in for the evening meal as that is when they strut their stuff on stage. I know I most regret not having them here for that communal moment of an evening, just to check out all's well. During absence, resentments can build up.

Well, you guessed it. We took Luke and Mark on for a period not exceeding 20 weeks, saying that it's not our practice to have people living here who don't usually eat with us. They saw some resentment here and offered more than we individually pay into the kitty by way of rent – 80% more! – saying that they knew what we paid, but they have an allowance and they're working rather than learning, and can afford it. They also showed such enthusiasm for what we were doing they'd love to cook for us and eat communally every Sunday at lunch time – would we like this? So it all came good in the end, and they did stay well into the summer, leaving as the Festival programmes opened their doors. And, I add with a greater perspective, they've been intermittent friends all our lives; but latterly have been living in California.

* * *

Autumn 1960 Festival Memories

In the summers, when the Festivals are on all over Edinburgh, we're spoilt for choice: do we all scarper to the South of England and parental home-spun life, go abroad on explorations and adventures, take jobs wherever we can to help support our next academic year, or – and this is the crux – stay on in wonderful Edinburgh while it temporarily triples in size with tourists and event attendees? The chief question is that of money: on paper, Lesley points out, we'd be best off letting the whole house to a well-to-do group of travelling players from, say, China, who can well pay much more than we do for the house, are in the UK on government grants, and bob's your uncle. There's a really good, if a bit under-the-table, market for this. Except, except. Always except! They must have the whole house on their own to have a place for the group to meet socially and relax together. So – what's the problem? The problem is that Quad are *so* into theatre things. Take Shirley and the Pleasance: this theatre may be about the only live theatre to stay open in Edinburgh throughout the year, but in the fuller Festival time of about six weeks it takes half-the-year's annual turnover. So all staff are on three-line-whips to turn up throughout the summer... Lesley is of course running between the two Box Offices – Formal and Fringe – a long quarter of a mile – and is wanted now more than at any other time of year. Derek, who's laid aside his work for the Tourist office, is not only stage managing at the Military Tattoo (he's been upgraded) he's also taking small bit parts on motor cycles, in a non showy way. And I? Well, less compulsory than the others, but the need for me in my position as Edinburgh Old City Walks Leader increases about six-fold, and I actually make reasonable money; well, a doctor wouldn't agree, but it's OK to a student.

So! We realise that we won't make as much as half the amount – adding all our emoluments together – than if we scarper and let the house intelligently. We even toy with the idea of moving say ten miles further out, and renting more cheaply, then commuting in, so we could kind-of get the best of both worlds. Actually, we keep the house on – laziness, possibly – and we hutch up our living space, with Del and Shirl each taking a tiny room (they normally have larger) and we let – somehow! – four bedrooms and our big reception room, us Quad, for our social space, putting up with a small front room, normally a bedroom, as microwave/toaster/ kettle/two-hob kitchen for these warmer months. We let to some street artists, who act dumb all day in their white-clown sad-faced imagery, but, when they get home, are as lively as a bunch of crickets. So sometimes we join them, and at other times they join us; but only occasionally, we're out most nights on duty here and there.

It's been a fun summer. I think I managed to attend sixty seven shows, or thereabouts. Edinburgh in August seems to quicken the step and add urgency and vim to our energy. If I wasn't on walks-duties, I'd call round at any one of maybe 50 different venues (there were many more...) and offer to help with anything for up to three hours, just to get me a free ticket for the evening. I could do that twice in a day and get to two shows of an evening. It would have been good to have done this with Lesley – or the others – but the exigencies of the day precluded such additional joys (i.e. everyone was so busy with their jobs and theatres that combining would mean the loss of that opportunity to get in somewhere free). So Lesley and I, in bed late at night, would wearily tell one another of our separate evenings' exploits, and often take a tip from the other to go to this or that Fringe show. Regular Fringers know how to play the month (well – Three Weeks plus week Nought!) and the whole thing, apart

77

from any of the other festivals – International, Film, Book, Tattoo, etc – is simply gigantic and, to give you a horrible medical simile, is a bit like cancer. The Fringe alone, having grown from just 6 shows in 1948 to the immensity of 1500 shows today in 1960.

*   *   *

Quad Reconsidered: Characters

Lesley and I, then joined by Del and Shirl, are taking stock of Quad, our friends foursome. We all own up to having had a lot of strain way back in February when everyone was poor, poorly, cold and hungry. We've all got to know each other incredibly well – even our silences are now enjoyed by each and no one feels under a social obligation to break them. Derek says he finds this quite profound. We are each aware of the selfish needs of all the others, and acknowledge them and feel they can each work with these – limitations? I comment on this: "I'm not sure that peoples' selfish needs are their limitations, although taken to extremes – rape, murder – I can see they become so." People are puzzled about this.

Lesley thinks: "I should be careful, Elliott, else we might not accept your selfishnesses if they become too gross."

She had a good brain, so, much later, careers advisers reported that she was clearly motivated to study medicine. It was a privileged girl who, at 15, arrived at Bedales, her father scraping every penny; but she started off as a day-pupil, as the family by now lived in Petersfield, her father working for the council. She's very close to her father still, and feels for him and his sad marriage all those years ago. Hermione is still running the house – I've been there with Lesley – and I think I detect that Lesley is very, very polite with Hermione, she recognises the sacrifice of those years to bring her and her sisters up, but this is a relationship with some residual strain, it's not a natural. There's a story in the family – said kindly enough – that Phil, her father, when he gets home, pats his wife and kisses his dogs. I think it may have been true.

Del – Derek Widmer – is the son of a family with a factory in the Cotswolds.

His younger brother Ned and he had seemingly belonged to a family that was quiet, industrious, and superficially happy, but very undemonstrative. No show of love or affection attended their arrivals and partings. Yet they fully acknowledged each other, and, had they been asked, would have stated that they did love one another; but that word 'love' would be hard to utter. It's altogether remarkable that such a lad – and Ned – should both find themselves at Bedales, a school which is not part of the main flow of education, even though it gets frighteningly good 'O' and 'A' level results. It all comes down to an endowed grandmother. She had herself been to Bedales, and was at the time of the boys going into the school, well into her seventies. She still had oodles of persuasion power *and* also loose purse strings where she wanted to make an impression. Yes, she was a personality, and needed her ego polishing every now and then. Mr and Mrs Widmer, Derek and Ned's parents, simply didn't have it in them to argue the toss, and so, for a quiet life, they agreed to send their boys to this – to them – strange school. Mr Widmer had wanted Derek to be trained in a trade so he'd be appropriate to take over the family business, but Del had, early on at Bedales, seen that he could better himself by reading medicine at uni. He was very quiet regarding sexual relationships and somehow we didn't press him.

Shirl – Shirley Shawley – is the daughter of a mid-European psychotherapist and an Egyptian money-lender, with her long red locks, and her penchant for dressing in bits of pink here and there, is our outstanding show-off, exhibitionist, fun-girl, and joy to us all. It's much less difficult to see why the now-single Madame Shawley (we think this may have been a name made up by herself to seem to have a semi-English background, and maybe she meant it to be Shaw, but something went wrong...) should send her only daughter to Bedales, than why Shirley herself had decided to read medicine. And I'm *still* not sure! But she says she had an unruly background, not exactly un-moneyed, as the Egyptian money-lender was frequently in touch and sent money orders as and when, but they frequently moved around and set up here and there, and she feels an ongoing instability from her background. So, early at Bedales, when the careers people get talking to you, she had happened upon the idea that to have a profession would be a more stable way to live. And so that had emerged after much sifting into a desire to do good for people and that meant reading medicine... I wonder. She is, we're gathering, very keen on the theatre in all its forms, and can magic up a lovely display of flowers from mere ferns and some daisies in seconds. She's also rather good at character acting, and can be an impersonating witch, empress, bag-lady, whore within moments of the request, usually making use of an odd curtain or mac that's lying around. Sex? We don't have time to talk to Shirley about sex. The very idea!

Finally, we thought that too much introspection would lead us to not enjoy each other's company for fear we would be keeping a weather ear out for psychological oddities. Rather, we should enjoy our group, help each other where we can, and not review again for a long time. Unspecified!

* * *

1961 Party Prospects

"I think you'll all think this is good news, I'm not sure. Please gather round. I've some info for you three and some others. Seems my aged father and mother have decided to throw – and that's *their* word – a huge party for me for my 21st birthday which is as you all know the 1st July this year. Parents are the very end, they give you the impression that the school fees completely cleaned them out and asking for money for our life up here has been a polite silence and now... they're going to spend thousands! But will you all please come? It's so very important that I have my best, my confirmed friends there! So do say yes, please."

Lesley: "God, yes, Elliott, we'd love to come, I mean where? Do we have to stay over? All sorts of questions. Do I have to climb into a dress?"

Shirley: "Yes, I'll come, Elliott, of course! Anywhere, I'll dress like a lampshade! I can fit in under the stairs for the night!"

Derek: "Invitation, please, Elliott old boy. Then I can see the details. Sounds great, I think..."

I say, reading: " 'In Wisbech, on the Brink' – don't ask what that is – 'under canvas and outdoor', wicked to do in a public space, that's the Aged Parents for you."

Chapter Fourteen: 1982

Inventions

"Derek – we've met before, haven't we? Or is your name – like Lesley and Shirley – so intertwined with Elliott's background that I can't tell a real meeting from a pastiche of recalled memories?" This is Sloane's weird longish intro to Del. She must be aware that to some extent I'd kept them apart, so Sloane could not easily propose that I should do less to help Derek with his business. "Not truly sure, Sloane – I've always been intrigued by that name! I've built you up into some sort of Mrs Danvers, shielding your precious Elliott from the vagaries of the World of Commerce and Industry – maybe so you can get his face-tints right for Newsnight!" A gauche attempt at a joke, I realised, but my intimates from differing worlds are clearly struggling to find a common basis for social exchange; no doubt it would settle down soon. I guessed I couldn't help much, so turned to choose a more esoteric wine at the back of the menu. "I guess my unruly mop of the blonde stuff is something you don't get just anywhere, especially on a bloke, so if you're a touch surprised, then we meet for the first time, and indeed hello again, and if not – we've met before; so sorry, can't remember"! I think this all very laborious and decide to break in.

"Del, you phoned – the matter of great importance. Shall we do it now, before we're gorging in prandial joy? Err, you can trust Sloane. Getting secrets out of Sloane has been described as a monkey puzzle with no monkey, a nut with no crackers." A sublime little smile to herself, Sloane seemed happy with these metaphors.

"Yes," says Del, "OK, well, it's all to do with this Patent on the *Nebuchadnezzar* project. Maybe Design Registration is enough. If Julian says we can't usefully get a patent, and DR seems like wishful thinking, then we may have to rely on a Non-Disclosures Agreement; which ought to be OK, but nevertheless the idea is then out there."

"Sloane," I explain, "we innovators do tend to regard the entire world as our enemy during the development of a uniquely new product, and commercial thieving is commonplace. Julian is our Patent Agent, and advises us without ever getting his hands dirty. He sits behind a desk and refers to precedent and the very exacting – but not very exciting – writing of copy."

To which Sloane, with as even a tone as she could muster, retorted: "Close now to teaching grandma to suck eggs. Perhaps Derek never told you, Elliott, but Del" – phew! She's used the diminutive at last. But they're getting no closer to a symbiosis... – "rang us about four years ago wanting to ask you to locate an excellent Patent Agent and Solicitor, and I passed on Julian's details. Julian had helped me with my Outdoor Car Picnic Rug about ten years ago. Nowadays he's a friend."

I exploded with joy: "Why, Sloane, this is great news! Is it still going well? Are you still receiving royalties? I *must* keep the bits of my life *unnaturally* separate. Never knew a thing."

Sloane: "For a self-confessed General Specialist, *very* separate! But I forgive you – this once! – you were deeply involved in the Glyndebourne Trust at the time, hardly came into the Orifice." Our perhaps naughty name for our office was a way of sharing a degree of intimacy and social street-wisdom with Del. "Yes, the product range did well in the UK and parts of Europe and is now made and sold under licence in the States and across Asia. So I have every sympathy, and some know-how, with your Consultancy's aims, Derek. For very good *other* reasons, I try to help Elliott live the life he's said he wanted, and I've frequently wondered at his deep involvement in Cotswold Concept Creations. It never looks like it, but he necessarily has to spread himself so very thinly in each area to fulfil his enormous diary commitments."

Food arrives; the wine we've been imbibing for a few minutes now. It's a Chateau Red with the crinkly glass bottle; actually Chateauneuf du Pape 1976, more main line than I usually buy. But reassuringly expensive. I often eat veal, to the disgust of some of my more-aware friends; nevertheless the *Saltimbocca alla Romana* is so out of this world, I reckon I deserve it occasionally. Del's gone for a really plump fillet steak, medium rare, and – when the waitress, the lovely Rosalie, asked him if he wanted chips, he glanced at his newly-developed, over 40s paunch and said "Duchess would be just fine" Sloane and I, exchanging slightly-smiled amusement, looked on. She ate venison. Broccoli all round. We could have had Samphire – Norfolk seaweed – for starters, but we'd all opted to have it alongside our main dish.

Sloane: "This, Del, you understand, is the little light lunch that Elliott and I enjoy together oh! at least three times a week!" Thanks goodness Del's ear for irony is switched on, as sometimes he can take these delightfully English no-smiles humorous nuggets a touch gauchely. But he's thinking hard: He says: "I wonder...I wonder..." a longish pause. "Out with it, Del, don't choke!" I say, lightly, wondering. Eventually, with obvious care, Del continues: "Would there be any mileage in – I don't want to upset your obviously really successful little ménage at the...err...orifice.. nevertheless I gather, Sloane you work part time for – or maybe it's with, Elliott. It may be that your brain is just what CCC is in need of, and if so, it would free up Our Leader to go on excelling in his many fields of endeavour?"

I decided to speak into the vacuum: "Take no notice of me, really, anything that gets your outfit properly, long term, back on the road should be considered. But I believe Sloane protects her Other Life quite jealously. She runs a stall in Camden Market on Saturdays. Apart from that I'm not privy to her life!"

Sloane: "That's the bit I guess I don't really *like* about you, Elliott. I could have said *all* that – and a little more, perhaps – for myself. But you will keep thinking you're God Almighty and plunging in. For the life of me I don't – with these celebrities – know how you don't burn your boats – well – *ALL* the time. But you don't. Oh, never mind. Del, you're probably on. How about I take a trip down to Burford this Saturday? Presumably I can see the factory and the CCC office then? And talk turkey?" Del: "Oh, surely, you'll be very welcome, I'll meet you at the station and take you to The Community first for lunch, we can see the Works in the afternoon. Err – I don't think we'll be able to do venison..."

Sloane pricked up her ears, looked sharply alert: "Did you say 'Community'?

For real or just like The Rectory, The Tennis Court – names for things that used to be...?

Del: "Oh, for real. Nine families, that's eighteen friends, all with or intending to have children, bought this magnificent old 35-acre estate, and it's been one of the best decisions of our lives. But not to talk about extensively over lunch – I can get quite loquacious about Taynton when given the chance. Most people enjoy their visits but say 'We admire you, but never, never for us, just couldn't.'"

"Yeeerrss" says Sloane, warming now to her subject and clearly now getting on with Del like a house on fire: "But, you see, this is what I do as well. In Muswell Hill. It's called simply Muswell. We were going to buy four adjacent terrace houses in Mornington Crescent, but that fell through. So – Muswell it is! Unlike you, we share the ownership of our building." She glances at – I guess – a now impatient looking me, and completes her sentence: "Look, this'll keep for Saturday, too. *Now* is a business lunch, yes?"

"Actually" I say "I live in a community too. It's rather large and has five or six billion rezzies now, and we call it The World. You may have heard of it. You two probably have wee population explosions too, but I have a colossal one across The Earth. About this afternoon, this is what we'll do:" I can't seem to help taking charge of things. It's the result of pretty well always knowing I'm right. Never mind. They'll get over it... "I'll have a quick B&B pudding, as it's ordered, then I'm going to scramble back to base to start to deal in one tiny way with the World Population Explosion. Do you know China is thinking of bringing in a law to prohibit couples having more than one child? Unthinkably fast progress, but what it will do to their society, heaven can only guess. I mean, at a stroke, to eradicate from the current dictionary the words: brother, sister, aunt, uncle, niece, nephew, cousin – it will be deeply difficult for them. But courageous. So I'll leave you two to talk communities and inventions for as long as you like – Sloane, please pay for everything with the firm's card – and pop back, Del, and we'll look at that NDA agreement you've sent across on the fax. Good company, I enjoyed it, bye."

The last of my pud in my over-anxious mouth, I turned to get up and go – and found myself face to face with two images printed probably deeper on my subconscious than my own mother and that monstrous Monica. "Hello, my darlings, Lesley, Shirley – how did you find me here?" Many hugs all round and some kisses, with polite handshakes for and from Sloane, and they sat down for a moment to catch breath and put some sense into all the maelstrom of to-ing and fro-ing.

Lesley spoke, her hair still brunette, but now more of a short nearly-boyish, definitely unfashionable crop: "Elliott, we all had an iffy get-together tonight, which Del seems, Sonya at Taynton says, he's forgotten, and which you didn't know about. Reasons too complicated and don't matter. So – we usually descend on either your Chelsea Base, or down at Taynton. And here we – hopefully – are! Please say you're on for tonight, Ell, else it'll be a threesome again."

Sloane said: "Either I get a word in edgeways now, or I'll be out of this conversation! I do know Elliott's diary, and he's definitely no longer going to the modern rewrite of Ibsen's 'a Dolls House', by Claire Booker, with Clement Freud, as that gentleman's poorly tonight and we've got the money back for the tickets."

Shirley's turn: "If it wasn't all so damn interesting, I'd say 'too much information'! But, what a life, Elliott, my love, you'll never cease to surprise us. So – we know you're OK, Del, as Sonya's not expecting you back till the wee small hours or even maybe a late breakfast."

Del, slightly confused, scratching his blonde mop vigorously: "This is all very well, jolly good and all that, overwhelmingly good to see you ladies as always, but I need to take stock. I was just then staying back in the restaurant to talk with my new friend Sloane here about an idea we've had for the betterment of CCC – and also of Elliott's diary. Is there any way we can jointly or severally work out how we can all be happy, but uppermost in all this is me getting to talk with Sloane?"

The silence was a touch deafening. Eventually Shirley spoke "I always hope, dear Del, that one day you'll learn to put these things more succinctly. Never mind, vain hope no doubt, and we love you. Elliott, Your Country Needs You, go to your orifice and do your bit for the World, and Lesley and I will go window gazing and even shopping in wonderful expensive Chelsea. Del and

Sloane can plan mutiny or whatever together, and we all – well, if Sloane would like to come too, maybe we'd all like that? – We'll all meet up at that South Ken coffee lounge we like at 6pm. Can you save the world in that time Elliot?"

"No, but yours is a good arrangement. Let's do it. Now!"

Chapter Fifteen: 1996

Deaths and Disclosures

In the garage beside the mews aspect of my office-and-abode, lies a 1965 Jaguar 3.8 litre. Jaguar boss, Sir William Lyons' maxim of 'grace, pace and space!' I find it fun to drive out on special trips to the country, to slip down to Brighton, or up to Wisbech – or perhaps to take a trip with a friend to Italy or Greece. Wire wheels, leather upholstery, burr walnut fascia! I understand from my mechanic that it's hard to keep in good working order these days. I don't worry overly about this as it's his kingdom, and he can take all the time he likes to get the auto running well. He worries that if I'm in Italy and I break down, then no one over there is going to fix it for me... Tant pis...

I scarcely use the Jaguar for my consulting work, as I have an electric car for that – also in the garage – and I think it's only right that I set the example here. When I bought this in the late '80s, there were so few electric cars on the road, so I had a challenge, and settled on a GM Impact car *prototype* – one of a very few cars available from General Motors to Those in the Know. I had it privately altered to run for 200 mile trips between charges by putting three times as many batteries in the car as was standard. This made for a heavier car than had been designed, but with plug-in house-supply electric juice, I had – for the time – an excellent if small conveyance.

This autumn day is a sad one. The Jaguar and I, with Camille for company and convenience, are heading up what used to be called the Great North Road, and by now is merely the A1. In due course of years it'll be more fully the A1(M), the Motorway! But for now, with not so much traffic on the roads, the A1 will do just fine. Wisbech is our destination, and it's to say goodbye to our father, now dying of prostate cancer; and of course it all depends on whether he stays the course in this nursing home until we get there.

Camille has stayed the night with me before we depart. We're still good company for each other, at least we are for the limited time we get together for these days, and so we're each looking forward to the journey, and will probably lunch at the Comet or the Clock on the way up the Great North Road.

On the open road, we've time to take conversation in a leisurely manner.

"How did you get on with Mother when you stayed over – and how was Father?" I ask.

"Well – Mother's much more independent these days. She's 78 now, but –apart from *looking* elderly – her back is good and straight, and she doesn't seem to have hip or knee problems... Yet! It's the confounded *independence* that gets to me, though. Remember, she used to be such a depressive, so dependent on Father..."

"I gather you're not promoting the idea that she should be more depressed? I guess it's a good thing – and certainly it is for us as Mother will shortly be living completely on her own. With you usually in Canada and me involved in a million things, we'd neither want her on our doorsteps – or crying down the phone for hours."

"No-no, I explained it badly. Of *course* I agree with you about her *happy* independence. It's just – I don't quite know how to put this – it's her remoteness, her coldness, her couldn't give a damn I'm staying with her – *that's* the stuff that's upsetting for me; and perhaps I shouldn't think about myself at all."

"Well, indeed, this may be the case. But I think you see a wider inference here, don't you?"

"Yes, well, I wouldn't want to think she was friendless – there's always bloody Monica, mind" a quick sidelong glance to me as if to say 'there's <u>always</u> bloody Monica' – "and there's no one else nowadays – the Elgoods have moved or died and there's no one else in her life. Seems not to mind, though. Just wonder what might become of her in say five years time. A recluse? A dementia case?"

"How about I reserve comment till I see her? But your comments are really wise and helpful." I change the subject a touch. "And how is Monica? Of course Ralph died last year, didn't he? Her approach to her 'pathetic' – as she called him – husband, may now have backfired and she might miss him dreadfully."

"As you know, Elliott, Monica has a Special Relationship with you, but no such thing with me at all! I've always wondered why that is... Anyway, yes, I *did* see her when Mother and I called in at the new Costa Coffee Shop, and indeed drank coffee! Monica passed us on her way out and kindly stopped for a brief chat. She did all the talking, Mother said hardly a word and I just chipped in a few comments while Monica drew breath!"

"Yes. Monica seems to have button-holed me into her life. I can't tell you how rude she was about Charlotte on the day of our marriage. Maybe she had a point there!" – we both smile at this – "But she has stuck up for me her whole life through; she's the reason I went to Bedales, for example. D'you remember, when dad had his clinic for failing old men and their bladders, do you remember that, at 5pm, Monica used to come and sit in the waiting room, waiting for him to usher her into the dining room – his consulting room. You remember – we used to watch through the banisters?"

"Yes, yes I do. Do you think they used to have it off with one another, right there in the consulting room, under his secretary's nose, so to speak?"

I ponder a moment; "Yes, this could well be the case... If you think what a drear Mother used to be, and the half-hearted Sir Ralph also, it could well have been a Weekly Fuck of Convenience. 'Thursday at 5 my dear?' 'I'd be so obliged, sweetie.'"

Camille and I let out a guffaw of coarse laughter. "The truth could be stranger even than that, Elliott!"

We now talk of general and her family things. How are they in Canada? How is her husband, Maurice and the children? The business? Satisfactory replies to all of these, and we draw into the forecourt of the Clock Restaurant for lunch. A lazy drawn-out sort of a lunch, we're fond of each other and don't much look forward to getting to Wisbech and all our parental woes.

I go the lazy way, via the A47; and we're soon there... Brinkmanship in parking is essential, and we walk over to the house to see mother first.

"And I was just going out! Suppose you'd better come in, <u>both</u> of you" says mother, her hair on end like a dog's – and the emphasis she puts onto the word both is impolite and inappropriate. "Your father's very, very ill" she adds as if we didn't know.

"Were you just going to see him?" I query.

"I was going for a _walk_" she says dramatically "Leaving _you two_ to visit _him_... I'll just get you a _cup of tea._" She bustles round her kitchen like a house-on-fire, cross and trying to smile at the same time.

"Mother, Mother dear, don't fret so," Camilla says plaintively, "We don't need tea if it's a bother..."

"And we thought we'd take you out for dinner tonight, if you'd like that?"

Brought up to a halt by my proposal, Mother tried to be nice. But it was clearly a great big effort. So we let her do her cups of tea; then we pushed her out of her own front door to go on her precious walk. Dishevelled, we got off to the hospital to see dad.

*   *   *

The Cottage Hospital Visit

The hospital was of that Cottage Hospital type, the doctors having done the most for him that they could when he was in the Peterborough Main Hospital some weeks beforehand. Here they can give palliative care, looking after his pain aspects as well as current drugs would allow. He was clearly uncomfortable and drowsy and hadn't a whole lot to say to us this late afternoon.

But we prevailed. To prevent any pain transmitting to his body had we, casually, sat on the side of his bed, we sat in chairs, with Dad having a good view of us both. I made the conversation, mostly, Dad being on the comatose side, and Camille being a touch reticent.

"Dad is there anything we can do for you, anything at all?" I asked at the end of my chat.

He forced himself to speak: "I'm ... worried ... about your mother ... she's so bloody independent ... and one day ... she's going to need people ... and I hope it's not you two ... what with Canada and London and all your busyness ... busy...ness.... " He seemed to trail off here, and it had been a big speech for him in his present state.

"Yes, Dad, I know what you mean about her independence," said Camille

"It's a bit devastating to come down and find her so bloody-minded, but we can put up with that. I don't suppose her friends can..."

"Hasn't got ... any" says dad, with slight shoulder shrug.

"No – that's what we were wondering – no friends ..." Camille says

"Well there's Monica!" I say, hastily.

Dad replies, slowly: "Monica is her own woman ... she's not a bosom friend ... she'll do in the coffee shop..."

"Oh well, we'll have to see how single life takes her – after your death, Dad" I say, breezily.

"We don't want to think of you dying, Dad. You'll be with us for ages yet!" Camille euphemises.

"Not so, I'm afraid, darlings, no ... I'll be shunting off ... this mortal coil ... any day now... But listen to your mother ... she has much to say ... about the family in Canada. I guess you'll hear more ... about this from ... Monica too."

"Monica? The Family? Dad, we do realise your health condition. I'm not much good at wishing people a good death as I fear I don't believe in God."

Dad laughs: "Nor do I, old boy!" he says, and brings such bonhomie into the room that we all laugh quietly. Soon our bedside moment has gone and we are away again, taking our leave of Dad in our own personal ways.

"Awkward," I say to Camille in the passage as we leave.

"Awkward for you!" answers Camille "I've nothing to say in these situations."

"You did fine – you spoke up OK."

"Anyway, it's mother for dinner tonight ...Where?"

"How about The Lamb and Flag over in Welney?"

"OK... well I don't know it Is it well-to-do and all that?"

"Just a very few miles towards Downham Market. Yes, very well spoken of."

*　　*　　*

Mother's Dinner

Mother is so impressed by the milieu of The Lamb and Flag – having never been here before! – that she is pleasantness itself this evening. Once started on The

Family in Canada, she doesn't stop. She can see that the two of us – especially Camille, who lives there – now (as if never before!) need to know about our blood ties over there.

While we are on our starters – she has an old fashioned Prawn Cocktail while Camille and I shared a Fish and Olives Board together – she tells us of the history of our great-great uncles who had all made good in Toronto. The Law and Banking and Farming – it had all been to the good of the family. The founding of the Dominion Bank – now the Toronto Dominion Bank – was their doing and we all know from the dividends we receive what value there is in these shares. There is another instance of doing something ahead of time: the purchase of maybe 100 acres of lakeside land some 60 miles North of Toronto, for purposes of providing summer houses for themselves and their families. Still going strong today, these houses have since been over-wintered, and are now fine to be lived in throughout the year; seems as though Camille and Maurice need to visit this estate soon now.

The main course (mother has roast chicken, Camille the duck and I the venison) is attended by some really fine red wine, which soon oils mother's larynx and delivery; and we are into her favourite Canadian cousin, who has sadly recently died, and her family, with her offspring about our age, and "it would be so nice if we could meet up somehow!"

"But, mother, no one told us about these people when we were a whole lot younger!" I expostulate.

"Well – they were all there, on the swimming dock all those years ago when we use to spend summers out in Ontario!" states mother, in a ladylike manner.

"That was so, so long ago, mother, dear," says Camille in a friendly way "and it would be nice to get together now, I rather think. I wonder if the ages of our contemporaries' children are anything like my girls' ages..."

"Which are your girls, again, Camille?" asks a bewildered mother, taken off her monologue track.

"Really mother! Hermione, Rosanna and Clarissa, who are now 14, 12, and 10 this year – your grandchildren! Remember, we brought them to see you three years ago when Maurice and I were touring the continent and England. You send them £10 postal orders each Christmas, but not for their birthdays."

"So much to remember, so much to remember!" says an exasperated mother; and, to be honest, we get very little more out of her for the rest of the meal. She has Treacle Tart and we enjoy Eton Mess together, and we sit in a happy-ish sort of strained silence, with periodic questions from Camille – who feels to blame for the shut down in mother's talkativeness.

* * *

Monica

The next day – after a mixed-up breakfast with mum, wherein she hasn't any of the normal breakfast goods in the house, and we make do with toast and butter – I call on Monica. In person. On my own. I feel I owe it to her, she having – however rudely – shown such an interest in me and my life, my wife, and my friends.

I ring the bell – a heavy affair with a chain and a clanger to pull on – and wait... Eventually there's a shuffling along a corridor and a winding of locks and withdrawing of bolts, and the door swings open to reveal Monica dressed in a fine – no, a superb – morning-coat-cum-dressing-gown. It's 10.30 in the morning and I would have expected Monica to have been up and dressed by this time. But then I reflect – she's now 83 years old, and perhaps she was out late playing bridge, or whatever. It's really none of my business.

I think feigning surprise at my presence, she nevertheless glides down the steps to hold me in a fine embrace; would that mother had had the grace so to do!

There's mad small talk going on between us. "Oh, but of course, you're here to see your dear father... how's your mother?...Is your lovely sister here too? ...Come in, come in, we must have coffee and croissants! Yes, right now – come on in, Elliott!"

And so we sit, in easy chairs, in her kitchen-cum-sitting room (that she doesn't call a Sitchen!) and we discuss – my father, my mother, my sister, my kids, my business, my leisure time; all, all, all about me. I realise that I'm being indulged; but also that she happens to love me. Compared to the reception we've had at mother's house, this feels good, and I begin to feel I wish we'd taken Monica out for dinner last night and not mother!

I ask her bits about her past, but it's the same as always about her now-dead husband Sir Ralph Mangold and her ineffectual kids.

I creep a little towards our childhood – infanthood, even. She clams up. Says she can't remember any of that stuff. She will let me into only a fragment of her past life with me and with Jack and Peggy. She says that it was great fun having Jack and Peggy around in Wisbech when we were all young, and how she admired Peggy for letting her, Monica, take a hand in, for example, my's schooling.

Then she drops this final note into the melee:

"Your dear mother should have the final say in what goes on in your lives. But… If she dies before I do, I may be able to intrigue you a little further…"

*　　*　　*

Jack's Funeral

The hearse and limos drive up to the house. Wearing black, Peggy and Camille and I leave from the front door. We follow the hearse, as does Monica and her two sons in the car behind. There is a scattering of further people in further cars of exotic colours, also following. It's a sad sight, this little procession of cars, following the men in black in the hearse ahead.

But it's at the church itself that the larger crowd is gathered. The Mayor of Wisbech, the consultants – Jack's recent colleagues – are here in reasonable numbers. We walk quietly through the thronged people, people making way for us, as we get to sit up in the front row, with Monica and her sons just behind us, and some distant cousins behind that.

At least it can be said that my father's funeral is dignified. It may not have touched so very many hearts; it may have been a rite of funeral and burial rather than an outpouring of love for the diseased. But it is that, it's dignified. And for the burial, in the same churchyard, there's a decided hush as the minister recites all those fine words: "dust to dust and ashes to ashes" and the group stays in silence for a good three minutes. The family leaves the graveside last.

Next, we put on a show of coffee and biscuits in the church hall. Nurses from his bedside are here, and they give forth lovely thoughts about what a good patient he has been. The local news was after me to explain what sort of doctor he had been. For once I swallow hard and fight back the inclination to say he was a wee-wee doctor to elderly men, and call him a Urologist.

Mother is more in possession of her senses than on some occasions recently. She leads the way, talking to neighbours in a proud and – I have to say it – a haughty manner. She makes no friends this way, but I believe she's no alternative. Her psyche is so set. I thank the undertakers, when they have done no more and no less than their job, but it seems the right thing to do.

Dad died about a fortnight after we had visited. So this is three weeks on, today, and Camille has been champing at the bit to get back home to Canada. We leave after a sad lunch with Mother and Monica and her young at the most central hotel in Wisbech. Monica gives me a warmer embrace than mother's minimal cheek-peck.

There it is. Buried now. We make our way south in the Jaguar, and are soon home.

Chapter Sixteen: 1982

Shirley in South Ken

South Kensington coffee house. As they arrived early, Lesley and Shirley delved over coffee deep into their current family lives – crises and calmnesses. At the moment, Lesley's man Garth – oh, they hadn't married, so no prospect yet of a red dress for me – was in a sea of mutual respect and sweet love that was a balm to all around them. They had little identical twin girls, Jonquil and Jessica – oh, how they wished they'd chosen names with differing initials! – now nearly 7 and so school was increasingly important in their lives. Lesley had specialised in neurology and was a consultant at three hospitals – the main one was Milton Keynes – all fairly near the little town of Tring where they lived in a now-bursting cottage. Garth was a graphic designer and ran an outfit from a small office, also, intentionally, in Tring, where he and colleagues – apparently – cornered a particular market I could never quite remember – nor readily identify if I was told. I'm supremely happy for her, my ex-lover, and to see her so at peace and suitably partnered is a joy. I am currently alone – well, not *quite* alone. But I feel no jealousy towards their idyllic lives at all.

Shirl (no longer Shirley Shawley) has a new handle: improbably, Carnt. After four years of bliss with Josephine in a lesbian relationship that took them all over the world for fun and fantasy, an unexplained event or tiff or happening in 1977 saw Jo off the scene and completely-disappear (did Shirl murder her? It was on everyone's lips, but so likely did this seem, it couldn't be mentioned, even by way of black humour...) Now she was suddenly with a male (of sorts), one Jerd Carnt, sharing her bed, and amazingly they got married in a rather messy sort of way; and immediately – if 9-ish months can be immediate – started and then continued as an annual ritual, to have children, After four, Jerd had the snip, and there were no more.

But all was not at peace in their sizeable Muswell Hill four-storey semi, built way back in the 1880s. They got along, were really familiar with one another, laughed incessantly, but somewhere between the warp and the woof of the fabric of relationship, it was held together by a constant rasping, an irritability, an unease and a perpetual criticism both had of the other. In social terms, Shirl should have won these combats with her eyes closed, as Jerd was – and intentionally—jobless and was a sort of semi-posh layabout, who cared little for the world and the people around him. Feckless? Perhaps. Evidence of children proved they made love at least once a year, but rumour had it that it was nightly, noisy and ended in shrieks. Whether these were of joy or pain or fear is unclear as observers were of the audio, slightly voyeuristic kind, who heard – perhaps they listened – through walls and no doubt exaggerated.

Anyway, Jerd did his bit, getting the – now – four kids up each day and out to nursery, playschool, preschool or school – my, how complicated our lives are – and collected them and gave them tea and then did all the baths and bed stuff, not so much reading stories as making them up there and then, quite often starting with "Do you want to hear about Fred the Ghost and what he did last night?" – but the scatter of clothes, undies, crayons, macs, plates, drinks and spills that greeted a moderately tired Shirl as she climbed the stairs to kiss them all goodnight, was a couple of evening hours of undoing and clearing up; which is why, we all suppose, Jerd usually cooks the evening meal – he'd never get fed till past nine if he didn't.

This evening, Lesley had said her bit in a minute and three quarters ("Yes, we're blissfully happy, the girls are progressing well at school, the sibling rivalry is settling down now they are in different classes, and Garth has won new contracts for his ...erm – you know – graphics work, so everything in the garden's rosy – except of course the garden, like the house, is too small for the four of us, now the girls are getting bigger and want space for recreation"). So she turned a concerned look towards Shirl, her friend since school, through uni and medical school, and ever since – along of course with Elliott and Del. "And how's life with you, my love?"

Shirley didn't start immediately. Then she drew in a big breath and started. Whether there were tears in her eyes to begin with, Lesley couldn't later remember, but they were certainly welling up before very long. "I should, Les, never have married him, he leads me such a dance, but even now, through it all, I love him to bits. Snip or no snip, it of course makes no difference, he's as randy as a rat with ten new lady rats – and that's just with me. But, somewhere, there's trouble and, although I know it, I can't pinpoint it. He's out at three or four school gates every day and – well, some of these young mums look almost *undressed* when they deliver the kids to school, so – well, yes, and not just one. I can't decide whether I'm relieved that he's not able to get them pregnant, or whether perhaps that kind of fear might have held him back a bit. But it's the feckless bit, Lesley, he *just doesn't care...* If I use words like morals, or suggest he shouldn't take advantage of such young women, he looks at me as though I'm trying to cut off his food ration. If he was attracted to kids – and I don't believe he is – he'd be in there, no second thoughts. I can't get a girl-baby sitter with anything approaching a nubile body, as he's in there; and so many of them *encourage* this.

"Oh! Shirl! I feel for you and also I feel so useless. How do you get out and live a life? Do you go out together without the kids at all? What about that choir you used to sing in? And you used to enjoy pottery. After your demanding job, I guess some recreation is in order. I always thought, with that wonderful mane of red hair and your irrepressible spirit, that you were going to rise above anything that could be thrown at you. Remember those days with Jo? You used to have fun then!" It was a risk, as Jo hadn't been mentioned these last few years, not since she'd disappeared... Not expecting it, she found Shirl in her arms, crying almost loudly, howling at recalled memories of her halcyon yesteryears.

So, with her sobbing friend in her arms, she took another risk. She asked: "Tell me about Jo. We all liked her so much. But since – was it '77? – you haven't spoken of her once, and we don't know why. Surely, once a friend is always a friend? If you want to, or it would help, do just talk about her." Shirley stayed sobbing a few moments longer but less fiercely now, and she was 'coming to', returning gradually to the old normal world.

"Lesley, I've said I'd never tell about this, but I must as I suffer such a lot from these thoughts going round and round in my mind. You see, I don't know where Jo is. She did disappear, yes, but as I knew there was a problem, and I didn't want my friends being questioned about it. So I didn't talk to you. One or two basics: did you know that Jo was Egyptian? And did you know she didn't have a visa to work in England?"

"err – I guess no to both of those. Perhaps you kept those things a bit dark, did you?"

"Well – yes – we had to, to keep up appearances. Then there was the accident..." Shirley trailed off, her eyes wet with memories; she looked half-vacant. Lesley comforted her, but said, softly "I think, Shirl, you're going to kind-of have to tell me the whole story. I had no idea all this was going on in the background to your marriage. What are friends for? Oh, never mind, just talk when you feel like it, Shirl.."

"OK," said Shirley, "this is it: when I met Jo she was in trouble to do with drugs. Just using, not selling. But when the police come round, they get on to your identity. And so Jo was 'found out' and given two months to leave England. But we scarpered and travelled and worked for cash abroad, and for a long time, no one was any the wiser; Jo was seen to have gone home to Egypt. But when we came back and tried living in Acton for those few months, we were hiding her behind my ability to be employed as a doctor, and so we might have continued for decades – you must understand, Les, that we loved each other and wanted to be with each other – forever. Now the accident. I could have killed myself! While I was out working, she drove my car – not insured, no licence – and ... well, it wasn't her fault, but if you're not insured, nor licensed, you'll take the blame. But not this case, it was manslaughter – only after we argued it down from murder."

*   *   *

Shirley's Distress

I suppose it was a good thing that Del, Sloane and I came in at that moment; and a doubly good thing that Sloane, an outsider, really, was with us. I read the look of concern and alarm on Lesley's face and Shirley's racked and tearful countenance. I could see that a lot of things had been said and probably tears had been flowing for a while now. We had never – or not without everyone's permission – brought an outsider into our Quad group of four before. I'd suggested it to a rather timid Derek, but they had had a great afternoon of sharing about both communities and designs, and I hoped the others would enjoy that too. So I stood there and simply told them this, in a quiet voice, and said I'd be really willing, the next day, to help with anything that I could so far as Shirley was concerned. Then I asked that we could please spend a pleasant evening on just this one occasion with the five of us, as Del had made quite an ally today and it was very interesting. So it was agreed and we 'stayed moderate' this evening, no big drinks nor night clubs, simply nice sofa-ey places to sit and converse as friends should who're fond of each other... Yes, the next day, I did see Shirley for a very long and difficult session, after which I called my friend in the Home Office and suggested lunch in an out-of-the-way place down near the river, right up Battersea way, where journos and MPs were unlikely to loiter. Our conversation, on the face of it, was what we normally talk about; but that alibi laid, we then talked of extraditions and laws and relaxations and so forth. When we left I had every expectation of success. But when Shirley soon was making the most extraordinary arrangements to spend a long time overseas, I managed to show surprise when the word Jamaica came up. Friends are for helping one another. Yes!

Chapter Seventeen: 1995

A Career Pause

I've decided to give up. For ever? Not necessarily.... To take stock and see where life's got me so far. Lesley's here – remember her? First met when she was 15, I was 16, at Bedales in those heady co-ed days; we were lovers and continued so through uni and med school and then... we parted, but always remained the strongest of friends – for company and for argument and for fun. Together, at school, we made a pact with Derek and Shirley – who were *not* an item – that we, called Quad after the place of our first success together, would remain lifelong friends and a support system – for whoever was feeling low. And, as we did at school and uni, we would meet to argue.

"Hey, Elliott – concentrate! Get those eyes off that PC you're slavin' at!" – she fakes an American singer feeling hurt – "Hey, honey! Show some respec' will you"?

"Sure, Lesley, I'll make some tea – what do you want, love? Earl Grey, Builders, Lapsang, Mint?"

"Lady Grey, if you please, kind sir!" She comes over to the sofa and snuggles into a cat-like pose in the sofa corner, looking delicious and fragile – it's very typical of my very good friend. I adore her still, years and years since we were lovers, but if you can keep the good bits going, there's such a charmed life ahead. OK, so her marriage has worked and mine hasn't. Tant pis. It's of no concern to us together now. How often do we get together? Once in three months, perhaps, no diary date, just when we feel like it but no stress, just us.

"Anyway, what did you especially want, apart from all your normal selfish pleasures, this time, Elliott, my sweetie? Oh" – she remembers – "this bloody book" – she apes me being big – " 'My Memoirs' – but, Elliott you're only 55 – I know 'cos I'm 54 – and you're about half way through your life… Footballers do this, only worse; publish their 'life stories' when they're 27; and then, published at 38, how drugs and drink has subsequently buggered them up; and then, at 49, how not all their money went on drugs and drink, the rest went on constantly de-toxing at The Clinic. If I was sort of famous as I guess you think you are I'd want to do one book and one only. Probably when you're 80. No?"

"For once you've found me out, doing what the world does, which as you know, I deplore. My technical publisher's put me onto MacMillan and they want to force an auto-biog out of me now. While I'm still popular, they say behind my back – well, to my agent then. So I've resigned from several Quangos, and told my direct clients I'm away on a sea voyage and can't talk to them for several months; and, anyway, I want to catch up with my children – Magnus'll be 22 by now, and Lillibet 20. And" (my voice gets very quiet here) "I want to try to see Charlotte again…"

"What's that you say? Speak up! You want to see Charlotte again? I *strongly* advise against this, Elliott, she'll tear you to shreds psychologically, and leave you feeling dreadful for ages ahead – again."

"Well, Lesley, she's my children's mother, and I certainly loved – or was it adored her – from a distance? Anyway, I *thought* I loved her for those few years. And I have the money and the time now to be … kinder – to see not only my best friends, but also those that life's rich pattern has thrown up alongside me along the journey. Remember Pru? Seeing her next week – for an objective review of life in the Edinburgh house together; also, as one of my partners with Isaiah, our dissection body. She's in the same field as you – well, here we come, that's it, you'll say a Neurologist and a Psychiatrist aren't within a million miles of each other! *But* – they clearly *are* quite close. Specialism, specialism."

"Have it your own way, I'm much more interested in this Charlotte thing. Tantalising Ms Green Eyes Plus Vacant Yogic Expressionless Expression – and No Answers, Ever. You surely remember? You were married to her! Now, Elliott, I know I sound like a jealous wife, going on about Charlotte, but you know I'm not that. I do this because I *really care* for you and your good fortune and happy life. BUT I can't just give up. I'll get Derek to call you up, he'll do it after a bit of stuttering. You've only ever had hell when you've tried to see Charlotte-with the-sexy-green-eyes. Men and testosterone!"

"You can ask him tomorrow. Del and Shirl are coming over. I just selfishly wanted you to myself for the first day. Then we'll have a good time with both of them too. No, I didn't tell you, I kept it a secret – a surprise!"

"Well – thanks for asking them. We've a lot to catch up on, the four of us. Quad... Who'd ever have thought such an alliance of friends would last nearly ... forty years... Shall we have a party for our 40th? When will it be? I guess the anniversary of that naughty debate – Mass Debating Society! I ask you! I'll hunt out the date. Do you know, Elliott, my twins are now 19! No doubt up to all the naughty things we did..."

"Perhaps one day we could risk all four of us bringing all our children to see how the oestrogen and testosterone go down across the mix. Mine at 22 and 20, and your two at 19 and Derek's boys now 19 and 17, and Shirl's gang – 18, 17, 16, 15! Wow! What an idea! – and can you remember Shirley's kids' names?" I throw down the challenge.

"Sure – here goes – Harebell's the eldest, now 18. Then there's Sorrell, then Delilah, and the boy Xavier brings up the rear at 15.... Your Magnus must be the eldest at 22, with your Lillibet coming next at 20, And Derek and Sonya tried the bit about bringing back names that have fallen into disuse through association – Quentin was OK, but I feared for them with Adolf, but all's going well, it's as if he's called Fred! And my twins, Jonquil and Jessica, have got used to having names with the same initial – for short they're called Jo and Jee... each at a different uni now, so they love each other again, like when young kids."

"Jo – which reminds me. Shirl's Jo. Glad we were such a help to Shirl over her Jo business: being in love carries all sorts of weird extra characteristics, but sheltering a worker from overseas and allowing her to use your car without a licence..."

"Worse still, covering up her exit from England. Glad that aspect never hit the light of day. By the way, what happened after you took over? So many years back now..."

"Lesley, you said at the time you didn't want to know! It's all of 13 years ago now – so… why not? I merely talked, very much off-the-record, to my contact at the Home Office. They have countless thousands who've defected, one way or another, and some they really do want to bring to book and the others – well, so far as the public is concerned, there's an ongoing effort to find them; but actually… you know… Anyway, I spun the story in such a way as to intrigue him – love-torn partner needs information so she can feel her friend is safe. It did the trick. People actually like helping each other out, makes them feel good when they go home. Within six weeks, we had an address in Jamaica, and you may have noticed that Shirley had that sudden urge to explore the Caribbean and was away some eight weeks! – far, far too long to trust Jerd for, and as you might have anticipated, she returned to mayhem and some other pretty young single women and their kids installed in the house. What happened after that was rather nifty footwork, and we must get Shirl to remind us tomorrow. Right. That's enough State Secrets. I'm cooking tonight. Do you still like you steak medium rare with parsley butter and exotic veg – I can do you beetroot and asparagus – OK?"

"Lovely, darling" and indeed she was speaking as it turned out of the whole evening – lovely it was.

My so-very-central London office was a masquerade, a facade, a Russian Doll set. It was situated on a quiet but accessible street with adequate immediate parking. Near the entrance there was indeed the posh, Charles Eames-chaired reception, press-button posh coffee, current copies of The Spectator, The Investor, The Whatever. And Private Eye. Through from this front area were simple services: loos, tiny kitchen and a room for photocopying, faxing and making up brochures. An office for myself and an office for Sloane. And an office for no one. Just might have been a partner or you never know quite what.

Through from all these 'front' services was a small business dining room with dining and lounge chairs, and a kitchen. It served as a boardroom or a bigger-meeting room, or a place for a special business dinner seating up to ten, and a cosy where Sloane and I spent many of our lunch hours, casually.

But now for the unexpected: through from all that, was another aspect of the building, curiously looking out now into a Mews. The scale was different and cottagey and lovely and very domestic. It was my home. Of course, Sloane knew of its existence, but she never ever went in there. Her's was a business relationship, and she held on to her private life and her perception of her roles very tightly. This is why I had not known about her 'community', Muswell, till our visit with Derek.

And it's in this 'home', in the cottagey bit at the back, that Quad used to meet. It's also where I, if feeling in the mood, might bring a lady home with me for the night. The entire premises served admirably for a General Specialist who couldn't see the advantage in wearing out shoe sole leather walking home; nor paying another private mortgage as well as the business one. Being already at home saved perhaps two hours a day, five hundred hours a year, and, if one has a forty year working life, then twenty thousand hours, which is a touch over two years.

And this is where all four of us, on the next day, celebrated love, life and ourselves – we ate, drank, argued, talked, slept a bit, had a wee walk; not far, just down the mews, came back and ate again. There came a point when I said to Shirley: "Yesterday, Shirl, I was letting Lesley into a few Home Office Caribbean secrets – hope you don't mind but it's such a long time ago. Anyway, I'd just said that on your return to England after your special, long stay away – Jamaica might have been involved – you had to take a firm hand at home 'cos of Jerd's behaviour. Then, what did you do?"

"Yes – well" reflects Shirley "I was on the sharpest of horns of a dilemma. Many things to consider. In the end, I converted the basement into a self-contained flat for Jerd and his entourage. He accepted the rules. He was to look after the four children on Mondays, Wednesdays and Fridays, during which time the internal access door would be unlocked, and none of his fillies was to come around on any of those days.

"However, he was allowed to do as he liked – fillies by the dozen, did I care anymore? – and during these times – Tuesdays, Thursdays, Saturdays, and Sundays – the interconnecting door would be locked shut and he had no access to any of our children on those days. I changed my job to casualty where long hours get your week's pay into three days a week's work. Every Mon, Wed and Fri I was off at 5.30 am, and got home typically at 10.30 at night. I got food on the way home, no nice suppers for Jerd, and very few late night kisses for the young ones. Occasionally, come the weekend, if Jerd is doing rather badly for fillies, we'll have supper together, and he and I can see the kids all at the same time. The system works. I've got some super kids, now aged 15 to 18, so nearly adult.

"Thank you, Elliott, my darling, for what you did 13 years ago. I think it was seeing Jo that enabled me to find the strength to do all this, and survive. Jo and I correspond, and chat on a thing called skype which some of you mayn't have yet heard of – on your laptop, picture of your loved one the other end, and you can chat for hours I think. I get holidays because Del and Sonya – thanks as always, Del, my love—take the four of them for a fortnight a year, letting me really get away. Jamaica soon! Not always, though..."

A beautiful silence fell, not one of us wishing to break it, we were so together. After a few minutes, when if felt right, Lesley said:

"Elliott and I were yesterday talking about all our now-mostly-grown kids and that Quad will soon be 40 years since the naughty Bedales debate – ha ha! – and we wondered if it would be good sense to ask all ten of our children to something with us – essentially a Day Out, a Break, a Happening, whatever. Obviously Del's kids know Shirl's quite well anyway. Just a matter of adding four more... Good idea? Not?" A long pause; and then everyone spoke at once:

"Why - yes!" "Why not?" "What a good plan" "Why didn't we think of this before?" "Too wrapped up in ourselves no doubt" "Where?" "How about Del's big place?" "Terrific!" "Done deal, then" "Well – OK Del?" "Sure, OK – summer though" "Happy about this, when Les?" "Summer's OK, best year, 1996, any date to suit – OK, I'll be the organiser – send me notes of your best dates then."

Now they changed gear and helped me with my Memoirs. That took a long time, down memory lane; my tape recorder taking the strain.

Another night together and then they were all off. Probably 36 hours was our natural maximum. 48 hours and there might be squabbles. Yes, even between such good friends.

*　　*　　*

Magnus Lillibet Charlotte

It's Tuesday. Magnus is here with me. It's not the greatest of relationships – my surprise departure from the marriage those 18 years ago, my apparent abandonment of the children, Magnus's mother Charlotte never ever giving a good account of their father.

"My dear son Magnus! Thank you for coming today! I've got a nice lunch for us to have here in a while. Haven't seen you in – is it three years now? How did you enjoy the last two years at Bedales? At least I've been able to finance these things for you three. Mother well? And pretty Lillibet – good too?

"I find it odd calling you Dad as we haven't been together much. But Dad – that was, as usual, too many questions! Is it what you usually do with people? Or is it you're shy with us and over compensate?"

"Shy, I'm afraid, sorry. You can't know how much I *want* to have a good relationship with you, but know I don't deserve it. I just hope that as I now age gently into the inevitable abyss – as indeed I have been – and you become a man of the world, we can do – well – just a little better."

"Yes, Dad I hope so; I kind-of enjoy your company but not until afterwards! Sorry, that's silly.."

"No – it's brave talk;" quietly, gently now: "Tell me of your dear mother, please Magnus...?"

"Oh, Dad – you know! I try not – any longer – to blame you, but something went out of her life those 18 years ago – well, from others I gather it may be longer, but I don't understand that. She's such a limp soul, with –and this is her take alone – apparently nothing to hope for, no future. She listlessly gets through the days... She might have been better off if you *hadn't* been supporting her, she might have had the gumption to get out there and earn it via her – so they say – excellent yoga. She doesn't even do yoga for herself nowadays. Her parents – Cedric and Florence – have been so endlessly kind – always going that extra mile – which they also were to you, Dad, is that right? Lil and I think they're both saints, never counting the cost, always willing to give. But – you know – they're really getting on now, really old. 79 and 83. But they still have the big house and big Christmases – you remember? But what of mother when they are gone? Uncle Robert's not really any help, although he tries to be. Not sure why. I do go on rather, don't I?" He smiles.

"Like father, like son? No, no, I love you to talk. You're relaxed, I like that. Come here more often. Anyway, I think I'm seeing Charlotte here on Thursday. Messages a bit mixed at present."

Magnus pauses; then: "Well, Dad, I shouldn't if I were you. You know how it's gone, Dad, every time. You get left in a heap of unnecessary guilt and remorse, and she swans off as if nothing has touched her. Your life is so important to everyone, we can't have you left in that way, for days – well Lesley says weeks, sometimes. Please just cancel."

"Dear Magnus! It was my soul-friend Lesley who was here a few days ago, and did her very best to get me to cancel. I know when I'm loved and cared for. By you two anyway... But no, as I said to Lesley, she's my children's mother and she deserves human civility – and my ongoing thanks for having cared for you two all these years. It's when you get to your kind of age that some women begin to feel very useless, their brood have fled the nest, and they've nothing and no one to mother. She needs kindness."

"Dad, if you do this, I suggest Lillibet comes round with her. Lil and I both drive these days and you've lots of parking here. But I counsel against the meeting entirely." And doesn't he sound very grown up? Smaller than me, neater and tidier – and thinner! – and with a wide smile and very charming; a very presentable young man. Glad he's turned out so well. I change the subject.

"So! You got a 2.1 from York. Architecture it's to be, then? Or – finally – architectural teaching and journalism? I suppose you'll have to see. And an attractive young man like you doesn't go about on his own, I guess? Some nice ladyfriends?" I shouldn't have asked, but I see him so rarely.

"Dad! Really! Does one have to respond to questions from one's dad like that?" But he's smiling the while "Have no fear, I'm hetero and enjoying it and careful. Err.. they say – it's a school fable really – that you re-started the Bedales debating society with a sign reading Mass Debating Society and got almost the whole school out! Is this true?"

"Yes!" I reply "and the people I did it with – Lesley, Derek and Shirley – are still my close friends, our 'Quad' group. We had the greatest of times. One day I'll tell you what the motions were and who said what. Memorable!"

"I wanted to say – I always try to see you on your TV shows and radio bits. I'm always immensely proud. I used to have to do it in private so mother didn't know, but now, who cares?"

"Fine. Good. I ought to tell you to prepare for my father's death shortly. A Wisbech funeral. Prostate, I'm afraid. Yes, our sex is good at these. Sad for my mother, though. She's batting on OK-ish."

After a pleasant lunch together, he was shortly away – to meet friends in a coffee shop somewhere near the Senate House. Good on him! Great to see him.

Thursday dawned all too soon and the afternoon arrived for tea for Charlotte and Lillibet. The conversion wasn't hard, it was non-existent. Lovely to see indeed very beautiful Lillibet, off at Bristol uni learning all about palaeontology and ancient history, and, normally, very good company, but with Charlotte there being 'not there' and odd, awkward and silent except for 'pass the sugar'. She didn't look at, nor smile at me once. Completely vacant. If I asked her a question, there was a pause every time, then Lillibet would answer for her. So – not much use for the autobiog I've been persuaded to write.

They were gone Inside 90 minutes and no particular harm done. I wasn't more than slightly depressed and I'd done my 5-yearly duty, sort of.

*　　*　　*

Camille

I hadn't seen Camille for a while. My sister still looked strikingly lovely and gracious as she walked in, wearing a skirt in these days of perpetual trousers. We sat with Earl Grey tea and shortbread and looked out through the mews windows to the drab day out there. We talked her life for a while – married Maurice, had three little girls – Hermione, Rosanna and Clarissa – now around 14, 12 and 10, I think – and spent much of her life in Canada, where Ralph seems to need to manage a lot of real estate, and at the same time run an inventions company in Montreal. (We'd tried doing a tie-up with Derek's firm, but things hadn't materialised, so we left it). This way I don't get to seem to see much of her, and she's such good fun. But now we have Dad up in Wisbech nearing his end. Any Power of Attorney to anyone? No, nothing she says, mother will look after everything. What about that big old house on the Brink, full of brown furniture nobody wants? Well, that's all staying and it will see her out. Mother's marbles all staying are they? She's not lost any yet that she could note.

So –what will Camille's movements be in the near future? Yes, I will go up to Wisbech to say my fond farewells and spend some time with mother. He's expected to die sometime in the next three weeks. Yes, Camille will stay in England till the end, unless that gets too protracted. If she wants a bed, a room, I can oblige. She said, occasionally when up in town, that would be lovely and we can have some dinners together. But she's many people to see all over the country and she's going round, bed-by-bed – "I'm even going to see Giles, that rascally cousin what nearly went into the River Nene on your 21st!" With warm love and good wishes, we said our goodbyes and I'll see her soon no doubt.

*　　*　　*

Pru

"Pru!" I say as she enters, coated up against the weather. "Have you come far? With STD dialling I forget where people *actually* live. Really lovely to see you!" We plan, later, to go to the little brasserie on the corner, but now we have an afternoon to get to know one another again. We had first met with dead Isaiah, the corpse four of us dissected at Edinburgh Medical School, and then we got chummy and she joining our up-to-8-sleeper student house for a year.

Since then she's been to my 21st with a memorable off-the-cuff reply to my mother. And then qualified and practices as a psychiatrist, and I've seen her about three times at gatherings and events. Oh! And she came to the Braziers public event and helped that day. So this is a rekindling of lots of old times. However, she wanted to talk about sex. Yes, surprising.

"Elliott tell me straight: are you involved or committed to a woman – a person – in a sexual relationship at the moment? No? I won't beat about the bush – anyway they're mostly shaved off these days – I like to come out with it so we know what's expected." I decide to leave Philippe out of the conversation for the moment – and no, I'm not *committed* to Philippe, I just have the occasional night with my Filipino friend, have done for years. "No, more's the pity – none – why?" I say, innocently and curiously.

"Elliott, I always fancied you and I find I *still do*. But you were with Lesley, then you married Charlotte and then – I don't know – we fell mostly out of touch. As it happens, I haven't been to bed with a man for a – now – very long time, and I'm getting – irritated at my – shall we call it condition? In plain English, can we come back to your snug tonight after dinner and can I stay the night in your bed? If you say no, that's honest, and kind of OK. But I guess I'll never have an opportunity with you again. It's sort of Now or Never. You decide."

Deja Vu.... Oh, it's such a long, long time ago... Out of the mists of the past emerges a tall, slight girl, we were probably both 14, can't remember.... yes, Caroline, that's it! My first time ever – but not her's. She brazenly asked for a bunk-up, a one night stand – because she wanted to notch me up on her totem pole, as all the girls thought that, one day, I'd be PM, and she wanted an early...memento? And I would only play ball (huh!) if she'd make it three occasions. Breaking all the rules of a very young lifetime, she eventually agreed. Is there a Caroline out there who's still hoping I'll become an MP and then reverse those letters to PM? Caroline could, now, be Pru...

Back to Pru and her proposal: it's kind-of marvellous that, these days, without prostituting herself, a woman can make this request. Not a blush, no sign of shyness. Just out with it. I do pause, though. It just doesn't seem seemly to rush in with a quick yes.

Slowly, I drawl: "Sure, Pru, that would be fine and lovely and I'd enjoy it. Stay a night or two if you'd like. I'm kind-of on a Sabbatical. Now, to change the tone a touch, how about a cup of tea?"

Tea was good and we remembered many things. Dinner was excellent and we laughed a great deal. Bed was best, no hurry, wide awake, nice long slow caresses; she had a sweet, very responsive little body, and I loved every moment of that night... In the bleary morning she got me breakfast in bed – and then we snuggled down again...

Pru stayed three nights and each new night was somehow better. Then she left. Never to enter my bed again? I wouldn't have missed it for a moment...

Chapter Eighteen: 1997

Dame Penelope Laird

Penel has asked me to her Lake District hideaway! In mid-September. Here am I at the age of 57, and I'm surprised to find that I'm a bit excited about this... She's a Dame of the Realm, no doubt about that; but she's no need to invite me to Ambleside – in that clearly she needs nothing from me except my company; and that's a charming thought. So, having buried my father last year, and finding things a bit easier on the consultancy front, I am happy to up-sticks and away. Train or Jaguar? I go for the showy way of doing things. The Jag it is. It's a Wednesday afternoon, and I'll take it easy up the motorways and get there about 8 or 9 o'clock. Dame P. I know from the Arts Council – and perhaps our habit of chatting on about this and that while proper business is in progress, has led to this invitation. Or maybe our trips to the cinema...?

She's a good fifteen years older than I – which at about 70 puts her in the retiring age for normal mortals. But she's turning out fiction at the rate of a book every eighteen months. She has to travel far for her subject matter. It's as a writer she's on the Arts Council; but also owing to her status as a National Conscience, for all her work in galvanising the population into picking up litter, into recycling plastics, into saving petrol by combining car-use, and into reducing the cc level of your car... Yes, where am I going to be with the Jaguar? Oh well... she'll have to take me as the unorthodox person I definitely am! I can't go all that way in the electric car...

7.45 and I arrive. Dame P is there at her half-and-half doorway, looking out through the top half and enjoying the remaining, sliding sunset. I stop the car a little way off and walk to the house, carrying my bag and coat. She gives me the greatest welcome and we embrace as do old friends. She's only about 5'2" and so this is a twisted affair! She's got up in a sort of Churchill siren suit, but prettier; eminently practical, with a bag round her waist to put things into, and today this includes a notepad and pencil, a camera, and – a cooking clock, a cookbook and a wooden spoon! Seems she's trying to add a touch of international flavours to her (normally) basic culinary skills... for tomorrow, anyway. But tonight we have a ham and chicken pie, and salad with potatoes and tomatoes. Simple fair, simple needs. My bottle of Merlot goes a long way to reviving our spirits.

"Your fine car made its way up here, did it?" she queries.

"Yes. Fine – but old!" I say.

"Well... that doesn't mean it's too old for service, does it?"

"No, no, certainly not. I'm fond of her and I hope she's many more thousands of miles in her yet... It must set your teeth on edge – to see I've brought her?"

"No-no, it's your thing... I don't mind what peccadilloes my friends have, now I'm in my 70s. But, having done the long journey in the – err – Jaguar, perhaps in the few days we spend together now, we can use my Mini for running about up here?" I indicate yes with a nod "Then we can use the time of year to walk the hills a bit?"

"Sounds perfect" I respond "have you any aims in my stay?"

"Well... yes! I'm rather hoping we can first check out that we get along smoothly enough – I didn't say brilliantly! – and then I'd like to persuade you to come on some of my fiction-busting trips overseas. As company and for conversation about my subject; AND about yours', of course, too... I expect to find myself at a loss most evenings after, say, I've interviewed half a dozen inuits, and I've taken aboard the bleak, never-ending flatlands where they dwell, it would be very good to have a travelling companion capable of more varied thought and stimulating ideas..."

"...Well, yes, but we know each other now as mates on the Arts Council, as occasional cinema companions, as a joy to talk to one another..."

"...*That's* why you're here for a few days now – to check each other out. If either doesn't like the idea, it's off, definitely."

"And – I was going to say before being so politely interrupted! – I'm not always the pleasantest company, especially when I'm fulfilling another's wishes; in other words, I'm a serious follower after my own path..."

"...And if I can keep up with the gentle interruptions, I'm aware of all that; and I hope to engender some common feeling for the peoples I visit to enable you to feel self-fulfilled."

"Oh yeah? How's this supposed to happen, then?" – said with a smile. "How do you think you're going to appease the will of a self-willed person like myself?" I chuckle to myself, hoping she is so able, as I'd love to travel with her.

*   *   *

The Deal

"I don't want to seem to have looked into your past, present and future too myopically, but it seems that maybe you've come into possession, recently, of information about your mother and her wealth? So, perhaps, on a trip to Northern Canada and Alaska, you might wish to look up the details of the trans-Canada train line, the CPR, which your great uncle on one side of your family is supposed to have financed, and your great uncle – still maternal, but on the other side of the family is supposed to have been the Chief Engineer. Will that do as evidence for the time being?"

I am non-plussed. How Dame P. could have reached this information I have simply no idea. But she has a point – yes, I *would* like, following some research, to follow up on the ground, the histories of these men. But definitely. How will it fit into Dame Penel's work plans, I ask, slightly baffled.

"Oh, I need to travel up the West coast of North America and Canada – yes, including Alaska – to research my novel which relives the lives of Early Man as he settles along the coast here. I need to spend some time in the Seattle area and then the Vancouver area. I thought you might join me for the Vancouver bit?"

"Penel! I can't say how impressed I am with your imagination as to what I'd like to do, and with your considerations as to how we might make this work together... I'm at a loss for a response, except that I'm warming to the idea, and guess our three or four nights here will produce a response from me. Trouble is, will you still want this after I've sullied you with my company?"

"Not much of a problem, there, I don't think; I'm even used to you farting!"

*   *   *

The Projects

So the deal was made, and I found, the following Spring, that I was chasing up my dead relatives and their involvement in the Toronto Dominion Bank and the CPR; and finding out that Uncle Harry had been Chief Engineer on the railroad for which Uncle Boyd – only in-law relations to each other– was Financier!

Now I meet up with Penel on Bowen Island – on the way to Vancouver Island, but smaller, prettier and, as the travel people say: "Within Reach –Beyond Compare!" This is a lot of buttering up by Penel to enable me to see that I'm getting my fill of Family Memories, as Bowen is one of the family names in the history bestowed on me by my mother during dad's last illness.

I get there by using the frequent ferry boat out of Vancouver; and 'weighing anchor' as it were I thought what a thoroughly beautiful place my forebear had settled in. In the few hours at my disposal, I slipped across to examine family records and the like just near the quay. No Bowens this way about these days! Just as I'm finishing up for the day at the family record office, up bounces Penel, in a very lively manner, and so we set off together in search of our lodgings at a small hotel on the water's very edge.

Penel has much news about her research. It seems that, in Seattle, she's discovered that Inuit had been as far south as Vancouver, the tribes of Aleut and Tlingit predominating in her century of investigation. Apparently this makes all the difference re communications back to Alaska.

I take these utterings as read and we move into our wee hotel. Separate rooms for the time being... Over dinner that night we discuss the many aspects of both our works until we dissolve in wine and laughter, and arm-in-arm move out to the splendid night sky over the Pacific; and eventually to bed.

*   *   *

Sadly...

In this way, Penel and I kept up an occasional, but usually annual or once every 18 months trip overseas, she always enticing me with nuggets of personal work I could do in each region. Perhaps my favourite was my visit to see Nelson Mandela, who wanted to be brought up to date with the World Population and Pollution themes advanced at Braziers Park in 1984... Penel visited me in London and me her in the Lakes. All this continued for about seven years. Yes, we made love, in a slowish manner, emphasizing our fondness for one another. But most of all we drank red wine and laughed ourselves silly every time we met. It was an odd coupledom, as, if you saw us together, you would have said: 'extraordinary couple, he so tall, she so short and look, they're laughing fit to gag!'

In 2005, Dame Penelope Laird, of whom I'd grown enormously fond, died after a short illness, to do with her heart and indeed all that breathlessness from all that laughing, at the age of 79. It was my position to read a eulogy at her funeral, along with the Chair of the Arts Council, and two others, unknown to me, but pleasant enough.

Penel's death put an end to my strange trips abroad, chasing up leads from a lifetime of work and contacts; and gave me the chance to actually cover the earth's fine places in my Round the World in 80 Months.

Chapter Nineteen: 1977

Making Omelettes

"Thanks, Taffy, you've put me on the right path. I said when I entered this 'open field' idea for a life-job, that I'd need all the contacts I'd made, and you having moved to Guy's has just given me that link with an income, that I'll so certainly have to have. Bye. Cheers!" Taffy Temple had been my tutor in Edinburgh, and now he's doing much the same thing down here in London. My actual interview with Guy's Hospital Research Department is tomorrow, but it feels like a dead cert. The Plan is patchy yet, but workable.

Leaving the family in Gloucester for a year or two, so I can get my feet under enough tables with enough people to pay a decent salary, Shirl – one of us Quad – is letting me use her flat in Belsize Park while she's off with her girlfriend Josephine on a round-the-world trip-of-a-lifetime, taking jobs here and there as they go. Of course, Shirley's a doctor, and she mayn't get that kind of work overseas, but she's a great social hostess, can get by with a photocopier and typewriter, and can cook a killer goulash. Josephine is in the PR and also the alternative therapies fields, so we guess these likely lasses will do well in faraway places. I am getting a two-days a week 'job' in medical research at Guy's, to keep the wolf from the door, and Cedric *and* Florence are very kindly running a series of coffee mornings, breakfasts, teas, and the odd dinner, at their Chelsea home, to introduce me to the big players and movers across the capital and further. They feel that, if I scintillate with ideas and intelligence at these events, then, little by little, people will want to take me on. And this 'take me on' means give me paid consultancy work – allowing me free-thinking outside the narrow limits of their bosses' instructions, outside their budgets, outside their temporal restrictions.

In one way it makes no sense. Next week I meet Melvin Bragg, who doesn't control the purse strings of any business account I don't think, but Florence found him at the Arts Council and asked him, and, as the South Bank Show is resting and he's already got his book to the publishers, he's kind-of free. Incredibly – but again what will I do with it? – I'm to talk to Jo Haines, Harold Wilson's press secretary, and it's a start. A very competitive woman conservative MP is also coming over – I gather she may stand for Leader of the Party shortly. She's called Margaret Thatcher. A chemist who invented soft ice-cream! I ask you... But again, she might see the great value of reforming the Patents Act – unfortunately a world matter. So she may come to nothing, but you have to start somewhere.

I haven't got consulting rooms at the moment. No way am I asking chairs, presidents, mayors, members, ministers and PPSs to the humble but delightful abode in Belsize Park. So I've taken out membership with the Institute of Directors – a very fine Nash building in Pall Mall. At this illustrious 'palace' one can hire conference rooms of almost any size, and also eat there in considerable style, and 'clients' can be shown in by their fabulous flunkeys.

No one has asked the only question staring YOU in the face: if I get no business, gather no moss, where to next? How and when do we say 'No!' exactly? In order to keep pessimistic thoughts away, we've all put effort into *making* it work. Lesley has said she thinks it's *absolutely* me, the right thing for me to be doing – not for anyone else, mind, nor for anyone else she's ever likely to meet, of course. But for me, an especially encouraging hug and "That's instead of flowers as I don't see where to send them, exactly!" It's true Del has taken more time to get his head round it, but that's normal, so his comment "Well... Elliott.. old pal... It certainly wouldn't be for me. But if it fits, wear it. Good luck to you! Do well!" Didn't really surprise me, and is pure Del all the way through. Shirley had been much more involved, owing to the flat, and so I'd had a couple of dinners with her, sorting everything out. These three friends of our Quad are coming with me all the way. I really love them. Yes, even doubting Del.

*   *   *

Charlotte

I'm driving back to Gloucester and our home. I've probably spent least time preparing Charlotte, little 3 year old Magnus, and tiny fifteen month Lillibet for the changes to come. Obviously, Charlotte has been involved, but, if I'm honest, a little icily, I think. Well – no ordinary wife (hey! – Charlotte is no ordinary wife...) would be easy about a husband giving up a suitably recompensed, five-days a week, job local to where she's living with two kids under four, for a London two-days-a-week job, admittedly at a higher day-rate than Gloucester; with all the absence and coping-alone stuff to go with it. Florence, being so keen on my scheme, has tried to put Charlotte more in the picture, but... Yes, I'll sell one of the cars – she can have her choice to go big and have mine, or save money and tootle about in her tiny tin. I'll use public transport in London and can hire taxis when needed occasionally. Trains back to Gloucester are very efficient, fast, comfortable – and allow me to read.

Frankly, in our last talk on all this, we were pretty deeply opposed. I said that I *had* to do this new life, else I would go mouldy, bad-tempered and begin to hate life. I pointed out how her parents were so *very* fully on my side, helping a ton, but this cut no ice. I begin to think that, apart from those at Bickley Grange, this may be the first argument in which I can find no compromise in myself, and where my usual, rather forceful, nature has – for once – failed to make it to the other shore.

I park in our small, quite neat, front drive, and lift the overlarge fan of flowers from the passenger seat. My key in the door; warmth and light and human happenings are all at once there. My darling little Magnus rushes over with a never-ending "daddy daddy daddy daddy, love you, daddy, daddy" and infant Lillibet – who I guess I don't know quite as well yet – looks up from her mother's arms and simply shrieks for joy. So far, so good. Then I look into those green and indeed wondrous eyes for my wife's joy and acceptance too. I have to say that the look back is still in my memory, in my heart, today. It communicated just so much, not a word spoken. In that look I caught suffering, accusation, regret, hostility, fear, non-co-operation, and a rather horrid overall snideness. How can looks say all that? Did I imagine it from my guilty heart? Well... Some, maybe, but it wasn't what I'd expected.

When she spoke, probably all of two minutes later, it was terse: "Flowers? So – obligations over? I'll take them. I've no other joys, no life. Bath the kids and do bed. Yes. *Now.* Dinner at 7.30." I tried to kiss her, she brushed me away. Both kids were getting the point – of the hostility, not the *actual* point – as really young kids can. I tried to put my sudden deep feelings of depression into my pocket as I carried little Lillibet and swung young Magnus up the stairs to the land of water play, bath toys and fun, pummelling towels and goodnight stories. It was hard to act the normal guy; but for their sake I did it, and I did it well; didn't *feel* good about it, nevertheless I had them laughing and falling about as usual. Thomas the Tank Engine, over, both turned their heads to the wall, and slept. But not until Magnus had hung onto my two fingers very tightly and said, "Don't leave us, Daddy, Please!" – and he thankfully fell asleep.

That evening is not my highest point in romantic memories. Yet there I was, with one of the most beautiful women I'd ever come across, I was legally married to her and she is the mother of our kids. It's a password to happiness and marital contentment. I guess, looking back, that, for reasons I've never extrapolated, Charlotte was never a communicator. So much of her life had gone by with her merely *looking* beautiful, and the world dancing to her attention, and now, now comes the moment when the supreme effort is, I'd agree, being asked of her, and she is failing on every front. I don't want to put it down to spoilt child, but if the cap fits...

Two things might surprise you: one was a really nicely cooked, and a quite hearty, dinner – all the things she knows I like, accompanied by – of all things – candles; along with slightly heavy breathing and a certain sullenness of demeanour. The other was her admitting me to our bed, and a memorable and actually very lovely night together, sex between us at its best, I'd say; and we had had our moments. Was it the pathos of the situation? Or was our timing, our conjoint body movements that night, in a heavenly symbiosis quite foreign to our worldly and verbal situation. Or – was this goodbye? Important to observe that we never, not once, spoke. And there is something about this argumentative self I have, that deals in words all the time, but all the time.

That night was like a cave painting, an original, naive happening, entirely without words. I've had to pause a few times since then to reconsider Homo Sapiens if s/he is without words. Are all my words merely constructs to keep people from intimacy?

*   *   *

Gloucester

I had to go into Gloucester the next day to 'tidy my desk' and sort sundry messages for colleagues taking over. Actually, all those I wrote messages to, joined me at 12.30 at the Golden Lion for a last pint and pie together. I'd only invited the younger ones. Good friends, men and women with eager, inventive minds, and fine ideas – all of them – for their individual futures ahead; just not *my* ideas nor *my* degree of risk; but good to argue with about it all. In 1977 we never used to have to worry about drink-driving, so we just did both. Oh, the breathalyser had arrived in 1967, but it didn't change many habits for about fifteen years...

About 2.30, with many cries and cheers and back slaps and hugs of goodbye, farewell, fear not, 'come and see us, but not for money', we all drew away from the car park in old jalopies, smart roadsters, motor bikes and one milk float – he I *did* admire for his early use of merely electricity to get about – and I made my way out of the city for the last time; well, for many a long year, anyway.

Aren't we incredibly complicated, us human beings? All morning I had been concentrating first on simple executive duties, and then hospitality and not-forgetting anyone, and yet, and yet, all that while, at another level, I had constantly been aware of the tiny vulnerable household in Birdlip, where even now they were aware, if not preparing for, my imminent return. I'd thought to have spent tomorrow – Sunday – with them, and make my way to London and my new life by train early on Monday morning. Something deep down – some folk call it the soul, others the conscience – was saying to me 'get out quick, get out quick, least damage, go now, get on with this new life'... I was made so miserable by this conundrum I was close to tears. My face was smarting, my conscience was very very guilty, but everything underneath everything else said *'you must go and do this new life'*. I called for ice-cream and lovely teatime things like marshmallows and chocolate for her and sweets for them. What tiny offerings! Pathetic man.

I parked quietly and took my packages to the front door. I lifted the key... Hey, I thought, everything's very quiet. I quickly went round to the garage. Her car had gone. Inside I found no message for me, just a dark, quiet interior staring back.

I waited in that lonely house, normally so full of life, for seven hours. It was 10pm, and no message. I had tried Beth – the other yoga teacher – earlier in the evening. Cheerfully (it was an effort) – "Have you seen Charlotte, Beth? Just wondered where she is?" Complete negative, kindly said, but no. Other friends I thought we had too much to lose socially by ringing. I spent the night alone there – how could I leave?

*   *   *

Magnus, aged three

Around 10 am, she drives in with the tinies, without a care in the world. Looked straight through me: "Thought you'd be gone by now."

"I've been so worried, I didn't know where to call or look."

"Well, that's an infinitesimal dose of what you're going to be giving me."

"I'm so, so, sorry."

"Yes, but you're still going aren't you?"

"Yes, I am. But I want you all to be happy."

"Oh stop your double bullshit! Bugger off to your 'New Life'.

"Charlotte, where were you last might with our children."

"Spent the night with Gareth, yogi. He's very sad for me."

"Oh... I see..."

"No you don't, but bugger off, now, will you?"

"I think I may just do that. Please remember my last word is 'sorry'."

Walking fast towards me now is little, vulnerable Magnus, tears welling in his suddenly-enormous eyes. He holds my trouser leg:

"Don't leave us, darling daddy, we all love you so. Please, please don't leave us. Daddy, Please!"

I pick him up, three years of a world's experience, and hug him close "You look after mummy and Lillibet, darling, I'll not be far away."

Charlotte now, slightly forcefully, almost grabs little Magnus from my arms. I let this happen. I'm so ashamed.

As I retreat now towards my car, my little boy is looking over his mother's retreating shoulder shouting and wimpering "Daddy I love you, don't go, Daddy."

I drive slowly away, an enormous lump in my chest. To my dying day, I will NOT forget the implication and the plea in tiny Magnus's eyes and those terrified words he spoke —"Daddy – don't leave us – I love you – Daddy."

I stopped en route at a cafe and in the car park I cried bigger tears and for a longer period than I ever remember. God, leading the life you want to is a precarious path for the sensitive soul. I eventually reached Belsize Park and slumped in and I regret spent most of the next day also crying. But, by Tuesday, I stopped feeling sorry for myself, rang Lesley for a 90-minute heart to heart, and then got on with life. But I did not forget.

Chapter Twenty: 1982

Communities – Taynton – Braziers – Muswell

How Del and Sloane persuaded me to come on this trip eludes me. I was very, very busy, and unclear how seeing a couple of real, live communities was going to help me to understand The World and its People. We'd lived in a shared house in Edinburgh and I probably had too strong a memory of six separate, open packets of butter/margarine in the fridge at a time, with little actual control of who used whose and when things went bad... No advocate of latter day Sell By, Use By dates, nevertheless applying the sniff test and looking for green bits was an inaccurate and inefficient way of housekeeping; Lesley had agreed!

Sloane was being invited (as was I, the introducer) to this old farm called Taynton near Burford where nine families had set up in some sort of community about – was it ten years ago now? – But they nevertheless owned their houses privately and each 'unit' had its own front door. What kind of community is that, I wondered? When, over these now several years, I'd driven down to see Del and the design development group, I'd made a point of getting away without a visit to his home; except the once, after dark, when design and marketing talks had gone on forever, and Del was expected home to child-mind while Sonya went out for her spinning class.

So I was invited to supper, and noted nothing communal at all, except for cries of "Do have some of these fresh veggies and salad, all picked from the communal garden this afternoon!" Which I put down to being like a group of friends co-operatively using a series of adjacent allotments.

And, for an Intentional General Specialist, all this just goes to show how narrow my thinking had got. Very regrettable, must watch myself. We arrived in Del's car – yes, community-livers do own cars – and at first view – now daylight – this was a place to die for. Think Cotswold, think that slightly green, but grey stone, used for all walls without exception, and wonderful vast stone-tile roofs, and not a plastic drainpipe nor gutter to be seen, it's all painted ironwork. An aspect of nearly all community living, I gather, seems to be a general untidiness, and we saw less of neatly edged lawns and pergola'd roses, and a good deal more of children's abandoned toys, mowing machines, barrows and rather jalopy-fied ancient vehicles that might move but perhaps were 'resting'. I could see that a degree of tolerance was required.

Hastening from one of the many Front Doors in this historic facade was the scurrying but pleasing form of Sonya, Derek's still-beautiful, raven-haired Italian wife. "Darling, glad you have got here – and Elliott, here at last in daylight, welcome! So...*you* must be Sloane, interesting name – you also live communally in London? Lunch will be about 45 minutes, enough time for you to come with me while I pick fresh spinach and a few carrots. Shall we have a little tour?" Her Italian origins showed through in the ways she made her sentences up and in some pronunciations.

Vaguely aware of quite a number of other 40-somethings and lots of kids from I guess 15 down to nil, presumably all communards – we were only introduced on our trip round if there was a reason. We 'did' the regular *short* route round, Del filling in on history or current purpose as and when. "You see these strange oblong holes high on those gaunt kitchen garden walls? We reckon – it's just our intelligent guess, mind – that there would have been a greenhouse along this wall, and, with wooden tilting panels in those openings in the brickwork, we guess they tilted on ropes to let the air in. Much cheaper than making watertight windows in greenhouse roofs. No, we'll turn left after the hens, that's the way."

Sonya, introducing: "Here is my wonderful immediate neighbour, Belinda. We share a party wall in the big house. She and I garden together, and over the years we've looked after each other's children a million times perhaps. Belinda, meet Sloane from London, and Derek's occasional business partner – is that what you call it, Derek? – Elliott." Belinda, clearly an English-rose, chats easily with us as she and Sonya gather vegetables. "London, Sloane? Where is your ménage, how big, all that?"

"A large house in Muswell Hill. We first sought four similar terrace houses, so we'd have equal holdings, but the ones we put an offer on in Mornington Crescent weren't quite the thing we were looking for. The place we bought is quiet and has a little garden, and is nice for the few children we have. You have – what is it? – 21 children in all?"

"Yes, that's not just us two mothers bearing them all!" – big laugh at silly joke – "It's about 2.5 kids average per family, for nine married couples. I and Neil have four and Sonya and Derek have just the two, so we average out!"

"Oh," says Sloane, "I'm much in awe of this project you've set up. However, we do eat round a table most evenings, so there's a communal kitchen, but each home – we don't use the house, flat, apartment words – has its own small kitchen as well."

"Very interesting – would love to see your place sometime. Hope you enjoy your visit." And she walks off towards the house, carrying a trug of veg and calling her collies, long blonde hair blowing slightly in the wind, a jaunt in her stride.

Lunch was a triumph of explaining it all to us. Sonya and Derek had had the forethought to ask Belinda and Neil to join them, with the slight disadvantage that there were now to be six children for lunch. I think I make a mistake here – I'm learning about community, perhaps. It seems that, having all six, they are so intimate they might be siblings, and they look after themselves, so little noise, really. Over lunch we talk communal living in all its forms and our hosts say they have an unusual treat in store for us for the afternoon. No, they won't tell us what.

After lunch – Quentin, 6 and Adolf, 4 going to Farm Reach next door for the time we're out – we pile into the car, Sloane talking to Sonya in the back, talking communal life. I have a chance to catch up with business with Derek; and that's all right to begin with, but I can tell he's not with me, not really. So I put it all to one side and enjoy the scenery.

Then Sloane and I start quizzing Derek and Sonya about where we're going on our surprise trip today. "I thought, Del, we were going right into Oxford; but you're turning sort-of South. Is this the A4074? Oh, well then we must be going to Didcot to enjoy railways; no? Or Abingdon and those kind-of-beautiful cooling towers? Are we calling at Wallingford for a re-enactment of the Civil War local battle there?" Somewhere, I'm a touch perturbed, and I guess it's because I do realise I'm a control freak, and I like to be the initiator of surprises and the like. So I'll sit back and observe and try not to mind. But I'm restless. Very.

Suddenly Del turns off to the left just after Ipsden. It's immediately a one-track road. Less than half a mile. Then a dingy entrance where there had once been a sign, and a deeply potholed drive that would take a few thousand to repair. Now, suddenly again, and charmingly, we're pulling up in front of a Country Manor House of quite some size and grandeur; even the un-mown lawns and poor paintwork and probably unsafe battlements – all these defects don't take away from the wow factor. It's a great place! But what is it? We are received by a couple who've clearly seen an age or two go under the bridge, but they're spritely, warm and smiling. I and Sloane are introduced: Glynn and Margaret Faithfull. Unspeakable possible truth – is this *their* home? We're walking into a baronial hall now, with sights of big rooms off to left and right. Drawing Room and Dining Room, each with a full curved end. When I notice that the dining room has three long refectory tables with benches and chairs, it begins to dawn on me that we're in another kind of community, a very different one to Derek's place at Taynton this morning.

*   *   *

Braziers Park

Tea and very home-made cakes are materialising, and I guess I must quiz Derek before I make too many faux pas. On my way over to him, Glynn Faithfull is there with the fullest explanations and I suddenly realise he's done all this explaining to thousands before us. Of diminutive stature, iron grey hair, he has the energy of a twenty year old. At a pace I can take in, he tells me that this is Braziers Park, School of Integrated Social Research, and it was founded in 1950 by his psychiatrist and philosopher colleague, sadly now dead, Norman Glaister. That Norman had had the – really! – outrageous idea of trying to be a tiny catalyst in *avoiding* a third world war, by using his Sensory-Resistive method in meetings… In so many ways it has worked and been inculcated into businesses and some of the services, education for example. Is it still used here at Braziers, I asked? Yes he said. Next or any Thursday I'd be welcome to join in, 7.30 after a 6pm supper, which would cost me £4!

Glynn really deserves to win, with all that front. He's certainly a fast mover! We all accompany Margaret on a tour (didn't we do *this* this morning? Will she be telling us about where they reckon ancient greenhouses stood, from evidence in holes in walls? Deja Vu? Yes, but not quite).

It's Margaret who tells us about Glynn's absolute commitment to this place and ethic, and to that end he's the farmer, milkman, egg collector, builder, electrician, plumber, painter – all that before considering his post of Convenor of Studies at the Braziers Park School of Integrated Social Research. He 'runs' the entire 50-acre place by a careful practice of asking everyone and then making the real decision! And he's the initiator and manager of the Foreign Students House Team, whereby Braziers is open to students from anywhere in the world to come and spend 2, 3 or 6 months here, helping with running the house, for a tiny amount of pocket money, and lots of help with the English language. Lastly and very importantly, he's a professor in the-Italian department at Birkbeck College in London, which he attends three days a week.

No wonder the lawns aren't mown… This 'institution', or home for a crowd of 15 or 20 very varied beings, has already lasted thirty two years, and, as it seems to live off fresh air and what the walled kitchen garden grows, it'll maybe last a very long time yet; and over that time, sundry accountants will say it's dead-in-the-water, and write their reports; and be wrong!

But I've seen particular possibilities. My work is so varied and wide spread. One item is the Environment, and here in the 80s we are concerned about the population explosion, concerned for how our burgeoning peoples will live off ever-decreasing farming land, as land is used up for housing, infrastructure and roads. We're concerned about Global Warming – which tends to be called the apparently much milder Climate Change, a misnomer. We have a concern regarding future generation of power and how we can avoid the folly of nuclear. We know only too well that kerosene and petrol are finite, and will one day run out; anyway, burning it in our engines is really heavy on ancient fossil fuels, we should be using wood that has just been grown and can be replaced by current planting.

Whether it's petrol or wood being consumed, how can we persuade people to use less petrol and less electricity, and get business people to invest in power from nature – wind, sun, tide, wave, waterfall; and technology to replace petrol as soon as possible.. I meet with Think Tank Chairmen and Foreign and Home Secretaries, and they seem to think I have the answer to everything! I suppose my publicity does lead that way a bit.

So, before we leave, I talk with Sloane, and then we talk to Glynn and Margaret, about having an initiating weekend using Braziers – they have lots of rooms where delegates may sleep, all old-fashioned but nice, homely rooms. We'd need a couple of marquees. The point of using Braziers is it so exactly represents the style of living we could all be thinking about – another pullover, insulate the house, turn down the heater, own vehicles together in small groups, go for smaller cc cars, try to combine lifts to save shopping trips so three or four people travel together. It's not a crying necessity now, but if we don't, our children are in for a much poorer lifestyle – and grandkids gravely worse.

Glynn is delighted, understands exactly, takes all contact details, and will be writing. We look round the house briefly – in the library there are hooks in the ceiling where young Ian Fleming's boyhood swing used to hang when this place was owned by the 007 writer's parents in the 30s! "What exciting trivia." On our way back to the Cotswolds, we stopped in Burford at the Old Maiden to eat. While waiting for our grub, Sonya said: "You thought, Elliott, that Ian Fleming's swing was just trivia. I'll tell you another story about Braziers and Glynn that's also just trivia. But interesting anyway." "OK, Sonya, on this day of rich experiences, I'll buy one more."

Delighted to have the floor, Sonya started: "Do you remember that very pretty singer in the sixties? Marianne Faithfull? Yes, Faithfull, *again*! Well, Glynn, by an earlier marriage, is her father. She lives in Ireland I think. Sometimes she stays at Braziers, I think. I haven't seen her – yet."

A pause. "Thank you, Sonya, that's a fascinating bit, trivia indeed, and I wouldn't want that kept from me! And thank you both for a lively and interesting day, Del and Sonya. I am coming round to see that community is quite hard work, but the joys can be immeasurable, I imagine. So – thanks for persuading me."

* * *

Muswell

A few days later, Del and I met Sloane at her Muswell Hill collective – they call it just Muswell – well away from trafficky bits, a mansion house of the style often served up as tall semi-detacheds, but this a detached house on a corner, no doubt in 1880-ish filling a planner's awkward gap. Slightly hilly terrain, a rather domestic-sized front gate led at lower level up and around the house to meet itself again, the garden now settling down to an almost level lawn. A driveway on another road led to an almost-underground car area, some of it covered. Sloane didn't own a car, she would hire one for a weekend when necessary.

The house-splits were curious, and I never resolved some of them, but individually they had all they needed, almost to excess. Four 'units' – called Flats (no beating about the bush here!) – and 13 permanent occupants in total – blowing apart the superstition about 13 sitting down to eat together. This was the evening when I learned that my office colleague, whom I thought I knew reasonably well, had had a woman partner, Marge, a slightly shy person, for many years. The others we all met at supper time, and – intentionally – Sloane and Marge were also cooking. We met two couples, one married and one as an item, living together these many years; and these couples had two, and three, children living in the house. But their ages were significantly older than those at Taynton, ranging from 17 down through to 12, with at least one romantic teenage thing going on between the lad of 17 and lass of 15.

Finally, and making everything so symmetrical it sounds like a fiction, there was a couple of co-habiting men, John and Josh. So – a mini-society made up of four men and four women, three boys and two girls – these were the wonderful, interesting, thinking, possibly introspective people we sat down with at about eight o'clock that evening. Who, I asked, had been the catalyst, who'd got it all together, how long ago, and had it been easy or difficult? Sloane answered for the collective: "John was the activist. He wanted to live with Josh, yes, but he wanted women and children in his life. He found like-minded people by working across a wide network of friends and acquaintances, surreptitiously 'interviewing' them, and not suggesting this project if they didn't come up to the mark. It took a couple of years. When together – this present group – we had to find the property. That was fun, but sometimes galling. Remember Mornington Crescent, everyone?"

We talked on, and it was one of the fullest meals, conversation-wise, that I remember outside of direct briefing meetings. Food this evening was vegetarian, but it doesn't have to be. It seems, they say, to be a gentler way to live, to try to travel lightly on this precious globe of ours; and anyway eating meat more than twice a week will, in the future, be impossible owing to the population explosion and meat taking the greater acreage to produce than veg and cereal crops. Thinking back to my Braziers event idea, I realise that just so many people are quietly getting on with a more responsible lifestyle. It's truly impressive.

"How would I have fared, applying to come here?" I asked the whole table.

Sloane took it upon herself: "You wouldn't have got past the first gate, Elliott! Sorry about that, but it's true. Yes John?"

John replied: "I never like to be what might be thought of as rude to guests – and we have had just so many guests around this table, every week. But we seem to be in Truth Park now, so I have to agree with Sloane – who, by the way, helped me a lot at the time, she really knows her stuff here. This does NOT mean that you aren't welcome with us tonight and many times I hope in the future; but actually living together – here – requires a certain kind of

character, a certain giving in, a certain quiet understanding that all is well..."
John's clearly thought of as the leader, even though the group is leaderless. I
fought off a childish response-feeling that I really ought to be angry at this.
There was a longish silence. Eventually it was broken by Jeremy, the 17-year-
old lad:

"Elliott, I really like you, you came across really well when you were
looking round the house earlier, but John's right mostly because I feel you are
a – err," was his courage going to fail him? "a *control freak!*"

Trouble is, he's right, and I know it; but I don't like acknowledging it.
Maybe, for me, this is the one lesson I can learn from all these communities. I
fight back the tears and burst out: "But that man at Braziers, Glynn Faithfull –
he's a control freak if ever there was one!" John allows several seconds to pass,
then says "yes, I know Glynn well, and you are right. But since about 1960,
he's established himself there with his then new wife Margaret and they've
had their three children there at Braziers, and he's seen to be the overt leader,
and, in his own way, he *is* doing a good job. But he won't last forever, and I
hope that Braziers will."

Chapter Twenty One: 1984

World Congress at Braziers

"Elliott – Sloane here – pay good and quick attention! – Many messages from or about your VIPs: HRH's bodyguard has many queries re security at BP. AND –he wants the morning slot if Diana is getting her's in the afternoon. The DG at the United Nations has problems between Heathrow and BP – oh! – all solvable. Henry the Kiss is OK but very private; you know he returned to government service this year, on President Reagan's Foreign Intelligence Advisory Board. Al Gore is on target to get here in time. Archbish Robert Runcie can get there, but his clerical team will have to stop over in say Wallingford – he wants a nice, good, private, hotel that the press don't know about. Hope to match him up with Archbish Tutu. And Tutu says to me that he so wishes that Mandela, still languishing in prison, could make this journey.

"Your –she's 25 – protégé from Exeter, Caroline Lucas, is keen as quicksand and messages us that she is co-ordinating the 5-MPs group – you know who they are – they'll arrive for the World Breakfast at 9 am. And J. Porritt CAN make the journey... Now for the detail – and I want answers as I go, please. Thank goodness you've arranged for Jeremy and Mia from Muswell to come in to the Orifice and help out, the phones are going mad – those extra four lines are essential!" They dealt with the detail for another 40 minutes and then she was saying "I think that's really all of high importance for the moment... and... Elliott..?"

"Yes, Sloane, you know I'm here, what?"

"Elliott – just in case I don't remember in the melee tomorrow to say this – I'm very proud of you and working for and with you at this time. Yes,

I said don't be so stupid, you'll never succeed... but you've succeeded beyond your *own* fantasies, I Imagine. So – a big Well Done and We're All Right Behind You, and in your Big Day Ahead Tomorrow. I will of course be there – Mia has offered to stay back here at this end to take the phone and stuff. Good luck today. And even more tomorrow. I'm blowing you a kiss!"

"Sloane, how very kind! I accept. Kiss and all... But tomorrow's '*for the World's ecology*', not for Elliott's ego. Yes, we've done well... So, very many thanks to you too, practically my partner in strategy.... Bye, love." We put our phones down, this very personal interlude moving both our hearts in a profound way. It's what I've been learning in these communities, it's accepting one another, warts and all, that's behind it all. Even us men have our feelings.

I'm actually at Braziers – I've had four more phone lines put in temporarily, BT do this for people holding exhibitions and the like. I've taken over Bedroom 1 – the largest – and I've got all my best pals working their butts off for the (private) **World Ecological Convention** tomorrow. Firstly, in charge of the office and of security, is Reliable Wonderful Lesley, taking a fortnight off from doctoring. I'll be getting Lesley to contact Prince Charles' aide re their security requests. She's sure to solve those without coming back to me. Dutiful, Determined Derek's in my office at present – also on a week's hol from the firm – and he's in charge of tents, house and equipment. And yes, Colourful, Creative Shirley's got a display table where she makes up wonderful flower displays – almost entirely using wild flowers, brackens, grasses and foliage. She has organised the signing system around the estate, everywhere. She's taken time off too, but I can't remember what from...

My sister Camille – still stunningly beautiful, now in her early 40s – is to be the chief receiver at the door, the giver of huge welcomes. Sonya and Belinda from Taynton have joined the Braziers' cooks to prepare sumptuous feasts, and John and Josh from Muswell are dealing with the many special dietary requirements for the VIPs and other visitors, not forgetting the press. The kitchen is rather full! Margaret Faithfull is sitting in the Inner Hall, away from the kitchen, available with advice whenever it's needed. (They do say that Margaret without her beloved Aga wouldn't be able to cope, so I've observed that the letters: a-g-a all come within the name Margaret. What, I wonder, will happen to that Aga when Margaret is no longer with us?)

The main tent is truly huge. Sad, of course that we can't rely upon Braziers for rooms to meet in. But the lawns are vast, the grounds huge, so all we have had to hire in are one enormous round circus tent, a smaller but large rectangular tent, and a host of mobile loos. And still with all this added infrastructure, Braziers *is* the right place to hold this event.

Glynn has been a masterful man in all of this. Little did I realise when I thought this idea up from those kernels on my first visit two years ago, that the Braziers family alone would be such a monstrous hurdle. With all the goodwill in the world, their blessed Sensory Committee is seemingly designed to *hold up* decisions, when in fact it's there to ease people's acceptance of decisions. But it's been Glynn – and Margaret, his wife, also – who, from the off have seen the long-term benefits of this congress to Braziers itself, helping to put this place on the map as a centre for such studies in the future......

Did you hear me say *'private'* congress? Well, it's a misnomer. Of course we want all the publicity in the world. But most of our visitors today would not have agreed to come had it been advertised ahead; it would have drawn journalists from right round the world on the day. So the BBC has agreed, exceptionally, to come 'privately' for the day and to report at the weekend when it can go public, and all the important people will be back in their countries and their homes.

* * *

The Braziers World Convocation

Sunday the 1st of July – my favourite day for nearly everything, but chiefly for being born, way back in 1940 – dawns mild and sweet, with a promise of being hot later. For now at this early rise of 6am, the almost-keen breeze keeps us on our toes. 6.45 Car and vehicle parking people from Braziers community, deploy around as agreed in readiness. 7am, as expected, a civilian-clothed police presence arrives, parking where told and also as per the rehearsal, and divides up into two-person units, usually a PC with a WPC, all as in the rehearsal, and situate themselves around the premises, un-noticed, with coffee flasks, picnics and rugs to make a day of it, it would seem. By 8.15, all catering people are in their stations, making ready, with Margaret, Sonya, Belinda, John and Josh organising people, foods and the stuff of it all – 500 mugs, tea cups, saucers, kfs, serviettes, salts and peppers... the list does go on, but efficiency is the rule here. (To get Sonya and Belinda, as I felt we needed both on the team, mothers and mothers in law had been dragged out of contented retirement to care for the six kids).

Nine o'clock: Camille and Glynn are at the Front Door. The Dining Room is open for a rolling buffet breakfast. Maybe the room can only seat 40 at a time, but not so very many are expected for breakfast, and some will come later. Those sleeping in the house – tickets for this advantage had been advanced to some press, a TV crew from (only) the BBC, St John's Ambulance First Aid, and organisers-in-chief. So 35 breakfasters were imbibing cereal tea and toast by 9.10.

Our big surprise was HRH. He arrived from his home in Wiltshire with an aide and two detectives around 9.15, and having parked in his special area, where a royal guard – his driver – would look after the vehicle for the entire stay, he and they made their way in for breakfast. It's one thing to say we all feel much more democratic these days, and quite another to sit happily alongside our future king and make casual conversation. Knowing how others feel, I immediate held out my hand and approached him saying: "Welcome, Sir, so glad you've been able to come. And I hope you'll both enjoy it and learn by it."

"And contribute to it as well, eh, Elliott? Ha ha!"

"Yes, indeed Sir, I should have said that too. Thank you. Coffee or tea? A cereal? Then there's just boiled eggs, toast, butter and jam. It's supposed to be a less affluent breakfast, just the basics, which is what this whole day is about –simple sufficiency. Now would you like to sit here? With Glynn and Margaret Faithfull – they're *dying* to meet you!" So I left Prince Charles in conversation with the most ardent anti-monarchists I know...

9.30: the big circus tent is opened up. It will fill up soon now. Camille's new focus for welcoming is now to be at the tent entrance, and she is joined by several assistants, some from Braziers – Cathi Llewellan-Davis, Sarah Wood and Hilda Salter; some from Taynton – Nina, Sheila and Judith; some from Muswell: Marge, Penny and Frances. Their men-folk had other jobs out in car park, informal security, entrance gate – which I'd seen to it had a proud new Braziers Park sign of such permanence that previous abuse was unlikely to re-occur.

HRH has now taken his place in the Great Circle – we had to have this round tent, so we could demonstrate our democratic, shared outlook. Bishop Desmond TuTu has arrived in time for breakfast, and been much lauded by Glynn and David Allen (the future Convenor of Studies) and now arrives at the tent, talks to Camille, to me, to HRH, and settles in a seat a few places to HRH's right. Robert Runcie, the Arch Bishop of Canterbury, is here now, with his entourage, speaking affably to everyone he knows and lots he doesn't. He, eventually, joins Tutu. Young Caroline Lucas now leads her posse of five MPs, two of them minor ministers, all now well-breakfasted, into the arena, and, after they've all done the affable bit, take seats around the circle. Representing his Ecology party, friend of Caroline, Jonathan Porritt arrives and immediately kind-of knows everyone. You'd think he'd never sit down. But he sits with Caroline. Jonathan's still grateful to me for taking over his programme when he had to be in Australasia with Greenpeace.

Now where's young George Mombiot? Hope he can make it, he also has a lot to offer. Roger Kelly is here from the Centre for Alternative Technology in Machynlleth – he hopes to be its Director shortly. He normally travels by bike, perhaps not today. The DG of the United Nations will be a few minutes late, I hear from an office runner. And the other DGs – Alastair Milne of the BBC and John Hoskins of the Institute of Directors, are now both here. The social noise is swelling, and it feels to be good, very good. William Rees-Mogg's here as a front row person, representing the printed word in journalism. Covering the arts, we have violinist Yehudi Menuhen, and architect William Rodgers. Probably he and HRH should keep their distance on this harmonious day... A financier – who, incidentally has helped us with costs today, and me with flying miles as I've criss-crossed the globe from South Africa to San Francisco in my endeavour to persuade this group to come together today. It's a source of some pride that, after running my General Specialism consultancy, I know all these people personally; well, except the UN boss.

Fifty people form the front circle, with a very few interpreters sitting just behind some of these. Then a complete ring of seats, for we have a crew of individually-asked members of the Press, who are all sworn not to write nor broadcast anything on this day until the Sunday coming – it was a ploy to get some of the big hitters here. They would have refused if there was a chance, with the fragile fabric of Braziers temporary security, that they be mobbed by journos and papparazzi. Nevertheless, along with official news reporter for the BBC, Sue Lawley, I see a cluster of very BBC faces, all of whom have been asked personally, who must have come independently and out of interest. Quite an achievement! John Simpson, Angela Rippon, John Humphreys, Michael Buerk, John Tusa and Kate Adie are all talking together, watching the spectacle with a touch of slight, light amusement.

*   *   *

The Programme

Time for the off. 10.00 am and a lot to cover.

My ex-father-in-law, Colonel Cedric Whitby, is Master of Ceremonies: "Your Highness, my Lords, Ladies and Gentleman, I am not the speech-maker, I am the introducer, but it cannot escape my notice that this day must be the most favoured day by eminence and influence since Brazier's founder, Norman Glaister, first set foot here 34 years ago. As the day goes by, with breaks for coffee and lunch, I do exhort you to look around this place. Yes, and notice how, although grand, it is also very primitive. It is Elliott Self's idea to bring the influential people of the world together to this place of peace, so we may appreciate for real what he is saying in terms of 'put another pullover on, save the electricity, try to use the car as little as possible, reuse old things, recycle, try to burn anything but ancient fossil fuels – laid down aeons ago and finite, and consider how we are going to fly aeroplanes when the oil runs out'."

"Speakers will be introduced one by one as their turn arrives. We have until lunchtime to make individual statements. After lunch there will be a – err – well-controlled free-for-all. So, this morning, minus a 30 minute coffee and comfort break, we have 150 minutes – and 30 delegates who wish to speak. With a minute's intro, this gives each speaking delegate just 5 minutes. I'm going to keep you to that. First up, a young man I very much admire, without whom none of this would ever have happened. Please welcome Elliott Self." Reserved applause.

After formalities, and into the hard message, I say: "..and dealing in my wide, no barriers, consultancy, I work with the decision-makers of the world, and I'm privileged to see the statisticians' and scientists' reports about our welfare in society now, and what, if we make no changes, the state of the world will be like in 25...., 50...., 100...., 150...., 200.... years' time. It's to my enormous regret that almost all the people I see are working on a five-year plan, or say till 1990. This is because of the vagaries of political fortunes and the term for most parliaments is 4 or 5 years. This period is USELESS if we are trying to SAVE THE PLANET.

"Today we will hear about the population explosion – I wish we had a delegate from China, where the greatest expansion is happening, but we don't. We will hear about food production and how this is approaching limits to feed the human race as more and more land goes into houses and infrastructure, leaving less and less land for producing food. You will hear how we will be persuaded to be, not vegetarian, but to eat meat only twice a week; as it takes much more land to rear cattle sheep and pigs than to grow cereals and vegetables.. We will learn about generations of puffing smoke and exhaust fumes, from burning antique carbon resources into the sky and affecting our ozone layer in the atmosphere, and about consequent climate change, or global warming. We will consider how we should make our electricity in the face of such evident dangers with nuclear, as yet very little power from nature's resources of wind, sun, tide, wave and waterfall. And, that other form of power, how will we as a global nation, deal with alternatives to motive power for cars, lorries and planes?

"I give you the day: Brave New 2085: 101 years. Will our children and grandchildren thank us for what we have done to leave them the rich, exotic, beautiful world we now enjoy?" Much applause, warmly now.

Prince Charles included in his statement "..at Highgrove, we manage our land well and ingeniously to take full advantage of natural life cycles. In the Princes Trust, we set young people up in business very much aware of what they owe to the environment. Wherever I go, I take with me the message – never of doom – but of putting a real effort into getting our globe right again...." a warm response. Roger Kelly spoke with conviction when he predicted that our next generations had about a 25% chance of making it through to 2085 alive and well; so it is imperative that we work together now. "The great charm of Elliott's initiative today is that it covers all aspects of our environmental and social future – other such gatherings are very narrow, and so their work suffers." Then Glynn Faithfull spoke. He told us of the opportunity awaiting us to put things right and about "this natural facility here at Braziers to be a natural home in the UK for such studies and healthy argument."

The DG of the Institute of Directors and the Chairman of the CITB both contributed comments on the urgency, and their fairly limited ability to sway their troops, but they would try hard. The United Nations expressed in such a courteous manor his joy at being here today. "It is a truism to say that naturally these subjects are rare on my agenda. My job is such that my aids regard a million other things to be more important and the acid test is this: Can I leave the environment for one more week? And the answer is always yes. But that doesn't mean that I approve this 'slipping status' of my agenda subjects."

*　　*　　*

H.R.H.

A very welcome coffee and comfort break at 11.15. A spooky helicopter is overhead; we think it's just the police, keeping a cautious eye on this event. I'd have advised not to do this by noisy helicopter, but there you are, not every decision in the world is in my court.

I find that Margaret Faithfull has been snooping in the tent the last 45 minutes and I ask her if lunch is progressing well. She says that, with all the help I've drafted in, she's a touch supernumerary, and so – just for once – she can have a peek at what's being said by the great and the good. She tells me she'll write some poetry about this day...

HRH is now off, to avoid running into his wife this afternoon. It's not so much the encounter, he tells me, it's the way in which Diana plays up to the press about their ménage. I thank him for his contribution, and he says:

"No, no! You are the one we should all thank! Terrific display of the breadth of human endeavour on show this morning. How you've got these people with such busy diaries to commit time is wondrous!"

"But, sir, you are a busy man – and you've come!"

"I haven't had to fly the Atlantic nor the Pacific to get here. Ha-ha. I just toddle up the road from Highgrove, a mere hour's trip. Mind you, by bike – as Mombiot and Porritt may advocate – and that man about the end of the world..."

"...Roger Kelly..."

"... Yes, yes, just the fellow, Kelly – well, I'd still be steaming across the Cotswolds if on a bike. Ha-ha" and with that, HRH was driven away...

*   *   *

Kissinger

After coffee, Mombiot and Porritt did NOT ask for us to bike into the future, when we reconvened at 11.45. They and Caroline Lucas looked forward to the Electric Car, hoping that the electricity to charge them and to light and power our homes could come from the energies provided by the sun, wind and tides.

Henry Kissinger seems to walk tall for an ageing, smallish man. His words – so European and of such tragic tones – are received very well indeed. He seems to need no microphone, his deep voice carries just so much conviction. He talks of the need for world co-operation and for compromise, for an understanding of the 100 year view and of the 5 year view..... Al

Gore – decades before his 'An Inconvenient Truth' film – is a spirited speaker fairly new to Global Warming, but with a zeal that ensures his relevance here today..... The Secretary-General of the United Nations, Javier Perez de Cuellar, through his interpreter, spoke so very tellingly of the Global Village in which we now all live; and its contradiction – the great need for travel to keep up contacts throughout the world......

Alastair Milne the forthright Director General of the BBC, spoke of the enormous responsibility on his and the BBC's shoulders, concerning the world environment, global warming, and the population question; he posed more questions than answers, but his contribution was invaluable for its style.

So, eventually, the lunch break was reached.

*   *   *

The Remainder of the Day

With so much conversation between so many famous and respected people gathered in one place at one time, it was hard not to feel a certain pride in the event. Lunchtime went well, with so many mixes – MPs with clergy, Guardian writers with the BBC crowd, Kissinger exchanging notes with Al Gore and the United Nations DG; the BBC's DG with Roger Kelly and George Mombiot, Jonathan Porritt with Caroline Lucas, Glynn Faithful with Princes Diana who has turned up for the afternoon session so avoiding her ex-husband.

And so it goes on. The goodwill and the excellent food, the wonderful environment and the crazy house; people are really amused to be here this afternoon.

So – what happened in the afternoon? How did Colonel Cedric Whitby get along controlling such a potentially divisive crowd? It was quite easy, really, none of those heavy political statements or protocols had to issue from this, the world's first-ever world-wide gathering for considering the portentous issues of over-population, food and fuel scarcity, pollution, global warming, and the many other aspects on offer today. Too much for one day too many issues... all of which I agree with, but one has to start somewhere.

There was an accord between many, if not quite all, for these notions:

- A neutral position on the notion of two parents producing only two children; with divorces providing exceptions.
- Intention to produce electric and hydrogen-fuelled cars widely.
- Intention to clear the seas and outer space from plastic debris.
- Intention to lessen the carbon footprint of our generation to reduce global warming.

How all this would happen was left unclear. It seemed reasonable to have such a simplistic accord, given that we have met for just the one day, and we haven't been surrounded by the scientist and specialists that can take these notions forward.

Dispersal was not so easy! Jonathan, Roger, George and Caroline wanted to give Braziers a definite walk-over, which they did together, with Glynn doing his best to inform them. But they already knew so much about the place that Glynn was, for the first time - probably in his life - completely at a loss to inject information! It was almost amusing to see this diminutive figure, with his commanding voice, unable to get his words out!

We – my assembled group of helpers, those that could stay – had dinner at Braziers, with the Residents. Sloane caught up with us for the evening. This day had been quite the most outstanding in Braziers' long and interesting history; and Glynn and Margaret are well aware of this. They see endless possibilities holding themselves out to be undertaken at BP, now our event has been held here.

I'm sure that Braziers isn't too keen on speeches, but I made one anyway. I thanked my sister Camille, all four of quad and their mates, and Sloane especially, having borne the heaviest weight of the administration. I also thanked Glynn and Margaret and all the Residents. And so comes the end of another day and we were soon on the road back to London and our various homes...

*　　*　　*

The Future

Kyoto... Bala... Copenhagen... Paris... As I edit this chapter, in the 2010s, it seems sensible to point out that many international congresses have been mounted on just these same subjects. They have the authority which comes to them through their pan-world advertising and clout. And they have hit the headlines like no other non-sexy subjects! They have certainly covered some ground, and have, each in their own way, been successful. But I must hold onto the fact that we had one of the friendliest, if shortest, of these 'contests' in 1984, in which Braziers was the magnificent background to our event.

Chapter Twenty Two: 2007

World Roaming – mostly with Pru

At last most of my consultancy work is set to one side, and I can see my way to doing some of this long term travel I've wanted for so long to do – well, so long since my time with Penel Laird, the Dame.

Travels with her gave me an appetite for seeing the world more fully. Back to my sojourn with Doctors Overseas and Medicine sans Frontiers? Back to my pacing across the world looking for men and women to represent the great World Population congress at Braziers? No. Not so much. There was more intrigue in the Dame Penel's activities, and I was not pressed for responses as I was with the Braziers hike, successful though that was.

*   *   *

South America – Machu Picchu – The Galapagos

Where to start? A degree of comfort seemed called for, but I couldn't see myself succumbing to all the World Cruising we now see advertised everywhere. I thought I'd take a continent and see what I could make of it. South America seems so attractive, its Inca civilisation and its Spanish invaders. So I went to Ecuador and Peru and, via Cusco, mounted Machu Picchu, and walked the Inca trail, passing Lake Titicaca, and the heights of these places is indeed fine and lovely if it's the views you want, but if it's your health that concerns you, think again – your lungs may not take in sufficient air at that height.

The Galapagos next: yes, I know these islands have been swarmed over by human kind recently, but I had to make an exception and see these strange Darwinian 'fossils' – and it was no particular treat to see humankind all over the place there; but worthwhile for me. Then down to Chile and Santiago, and to realise that there aren't any roads the length of Chile at all! I had wanted to rough it through Patagonia to Tierra del Fuego – the natural island at the foot of the continent, barring the way to Cape Horn and Antarctica.

*   *   *

The Antarctic and Argentina

So, rough it was, and I caught a Luxury Liner (as I said I wouldn't) to see Antarctica, and back to the Falkland Islands before returning to northern Argentina and Buenos Aires and a night of fierce tangoing with a lady from those parts who reminded me what I'd forgotten – a lady companion for my trips. Anyway, she showed me Montevideo and the Iguazo Falls (wondrous sight) and also Rio de Janeiro; by which time I'd had enough of South America to bore my friends silly with photos and anecdotes, and so I repaired unto England once more for a breather and to take on a bit of consultancy work. Sloane still did about two days a week for me, and she had a monster list of priorities...

A couple of months and maybe half a dozen heavenly lunches later, and I was all aboard a new adventure, this time to South Africa, Madagascar and Kenya, with all their wild beasts to view. This time I took the precaution to take Pru with me – to heighten conversation at dinner time and (hopefully) to be a comfort in bed. You remember, the girl I shared a dissecting corpse with at Edinburgh Medical School, and who shared my bed at her request when I was doing my Leave of Absence and writing my memoirs, mid-life? I may now be 67, but there's still life in the old dog. Anyway, she agreed, and so we set off for Cape Town aboard a Tall Ship, the Tenacious, prepared to do 4 hours on duty to 8 hours off, for a presumed 40-day crossing (you'll know when you get there!) and calling at South Georgia in the Antarctic for the second time this year!

"Sounds like – fun?" said Pru, aghast but keeping it mostly to herself. "If it's your way of doing things, then I'll come along and sing to the same tune..."

"I think we'll love it," I said – "remember they take disabled people as well, so we'll be lining up on the ropes with guys and gals in wheelchairs."

*   *   *

South Africa

Some of us were allowed to mount the masts and rigging to see to the settings there, and Pru and I, each of us 67, were allowed to do this – on calm days, in daylight! The evenings were full of dominoes and cards, of chat and conversation; and the crew were a heady mix of friendliness and story-telling. South Georgia was a white-out and thus not too much story, except for the wonderful Adélie **and** Emperor penguins, which swarmed around the landing stage.

Cape Town is an old fashioned city, overlooked of course by Table Mountain, but with wonderful beaches, and a good line in Olde English Pubs; and a sense that they _are_ England but for their sweltering heat! We passed time pleasantly enough with the friends of Pru's aunt Priscilla (yes, I did ask whether their naming tune had another groove apart from Prudence and Priscilla – to which Pru said "You can't object to a Horrace and a Quentin in the old generation if the new lot has a Jonquil and a Tristan..." and with that the conversation closed. We also stayed in a hotel of simple means by the sea, where swimming and snorkelling were easily on hand.

I also managed a visit to my old 'friend' Nelson Mandela (having met him the one time on a trip this way in about 1999, concerning World Population and Pollution). He gave me a ticking off for not continuing to follow up on this work in my current to-do list! I said that I'd had the inspiration to do that first World Congress, but now that Kyoto was in full flow with its 1997 Protocol, and Bali was trying to do ditto, and Copenhagen planned for a 2012 event, I could see myself as one of ten thousand voices, crying in the wilderness...

*   *   *

Madagascar

Madagascar was as much a surprise as anything. A micro-Darwinian enclave! Madagascar split from the Indian peninsula around 88 million years ago, allowing native plants and animals to evolve in isolation. Consequently, Madagascar is a biodiversity hotspot; over 90% of its wildlife is found nowhere else on Earth. The island's diverse ecosystems and unique wildlife are threatened by the encroachment of the rapidly growing human population and other environmental threats.

I had some conscience difficulty over what to do about travelling in Madagascar – with Pru. Reading so much about the criminal attacks in the daytime, let alone the nights, it seemed better to travel with a reputable company, which would know the ropes. Perhaps against that, I've taken a fancy to the wee hotel L'Heure Bleue, on an island – the Madirokely Plage! – on the island of Nosy Be!!! And the town of Hell-Ville!! Just too unlikely for words… The tourist runes runs: 'Nosy Be lies off the northwest of Madagascar and has a near-perfect climate – sunshine with brief showers that are often at night'. Here we can –and did.

So I fix up with a company that does mostly private trips, and is prepared for us to stay at the L'Heure Bleue. Our guide is Dirk. So far, so good. And – what do we do at L'Heure Bleue? We spend the first few days soaking up the sunshine and swimming in the Indian Ocean. It's here that our sex life really takes off, having been a bit on the exhausted side on the Tenacious – the tall ship where we had to take duty turns with the rigging; and in South Africa we'd been with friends rather too much to indulge in the other. But here, with such idyllic weather, such perfect food and such a luxurious bed – we 70-year-olds could really indulge one another… and we do!

The restaurant serves excellent Malagasy and French food, with an emphasis on fresh seafood caught by local fishermen. For puds they leave us out mangoes, passion-fruit, Madagascan cocoa and vanilla.

There comes a time when we grow tired of doing nothing except eating, drinking and fucking; we look out to see what Nosy Be can offer by way of wildlife and long walks. We'd noticed heavily-loaded dhows and pirogues sailing past, delivering to villages. We'd also seen ghost crabs scuttling – sideways! – up and down the beach. And we'd observed frigate birds soaring overhead, their immense wingspans dwarfing other birds in the sky. Under Dirk's advice, we now potter about on bikes, through tiny villages, catching sight of black lemurs and giant tortoises, and, out to sea, dolphins, whale sharks and humpback whales. We snorkel down to see marine life such as parrotfish, turtles, groupers and stingrays. A new guide, called Nana, takes us on a seven-hour night trek, observing diverse wildlife. We hear the haunting call of the indri across the Andasibe rainforest at almost dawn...

There's a problem to Madagascar: no air con, and no telly, as these will limit the electricity available for 'more important' functions.

But there's another longing that I have and that's to overnight in Camp Amoureux, in their En-suite tents in the heart of Marofandilia, in Kirindy Forest. Of course, it's nowhere near Nosy Be! It's sort-of half way down the West coast of Madagascar.

Once there, Pru and I go on day- and-night-walks to see Lemurs and their like. We find the smallest mammals, including Madame Berthe's mouse lemur, mostly at night. From more of a distance we get glimpses of the larger nocturnal lemurs: the pale fork-marked lemur and the Coquerel's giant mouse lemur. Madagascar's largest and most formidable carnivore, the Fosa, reputedly lose their fear of people during their mating season in November. Site-faithful females return to the same mating tree annually. But we aren't troubled by this, it being August. So we watch timid Fosas sneaking in the gloaming. We're amazed at the largest rodent's baby-kangaroo hops around the baobab forest – the size of a hare. Turning in at about 2am after so much nocturnal prowling, we're too exhausted to take much interest in each other, but look into each others' eyes, thankful of our expedition together.

*　　*　　*

Kenya: January 2008

Kenya is just across the Indian Ocean...! Based in Mombasa –a suitably proletarian base for us to hide behind – with wonderful views out over this

Ocean, remarkable sunrises – which we occasionally actually see! Swimming in the sea is a whole lot more crowded an activity than we'd had in Nosy Be, so we stick to the swimming pool at this hotel. Food is excellent here, but we gather that the local restaurants are a little below par and also not particularly clean...

Tsavo East and Tsavo West are our nearest National Parks where wildlife is found. We use these local places as our practice grounds, travelling over uneven roads and tracks is hard on the rump and very tiring, but the crocodile, hippopotamus, elephant, giraffe, zebra and many types of deer we see, make up for all the discomfort. Thank goodness I'm not trying to photograph it all – sticking our heads out of the top of a Range Rover is one thing; trying to do this with a camera in your hand is quite another. But we are 'hunting' lion and leopard and cheetah; some big game kills – and we're not so likely to get these in the Tsavo area.

So the Amboseli and the Masai Mara game reserves are coming within our sights; at a greater distance – nearer Nairobi, which is no good thing – but far more likely to bring us face-to-face with some kills. But much nearer to Mount Kilimanjaro! Spectacular and beautiful views from our chosen Park Lodge: the bijou Segera Retreat, with just 6 timber-and-thatched villas to hire. We find that we can fly – by helicopter – to our chosen Lodge. So we arrive, cheerful and spirited, _not_ after a long drive over terrible roads... We quickly sign ourselves up for leopard, lion, and cheetah game drives over the days to come, and find that very afternoon that we are joggling over rough terrain in a Land Rover in search of our prey.

*   *   *

Big Game

On 20 000 hectares of land, Segera is situated in Laikipia, one of Kenya's richest ecosystems; its abundance of wildlife is breathtaking. The area teems with birdlife. It provides an important corridor for the east-west migration of elephant and others. But we are firmly on a Lion-Leopard-Cheetah mission;

and what do you know? A little before sundown, we happen across three cheetahs, two of them cubs, with their mother, who stands guard over the two frolicking young ones; our co-riders are clicking cameras for all they're worth. It's a fantastic sight, so close to sundown; they're not after a kill, they're having some downtime.

Bright-eyed from our find, but sleepy in body and soul, we make our way in semi-darkness back to the Segera Retreat. A late supper of a beef curry is available and we gobble it up. "How was that, for our first day out?" murmurs Pru.

"Pretty damn good" I reply.

"Do you think we're likely to go on scoring as we have done today?"

"Dunno... Who can tell? We can but try..."

A delicious night, adjoined by the bleats and cries of wild animals almost in our presence, is ended by a bird trying to make its way into our room. We have no idea what this exotic bird is, but by the racket it's making on our window pane, it's probably very hungry.

We fetch staff – the same guy who was on the night before at 11pm – and ask him what it is. He laughs a little and says "yes it is Lilac Breasted Roller, one of the commonest birds in the country" and he opens the window and in it flies, heading for the dining room, where no doubt many breakfasters will be feeding this little mite.

Out in the Land Rover day after day. Today is desultory, very hot and very humid. We haven't found any of the game we're after. We're just on our way home – oh, plenty of elephant, deer, giraffe and the odd hippo, all very fine and dandy, but not quite our number. It's getting dark now – which happens very quickly in Africa – and then, unannounced to the driver on his mobile phone – we see them, across the twilight into the sunset.

It's leopard! A slinking, probably female, adult, no doubt with a thought to the hunger needs of two or three cub leopards probably hiding in the long grass, is making her way incredibly stealthily towards a young zebra. Needless to say, the engine was switched off as soon as the driver espied the drama ahead. Now the leopard advances, very, very slowly. The young zebra, oblivious of its impending doom, is feeding from long grasses, and his mind is on nothing more than lining his stomach. His mother and the zebra herd are a little way off, mother clearly trusting this young cub to know his stuff... The leopard nears his quarry. The quarry is attending only to the grasses. Suddenly, the zebra raises his head as if to gather where his herd is; this awakens the leopard to start a dash towards the zebra, which sets off as fast as he can run towards the herd, leopard is in no mood to fail in her mission. Her 35 mpg spurt of speed differs from the zebra, not being an adult when he could run at 40 mph, can only muster 25 mph, and zigging and zagging at that; it's the leopard's incredible jump forwards – anything up to 20 feet, but here she'll only need about 12 feet, and the zebra cub is caught and strangled to a quite quick death.

Leopard brings zebra to the cubs – just two, we see now; and they have been on high ground and able to see their mother in action; good learning for the cubs. All now set about a good feed, which we can't see properly owing to the failing light. But we've had our fill of this kind of 'delight' and it's time to get back to the lodge for a carnivore dinner of bison steak.

Pru is overwhelmed by the kill. She's very quiet but also full of joy at our 'success'. I guess she's concerned for the wee zebra. It doesn't seem fair for this poor little beast to have suffered so. At dinner, she goes for a vegetarian dish – an eggplant moussaka – but I'm afraid I have the bison – actually the Thyme-rubbed Bison Rib-eye Steak with red wine reduction and wild mushrooms! Absolutely delicious! But so is Pru's Moussaka, as I try a bit of her's too.

We sleep excessively well after our dinner and our experiences of the day. Next morning, no bird at our window, but a Pru anxious to make love this majestic morning... We take a day off from being thrown around in a Land Rover, and take gentle walks around the lodge, swimming in their pool and lounging on the poolside, reading.

Next day, we're as bright as chicks, and as lively. Lion has been sited maybe 20 miles South West of here – and if we are to get a glimpse of this most kingly of creatures, now is the time to go. So we're lively and expectant as we get aboard the Land Rover for this, our potentially final drive. Driver sets the pace and we're heading over this rough ground and jiggling around in our seats. We've gone about 7 miles, and we come across, not a lion chase, sadly, but a lion meal. A lion-feeding off a buffalo that the mother had killed previously.

We settle down to watch progress – mother lion rips the skin off a foreflank and exposes the meat, and the cubs, four in number, come to help themselves. Incredibly communal as lions are, there's no fighting over who has what, there's enough for all... It saddens me that we are probably not, in our time frame, going to be able to find and watch a lion hunt, where lion uses its entire family – barring dad and the very young – in their attempts to bring down giraffe, buffalo, or whatever. It's an incredible feat, how these alone of the big cats do this. And dad, the male lion, stands aside and lets his 'women' do the work.

It was a matter of moments to get our stuff together the next day, helicopter back to Mombasa, and spend one night there before flying home; a really good holiday and a lovely companion to travel with. Back to her psychiatry and my consultancy – but only three months, as I would soon be off to Canada to share some time with Camille and Maurice and to go on a trip to the Northern parts of Canada with Camille on our own.

Chapter Twenty Three: 01.07.2021-!

Eighty (One!) Not Out – Burgh Island

Bother this Coronavirus, making it impossible to have a great party on the actual DAY of my eightieth birthday; we've had to re-arrange this for 2021, a year on from my actual 80th. Never mind, it should be good...

I think most everyone is coming. Biggest beano of my life. I'm eighty a year ago today - and blooming. Blooming well, that is. No significant arthritis, my bladder only gets me up twice a night, and my normal reading specs are OK for most things, no cataracts, nothing. Still driving, though not quite so much, nor so far. Can mount three flights of stairs without over-puffing and can walk five miles on the flat with ease and up hills with a bit more difficulty, but I get there. No replacement joints – yet!

It's supposed to be a treat, bringing me down here to Devon on this wee island where the only hotel is dressed up to the nines in Art Deco and Noel Coward detail; not really an island as the sea comes swelling around and closes it off from the land twice a day, so a part-time peninsular, part-time island. Burgh Island. Arranged by Magnus and Lillibet with help from Camille and from Quad – all four of them – all also achieving the fine age of eighty last year, Camille in 2022.

Of course, my parents, and feisty, irreverent Monica, and my ex-wife's parents also, have gone the way of all flesh; my father, the urology doctor, to his 'favourite' organ, the prostate. I wonder how many of these awkward little squid-like male organs he'd operated on. Mother via a clear brain till Alzheimer's took a hold late and fast. Monica, active into her nineties, by mistake then fell off a Derbyshire crag. Too many years in the flatlands of the fens had made her incautious. Her funeral was – somehow – more significant than either of my parents. Without Monica – would I have gone to Bedales, met Quad and Sex as I did, had the courage to set out on my own, leaving my wife and children as London called. Would I? Probably not. Monica, I owe you so much.

I'll just walk down to the headland and see if the boat-tractor is bringing people over. Oh, at eighty, you normally have a lunch, not a dinner, as old people fall asleep in the evenings, as bladders are short, as visitors have to travel either home or to hotels afterwards, as stomachs are not as big, nor stretchable, as they used to be. But we've done it differently. 'Gather on the island during the first morning, take a light lunch here, and in the evening – but early, like 6pm – we'll have The Party; everyone to stay the night. Tomorrow there's breakfast, a light lunch and then off' – so ran the invite description. And who's paying for all this, hotel overnights, all meals, drinks? Throughout my life, I've had money and been generous. But, by now, an event of this magnitude is more than I can do alone. My son Magnus is a banker – yes, it's still a rude word, wanker less so – but anyway he's footing two thirds of the bill, I one third. Here's to the HSBC !

Yes, the great blue squat-giraffe-bison-like vehicle, used for delivering people to this wee island-peninsular, is travelling over now. I can see the muffled – even in July – bodies of the full Quad gang, all old now, with a smattering of their spouses and kids – kids who now range from 48 down to 41 – how the great whirl of time keeps on churning – and their spouses and kids 'upon their backs to bite em'. It'll take a couple of hours to get the mob I see on the other side over here. Magnus and his wife Dot, and Lillibet and her man Wolfgang are here already, brought me down yesterday and have taken a longer hol to be with me. No, I don't deserve it, but I do like it. To have one's family around one when one's old is charming, delightful, warm, good. Their mother is rumoured to be coming, but she doesn't know how – yet. She's old and glacial now.

So many of my girlfriends will be here. Spoilt for superb choice. There's Lesley, of course, my life-champion. There may of course be glacial Charlotte, my ex-wife. There can't be Penelope as she's passed on now; she was a special lady. I'll be remembering her this couple of days. There'll be little Pru, my surprise sexual oasis in a desert of dearth, 15 years back. There won't be Philippe the Filipino, as we've lost touch and she never really had the language. And I? I am on my own... What a feast awaits me!

After a coffee on the back terrace with Magnus and Lillibet, I join the early light-lunchers in this fabulous art deco restaurant. I sit between two tables, with Quad Originals on my right and Camille and Maurice – over from Canada – on my left. Gentle chatter, remembering always the possibility of advanced deafness, we exclaim and explain and engage and entertain each other in that way the human spirit has of being outward to one another. Waves of the more-active middle generation come over and offer me felicitations for the day and for my future.

I guess that the event we held way back in'96, at Derek and Sonya's Cotswold communal farm, for us four Quad, our spouses/partners, and all our children – who were then 24 down to 17 – was the start of these wider family Quad events. It paved the way to everyone knowing, accommodating, trusting one another, eventually to arrive today at our Burgh Island celebration. I want this to be a celebration of 'Quad at 80' – well, Del's last year, and Lesley and Shirley are this *actual* year, but we can't all keep tearing round the country for each birthday. And today it feels has started with a wow. And the great grandchildren level? Oh, 21 down to say 8. They shriek over and away again in no time, but exhibiting the kind of bonhomie that arises from places where you are trusted. They seem very pleased to see one another. And it's a fun island.

Leisurely light lunch. I sit with Pru and Camille and Maurice and Lesley and Garth – 6 of us is enough for the table, as Garth, Lesley's man again (after a brief break) has gone fairly deaf now. To put the cat amongst the pigeons, I asked Garth whether he and Lesley were shortly going to announce their engagement to be married – he totally misunderstood me and thought I was talking about being enraged and harried, and so asked if I'd be able to relax later and feel better... I reflected that humour can be one of the casualties of old age when hearing is very dim. So, through Lesley, I asked if I could be released, from today forward, of the promise I made to her at Bedales, that if she ever got married, I'd put on a pink dress and be chief bridesmaid – she had so honoured my wedding, she'd brought the house down with her humour during her Best Man's speech... People remembered...

Camille talked to Maurice quietly in his ear. Eventually his frown went. But not his demeanour; he's a sick man, not long for this earth. It seems that cancer has caught up with him and maybe this is the last time I shall see him. Poor Camille!

Poor Garth! Most of the others remembered the event well, and chuckled tons, but he – being deaf and not having been at my wedding – got not much clue. However, Lesley stood up and brought a dinner knife slowly down onto my shoulder and said "I dub you, from this day forward, the freedom to enjoy life without bridesmaidial restrictions of any sort, ever, and you can also have the freedom of this Island for evermore." I imagine Lesley was still trying to explain to Garth in their room afterwards... Ah well...

Then a short kip. My room has a porthole! What joy...

*   *   *

The Evening

Men in Noel Coward hairdos, bow ties and dark-dark suits were at two grand pianos as men in Noel Coward hairdos, bow ties and dark-dark suits made us cocktails at the bar or at our table. Ladies and Gentlemen came down the curved stairway, with the fountain in the centre and one piano to its side... The Reception. Not too formal, but all the ladies, even at their now advanced age, wore long dresses, and a touch of glitter from real diamonds; all the Gentlemen wore dinner jacket suits. Some tried for individualism with a loud bow tie, but most wore everything black: tie, cummerbund, socks... And still that piano tinkles pleasurably on...

All my generation was so dressed as were our children's generation. The children's children – remember? 21 down to 8-ish? – wore more colourful clothes. But all were smart, slightly formal, certainly special. Small talk and champagne and canapés flowed for a long while ... probably 45 minutes. Everyone's here. Even a select smattering of those of my clients and big-business and arts and culture friends – I say and mean a select few – were dressed rather perfectly. Still no Charlotte... My thoughts wander.. Magnus and Lillibet have in recent years tried to persuade me not to worry about her, she's who she is, and that's that. Nevertheless, through all these decades, I do feel a fearsome guilt... Let it be, let it be. Magnus's and also Lillibet's children, Oliver and Catherine, Peggy and Jolyon, are all trying to get me to choose an olive or a cheese straw or a devil-on-horseback and we are enjoying my uncertainty together...

A melodious gong tells us that dinner is ready and would we take our seats? I am to swap with Magnus and his wife Dot so I get to sit with at least two groups, possibly three, as Lillibet and her Wolfgang are also poised in the swap routine. So – starter at place one, main course at place two, puds and cheese at place three. Seems good. Well organised, Magnus, all round.

So I join Derek and Sonya and ... wait for it ... Shirley and Jo! – yes, back from Jamaica these days, and only 74! Oh, don't ask me how. I look around. It's 67 years since I met Derek and Shirley. How Quad has fared! And now, at 80 - or 81! - aren't we well and happy? The asparagus and smoked salmon just walk down my alimentary canal, no problem. "And how is the community now, Derek? Still going strong, although you aren't so strong?"

Derek had an interesting answer: "We've got an idea. You'll know that we think Taynton's the best thing that ever happened to us, barring finding each other in the first place. But now we're getting old.." – here we have one of Derek's trademark long pauses – if left, he may never come out of them.

So I say, to goad him: "Yes, Derek, where do we go next? You and Sonya are moving?"

"No, Elliot – YOU know what we intend! We've been thinking along the lines of Succession Planning." Yes Del, but that doesn't give us the meat your audience wants.

Another, I hope, friendly kick: "Well, that might just mean that you're going to die, like all of us, and you've found a plot – is it to be standing-up burials at Taynton, figuratively to show you are still talking to each other?"

Del: "Even though it's your birthday, Elliott, you can go too far... What was I saying?"

Sonya: "I think I'd better have a go, although Elliott is quite an expert in this field. Two things: The first, we want to build a leettle cove of leettle houses down the front drive somewhere, yes a green field site, I'm afraid, to which we could retire and live out our remaining lives gracefully, looking after grandchildren till our children need to look after us. The second, we attract either Quentin or Adolf back to live in our huge draughty house and do most of the farm, hay, wood and garden work – oh, and hens and sheep and pigs and stuff. These many years at Taynton have been such a success, and it's the young who enjoy it now, and perhaps other communard families will also do this swap with one of their kids; or more... We already have Belinda and Jude saying they'd love to live in the tiny, heat-able units, and persuade one of their four to live in their huge draughty house, too! Whether it'll be Mat, Mark, Lucy or Joanna, we're not sure."

A silence. Awkward? A Bit... So I clap, "Well done, Sonya, speech-maker... and now the arrival of your next companions, Magnus and Dot, tells me I have to move to Table One!"

And at Table One we find Lesley and Garth, and Camille and Maurice, and Pru. For Lesley a long gaze of our lifelong joy together, for Pru a wink, which I think best expresses our short sharp sweet joy. I wonder whether I should have spoken so demandingly to Derek; my face may indicate a touch of this:

"What's all this, dearest Elliott on your 80th birthday? Looking a little bit down?"

"Lesley, I just had to put the crank handle into one of Derek's stop-stop stories. I promise I won't do anything else wrong."

Dinner continued to be perfect: Venison, done with wonderful sauces. A well-oxygenated prize Burgundy at room temperature.

The third table had BBC and Arts Council good friends for many years – which Lillibet and Wolfgang had obviously engaged in fine conversation from the comments that followed our arrival about my intelligent and beautiful daughter and her interesting, original partner (which meant they'd fathomed her but not him!)

Speeches were a joy, too. My son, my sister, my longest friend and one-time lover – representing Quad, and one only from my past life of business and cultural affairs: Melvin Bragg. Kept down to seven minutes maximum each, they had to be pithy and quick – and were!

*   *   *

The Crucifix

Out on the Quarter deck – no we're not on a boat, but owners of places like this like to bring in sea-connections wherever they can – we surveyed the night, balmy scene. 30's music below with middle-aged and young writhing in almost sexual ecstasy.

I have my cognac in one hand; warmth, friendship, love… Who can take this pleasure away?

And then I saw it. Saw her… Hanging from the yard-arm of this now-ridiculous quarter deck, barely thirty feet away. I suppose it was – well – several nanoseconds before we could be sure. But an instant later we were sure… It was my ex-wife Charlotte, spread-eagled in death in the Quarter Deck sails…

I turned away into the building and said to a hostess "deal with that" in a rather sharp manner and sought the company of Quad. I said: "What we've all seen out there on the yard arm on the quarter deck was none other than the body of my ex-wife, Charlotte – who I left 43 years ago, and who was invited to this event, but never replied properly. Now I remember her last email said: 'I'm sure you'll enjoy my presence at some point'. She came here to commit suicide in front of us and all our guests." I realised that the grave is going to be no insulation against the guilt I still feel. It will last the rest of my life.

Chapter Twenty Four: 2001

More Deaths and Disclosures – Peggy Self

2001. Another ride out for the Jaguar, again with my sister Camille as my passenger and conversationalist. We're attending the funeral of our mother. Peggy has kept up her ownership of the Brink House in Wisbech – which they must have owned since 1940 – and now, at the not unreasonable age of 84, she has died, just a few days ago; although we regret that it was three days of milk bottles on the doorstep that alerted the Social Services to her death...

No friends, that's the trouble. You couldn't expect Monica to keep an eye open; not forever, anyway. Never mind, let's give her a good send-off, we're saying... and so this is why we travel to Wisbech today. Social Services have found mother to be a really difficult client or patient. High-minded and dismissive, she was not tractable to their kind of care and observation.

Recently, not so sure of her footing, she nevertheless would go out walking, and could get stranded anywhere say 2 miles from home and with no alarm on her – she refused to wear one! Alternatively, she would also lie back at home, apparently too depressed to go out or feed herself reasonably. Much as she had when we were youngsters at home...

And the feeding herself was one if the difficulties. Peggy would get in mountains of shopping and then let it go bad in the fridge. By the time she came to eat it, it would be more than just 'off'; and she would still claim that her nose for the smell and her eyes for the colour were much better tests than the 'sell by' or 'use by' dates stated on the products... When we visited – not often, we're afraid to say – we would throw out much of the 'off' food and lay in new stuff. There must be a real problem for those who are left, after family has left home and the partner has died, to form a sensible eating plan, and to cook for oneself, often a dispiriting process.

Camille and I have been in touch with mother on a regular basis. Not that this helped particularly; she would be distant and curt – even rude – on the phone. Camille ringing from Canada has had the hardest time, making sure her calls were within sensible social hours in the UK. I'm afraid I would ring about six in the evening and if that found her in, then OK; I didn't try to get her hour after hour.

Here we are now, at the same church where we buried Jack six years earlier; and the hearse has arrived and so we go in. There are fewer people than for Jack's funeral, partly because everyone is older or has died off, and partly because she wasn't a professional woman, and hadn't cohorts of colleagues there to say goodbye.

I have cajoled Monica into doing a brief Eulogy for mother – and she came up trumps, saying what an excellent household she had held together for 60 plus years, and what a good mother she'd been to her two children, and an excellent wife to a very busy doctor... Church and burial soon over and the coffee thing afterwards going more simply this time as mother wasn't there to add that haughtiness...

* * *

Monica Says It All

Monica slipped me a note about visiting her on my own; which I did the next morning. The same sort of reception as last time, probably the same morning coat, and the same coffee and croissants in the same sitting room/kitchen. But a different approach from Monica.

Pleasantries were soon over and we sat for a moment. Then Monica started. It was as if she was giving me a prepared speech from long ago, but with the terseness of being very much in the present.

"Elliott, there have been some secrets held back from you till now; or maybe you've guessed the truth all along? Dear Elliott, I am your mother, believe it or not...

"Now for the potted history:

"Maybe you didn't know that my former surname, my
maiden name, was Smithers? Ah, yes, I see you're reacting!
You remember that your mother had a friend and colleague
called Monica Smithers with her in Canada... Someone
with obstetric skills, supposedly to help Peggy. But I was
the pregnant one! Anyway, so I, pregnant with you by your
father, on the very eve of his marriage to Peggy, intending
to pass you off as Peggy's child... What could they suggest?

"The family in Canada was their best solution. So, at
three months pregnant - and I was not showing it much -
Peggy and I left these shores for an 8-month stay in Canada –
where they all knew the secret! – and made us really at home
and were so, so friendly to us! We really had a good time
there, keeping in touch with our common lover, your father,
by phone and by letter.

"He slaved away at the Peterborough Hospital the while,
making up for my lack of presence there as his assistant
(wartime was not a good time to get replacements!) he
worked doubly hard. He owned the house Peggy has recently
been living in, right here on the Front; but he hardly got to
it, poor man, he was so hard at it at the hospital.

"We returned with our infant – you! – in late summer
1940 to eager arms and a loving Wisbech community.
Wisbech accepted that the child was Peggy's from the
beginning; she and I were good actors! The next year I found
a floundering Sir Ralph, potty for some woman to bed, and
so I took him on, on the basis that we could continue to live
in his parents' old house here on the Wisbech Brink – so, of
course, I could continue to be close to your father.... with
whom I kept up a relationship through thick and thin.

"Oh, yes, it was me in the Waiting Room in your house each Thursday afternoon, after all his old men had gone. He'd take me through to his consulting room and lock the door – although the secretary knew all about the arrangement; and we'd make love there and then upon his couch... I think you young children noticed me there, didn't you? I remember the childish screeches up those stairs!

"I always wanted to keep Peggy from being jealous; but of course she was, and that was on my mind as I was giving the eulogy to Peggy today...

I seem to have come to an end of my little speech, Elliott my dear boy..."

I was almost speechless. I suppose I must have thought about this as a possibility in my youth and as a young man, but never, not in recent years, never at all. I said I couldn't really comment at this moment, but as Camille and I were staying the remainder of the week to sort the house out, I'd be back to talk things over with Monica on another day.

Most pressing on my mind was whether to tell Camille about this great revelation...

*   *   *

Camille's Reaction

I decided that I should tell Camille; and this I inappropriately did over a couple of steak-and-kidney pies at the local pub. Her reaction was one of stupefaction. She was at once angry and tearful and resigned to the situation. She showed some distance between us, now, as we begin to shrug on the mantle of being half - rather than full - siblings. She wondered whether the 50/50 split in the will was still appropriate, and I said that all dad's money had gone to Peggy and so I'd be inheriting 50% of those moneys.

"But it's Canada that matters," Camille snorted loudly. And I saw her point.

"We'll come to an arrangement, then" I said. And so the evening went on.

My swift talk with Monica proved less effective than I'd hoped. So much for family life.

We drove home much earlier than planned, on the Tuesday, mostly in silence.

*   *   *

Other Deaths

In 2007, at aged 95, Monica died while hiking in Derbyshire! She had been 'dared' by a gentleman friend into taking this trip across the moors and had slipped and fallen above Hayfield, as they tried to traverse the deep valley of the River Sett below Kinder Scout, a high plateau that stretches across the eastern horizon like an enormous beached whale. She fell 300 feet to her immediate death. The friend with her, Ross Campbell, did his best to stop her fall, but was left with the only possibility open to him, to descend to the valley to the point where she had fallen, and then call the alarm. They had been attracted to Kinder Downfall, a waterfall that varies from a trickle in dry weather to a cascade that blows back on itself in wet and windy weather. Fascinating! And they had seen this back-blow, so had really completed their mission...

I couldn't make her funeral, much as I would have liked to, owing to my being in Madagascar with Pru. However, Camille has 'forgiven' me for being only her half brother, and we get on famously as we always used to.

Col. Cedric Whitby – my ex-father-in- law - died at 100, in 2012; and his wife Dame Florence Whitby, died at 102 in 2018. They had both been of enormous assistance to me in setting up my consultancy and with introductions, and I felt a great kinship with them; but there was the problem of Charlotte, the green–eyed Yoga-teaching daughter, my ex-wife. So, for each of these funerals, I crept in the back at a late moment and felt I had honoured their lives.

Chapter Twenty Five: 2008

Roaming with Camille

Canada: The Fall

Departing from Maurice and their youngest daughter Clarissa (who's now 25 and home between jobs) – it's been a delight to see both Maurice and Clarissa in their home, a relaxed setting, these past two weeks – we're now setting off in their car for the Algonquin Park, on the shores of Little Joe Lake, and the finest of all Places on the Lake, the Arowhon Pines Resort. This place simply surpasses other resorts by just being excellent. Open from June to October, the venue only caters fully – that is to say you get breakfast, lunch and dinner in with your overnight cost, which of course isn't cheap; but it's not expensive either, so we go with glad hearts.

In the UK, I had read the following from their website: *'At Arowhon, you will find an Algonquin escape with just enough rough edges to be genuinely Canadian and just enough soft cushions to provide the peace, relaxation and comfort you're seeking. A small, summer resort nestled inside Algonquin Park'.* and *'The on-site recreations include Tennis Courts, Golf Course, Sauna, Water Activities, Fishing, Canoeing, Kayaking, and Hiking'.*

Camille and I have chosen to go for a three-night stay in a log cabin, where we can save money by sharing a cabin! How Camille and I, as siblings, are going to take to this, the first time we've slept in the same room since our childhood, I don't really know yet; but we'll soon find out! We should at least enjoy the restaurant! The dining room itself is beautiful, it's a hexagonally shaped log room with a huge open fireplace in the centre; the food is by waitress service.

So we are very unlikely to become bored by our experience. Our first evening, after an excellent dinner, we went on a wolf hunt; well, not so much a wolf _hunt_ exactly, more to hear them howl. It's an eerie and magical sound, and sends shivers down both our backs, and we are glad to hear also the sounds of birds ending their day, and small mammals scuttling about – some of them starting their 'day'! On days that followed, we're led by the waymarked forest paths; along with our kindles and a good read, we were well away...

Above all, there is the reality of The Fall all about us. It's endemic and all-consuming. I suppose, with an Englishman's phlegmatic point of view, I tend to regard the Autumn as a Brown Study, but that's because of the amount of cloud cover we get in the UK. Here in full sunlight every day, it's a Glorious Golden Light that we receive from all the trees; it's so lifting to the spirit. Together with Camille, we crave it and love it! It's the reason we've come here and it will be difficult for each of us to leave.

Actually, by the last day, the last lunch, I'm beginning to feel like a person in a mental institution. Our usual waitress, dressed rather clinically in white, with a special smile, comes up to our table and asks: "How are we today, then?" I'm overcome by this feeling of Being Cared For, and I shy away from answering, leaving Camille to cope with her and our order. I've shared with Camille my feelings about the dining room, so she understands. Our stuff is in the car now, as we have reached the dreaded checkout time. It's a matter of moments before we are on the road...

How did our sleeping in the same room go? Well, it was Just Fine! any body shyness was eradicated on the first evening, when we both undressed with a certain privacy, and yet without barring anything from sight; not that we were looking, mind! She's 69 and I'm 71, and it's all plain sailing...

Pushing out into the main Ottawa-Huntsville road, and turning right for Huntsville, we are still surrounded by The Fall – wonderful autumnal colours are simply everywhere. Next on our agenda is to stay two nights with the Bolsovers – our mother's Canadian family – who have remained up here at The Lake at their estate to welcome us a couple of weeks after they would usually have moved back into their winter quarters in Toronto.

*   *   *

Perch Point, Lake Simcoe

So we turn South and aim for Lake Simcoe, near Barrie, to Perch Point, and a collection of about nine houses, all in the ownership of members of mother's family – laid down as a masterpiece of family living in about 1850, when of course the houses could only be used in the summertime. Gradually, over the years, owners have done them up to over-winter them; and here and there another new house has been added, always with the same family owning them.

It's a bit like Taynton, but there the relationships between householders are merely of a friendly nature, no one's related. And the Cotswold view, while terrific, isn't quite what this territory has with its lake views. There's scope to swim and run boats and so forth, and everyone in the summertime tends to take coffee of a morning on The Dock, a wooden wharf which extends into the lake water a touch.

We're greeted warmly by Natalie and Ben Bolsover, where Ben is the family member, and Natalie his wife; they're about 70 years of age, as we are, and the reason why Camille has befriended these relations is because of just that, their age compatibility. Remember, Camille and Maurice live in Montreal, and so have had the time to make friends with these and other relations.

They are sorry, but their children have long since fled the fold, and return only with spouses and children to celebrate the central summer months or Easter or Christmas; but for Christmas the young are very unlikely to come to the Point, as the snow would no doubt defeat them; hence the Toronto house.

Ben and Natalie can – and do – walk us round the estate (of some 80 acres) and we take delight in seeing how they have just <u>so</u> much space each; not much chance of neighbourly arguments breaking out here... Dinner's at home tonight, and Ben's cooking. He's made a marvellous beef casserole, with mushroom and broccoli accompaniments, and over a glass of the fine Claret we've brought them, we get down to some conversation. I open with:

"It's indeed wonderful how you can carry on year after year living here, with the same neighbours as your friends, also your relations, and it doesn't seem as though you are about to move out..."

"No, certainly not!" says Natalie "we just love it here – and remember, we have our own friends who come down and stay with us here, and we have another house in Toronto, so if Ben is running late with business, he can stay over at our Toronto house."

"Yeeerrrs... I quite see all that... But, tell me, how fragile is the basis of all one family living here?"

"Oh," Ben speaks, "Now you come to speak of it, it's fragile indeed. We've lived here, including our family before us, for about 160 years now. And Natalie and I have ourselves been here for about 35 years. I don't think any of our children will want to take this commitment over when we finally give up. So I fear it can't last."

"Do you have private deals? With your own children, this would be... I was thinking" Camille speaks.

"Mercenary matters overcome us all! Till maybe 1970, there was a real feeling that the house you owned was important, yes; but values since about that time have rocketed, so we would be looking for about Can$1m for this house, and the open market is probably the only answer.

"As it is, our neighbours Carol and Lucas are currently looking to sell their bit, and, you know, it's not the deal it was now. If they *do* sell on the open market, we can expect fences or hedges along the sides of their property, and a real struggle to see this as one estate thereafter. And there are new lakeside dwelling taxes to cope with..."

"So we'll drink to the present and the next say ten or fifteen years – the time we've probably got left," says Natalie.

"Yes, let's. Here's to Perch Point and all who sail in her!" I say, and the others accompany me, and we chink glasses together.

"Mighty fine wine you've brought here tonight!" says Ben, in an effort to change the subject "Tell us all about your Algonquin extravaganza."

And so we told them; and showed photos. This led to my sharing my other Around the World in 80 months so far and then they asked the impossible: where to next? I said I had the US, and India and the Far East as lines of sight.

How did I choose which friend I travelled with? Who wears the trousers in the decision making? And that's where Camille came in.

"He's been very pleasant about it all so far. His suggestion was to see Canada in the Fall, and would I like to come with him? I jumped at the opportunity of having not only a friend but also my brother to go with. This, Perch Point, was my suggestion, and thank you for agreeing and for staying back here to meet us. His is the next bit, and I can't say how it's going to finish, as we haven't decided yet!"

Idyllic, they both think, and somehow sound as though they mean it. An early bed – in separate bedrooms! – and we spend the next day leisurely enough, and the following evening, we take them out to dinner. The next day, after an early breakfast, we are off again on our travels.

*   *   *

In search of the Aurora Borealis in the Yukon

It was a matter of a couple of hours to slip down to Toronto, call on a friend of Camille's who's going to look after her car in our absence, and for this friend to drive us to the airport. Our trip to Vancouver was easily accomplished, as was the next step, to Whitehorse in the Yukon, the Northern-most territory in Canada, and for us to transfer to the first of three places to stay overnight, this one being the Northern Lights Resort and Spa.

We've bought a seven-day holiday in the Yukon, with the intention of seeing the Aurora Borealis, or Northern Lights, which in October we have a really good chance of viewing. Partly to enable this, we are moving our hostelry after three nights to the Aurora Inn; and for our last two nights, we will be at the Westmark Whitehorse. So, how are the Northern Lights playing up?

Exhausted after our 12 hours travelling, we are glad to hear that the Aurora are not going to show off tonight, and, after a hot but decidedly ordinary dinner, we head for bed, to read there if sleep doesn't come. But it comes for both of us, and so we are happy and talkative at breakfast, and wonder what to do in the days up here. Especially today: a spa and reading day it turns out to be. Night two was also indifferent, so we played dominoes with newly-made friends in the bar.

Nights three, four and five were really terrific for the Aurora Borealis, and we strained our eyes till past midnight, enjoying the changing skies: strong greens and greys seemed to proliferate, with touches of yellows thrown in; and the last good night was purples and mauves. For three nights in a row, this was really rich, really intoxicating. Nights six and seven were a poor show, but no problem for us; we'd had our fill and caught up with new friends.

Back to Vancouver, where we stayed for a few uneventful days; Camille remembers the temperate climes of England from its temperate, west-of-land-mass, weather and says, if her husband predeceases her, she'll most likely move back to England for her declining years. Flying to Toronto is no hassle, and then we pick up her car and drive along Lake Ontario to Montreal. My return plane to the UK is in two days time; so I was soon safely home – and, of that that Sloane had left me, opening three months' post…

Chapter Twenty Six: 2019

Quad's Grandchildren

This time the event's being organised and run by Lesley's and my children – Jonquil and Jessica, identical twins, and my pair, Magnus, and Lillibet, all about 45. Once again we're at Taynton, in Gloucestershire, at the welcome of Derek and Sonya, with their sons Quentin and Adolf, who now own the business and the house respectively.

Oh, it's so exhausting going through the ritual of names for all the grandchildren! Suffice it to say that Magnus and Dot have Oliver, now 19, and Catherine 16; and that Lillibet and Wolfgang have Peggy, 20, and Jolyon, 17. Maybe we should have had this party a few years earlier? But wait a minute – there are all these young ones coming along – down to Shirley's fourth child, Xavier, who has sired two children, one a forward young lady called Gabrielle of 12, and one a young assertive lad called Paul who's 7 years old. He's got a young cousin aged 8 called Sarah, the younger of Delilah's two kids. And Camille's youngest three grandkids are 8, 8 and 6.

Surpassing all of these is John who is 26 and is the issue of Shirley's eldest, Harebell, who had a school pregnancy at age of 16 and decided to take it to birth and look after the child...

So today is a mix, a real mix. Magnus and Lillibet are good friends with Jonquil ánd Jessica, now these two have stopped flirting with Magnus so outrageously; and tolerable friends of Quentin and Adolf, who are themselves good acquaintances of the Shirley four, as she used to leave them at the Community for three weeks a year and go overseas to see her lover Josephine.

This was in the bad old days when Jo was barred from England owing to slight crimes she'd committed in the UK.

I'm actually here today, and so are my old love Lesley, and the rest of Quad – Derek and Shirley. We're sitting this one out a bit, drinking spritzers on the poolside. Yes, since 1996 when we did the *first* party for our children, some 23 years ago, the good people of Taynton have put in a swimming pool, and although it's mostly for those of my age just to look at, it's indeed a wondrous spectacle, much enjoyed in use by the young and middle aged.

There's a follow-my-leader going on at the moment, led by my son Magnus and by Jonquil. They lead a mixed bag of youth around a thicket of a hedge which keeps the wind off the pool, and thereafter through everyone's houses and up into lofts and down into hay barns... It's the sort of thing that you wouldn't imagine working, but Magnus and Jonquil have got the message for this party: mix 'em up, make 'em laugh and Bob's your uncle. It's the strangeness of such a big place that gets to the young ones and a romp around is a good idea.

But not maybe for some of the bigger young people. I find, in the role of Grandpa, I'm indulged a little – well, we all are, we Quad. And so, on their second lap by the pool, I get both Catherine, 16, Magnus's daughter, and Peggy, 20, Lillibet's girl, on my knee – as if that will hold out! After appropriate tickling both literal and metaphorical, I sit to hear how their lives are going.

Peggy's at Keel University, and reading law and English. Catherine's just leaving school, having attained good GCSEs, but determined to get on in the world and not faff around with As and Uni.

Peggy explains: "I'd like to become a barrister, Grandpa, and then I could argue with more than just my dad, who's very good at arguing, but I think I'm better. What do you think, Grandpa?"

"There are two questions there, my girl! One is: are you better at arguing than your father? And the other is: should you become a barrister? I guess it's the second you'd like me to address, yeah?"

"Sure, Gramps – but you can say whether I'm as good as Dad at arguing, as well, can't you?"

"Yes, I could – in theory! But, young Peggy, you'll need to spend a few years at your training, you know, and it's not easy being a barrister for the first few years. There's a pupillage to obtain by gentle letter-writing; although you, as a girl, are much more likely to succeed here —"

"...that's very sexist, Grandpa!"

"Yes, but there it is, my girl. See it like this: a barrister has to put up with you in his chambers for six months, adding absolutely nothing to his practice whatsoever. A real drag for him. But, if you're a girl and willing to make the tea and so forth, think how much more attractive that is as an offer!"

"But, Grandpa, there are now so many female barristers that your argument is absolute balderdash!"

"Not so fast to conclude your case Ms Self! You'll now find that just 35% of all barristers are women; and these tend to be the more junior barristers who wouldn't take pupils; but also that women at present exceed men in pupillages by a considerable number."

"Are we having a battle, Grandpa? I thought you were always so kind towards me and Oliver..."

"And so I am, my darling girl; but you asked me as an equal to fill you in a bit on being a barrister. I can say more about this if you want?"

*   *   *

Barrister and Barista

Catherine finds her voice now: "Gramps, I want to ask you a question, too!"

"OK, go for it, young Catherine – you're leaving school now, I gather from your parents, and you're going to earn lots of money without the aid of A levels and university, right? What are you going to do?"

"Well, like Peggy here, I'm going to be a barista, but I'm going to get the basic training in 3 to 4 hours, with perhaps a few weeks on the job, to become a fully fledged barista. So, stuff your pupillages Peggy, and all those long years of learning and come and join me at Costa's in Hammersmith – it's not just making the tea I'll be doing, its: 'Double shot skinny caramel flat white for you, Sir?'"

"No, no, silly Catherine, I'm going for a professional job where I'll have to defend people in court when they have maybe broken the law, and really need my defence!"

I quickly reply: "I think you're both following what you want in life which happen to be called by such similar names – Barrister and Barista, the second has only one R near the beginning, and an A at the end. I know a few barristers as I used to work so close to the law; and I know a few baristas as well, as I love coffee, and the heart the girls display on the top of my cup of cappuccino. Never mind the argument, it's all in a day's work."

Magnus is at hand now and they want Lesley and I and the others to talk about why we started up Quad and no doubt lots of stories from Bedales and Edinburgh.

And then there'll be a barbeque and a bit of light drinking and soon we'll all go home, satisfied that another party has gone off successfully.

Chapter Twenty Seven: 2009/10

Late Roaming with Quad

The Far East, the United States, and India

In 2009 and 2010 I made trips with each member of Quad. I visited the Far East with Shirley, to explore her sense of fun and colour, her innate rhythms of life, her inner self. We went to China, to Beijing, to Shanghai, to the Great Wall and to Xiang and that immense underground bodyguard of life-size soldiers. Shirley was most taken by Chinese dancers and athletes. Then we took a train down to Hong Kong, and explored the islands there, including a day-trip to Macau, the Chinese gambling centre. We progressed to Singapore and Malaysia, Kuala Lumpur, and Thailand.

In the second half of 2009, I went to the United States with Derek. He's not so keen on countries where English isn't spoken, and we'll forget that GB Shaw said that, of English 'in America they haven't used it for years!' We visited New York and Washington; and then headed for California and Nevada, to try our one-night's luck in Las Vegas (a failure); to descend into the Grand Canyon and survive (a success), and to visit the cities of San Francisco (I couldn't get Derek to lift his eyes off the trams and their tracks) and Los Angeles. And then home again, Derek quite stunned by his experiences.

In 2010, Lesley and I go to India. This comes last as I have been savouring it. Since her partner, Garth, had walked out on her in about 2004 (to spend a few years with a man friend, only to return to Lesley, crestfallen, in 2016) we'd had the odd night together, and had (I believe) found this rekindling of our teenage and early 20s passion for one another, exhilarating and confirming.

So, India. It's going to throw us into close contact, and we both say we welcome this. We start with a holiday in Goa, where those long days and idyllic nights stretch out before you like it's forever... And it is the stuff that dreams are made of; and if we never had a honeymoon, then this is it, right here and now. Long lazy evenings into long caressing nights into long lank days... Would we be for ever thus... Ah! well, life doesn't seem to go like this, not for every day...

Now comes the hard stuff: India itself. We take a mixture of trains and buses to get around, and we use 3 to 5 star hotels, typically. We try to travel by night sleepers, to avoid overnight stay costs and to maximise the time we have available in the destinations.

We're both amused and amazed and sometimes quite frightened by the road use when we're on buses: the constant jostle of traffic, made of lorries, buses, tiny 3-wheeler tuk-tuks, pedestrians and cows! The way in which a two-lane traffic queue can keep up its speed of say 40 mph, pushing and shoving, three tuk-tuks taking up the width of one lorry or coach, each very close to one another, and then against the traffic will come a van or bus and the traffic veers over to the right to avoid it.

"What are they doing, driving against the traffic like this?" Lesley asks our driver.

"They not having much money. Cannot afford fuel for to go round long way. Easy like this. Can do."

But how our bus approaches a T-junction is truly amazing. The driver, without pausing, surges into the traffic which has to give way. Is it the relative size of our bus? Well, no, as the mini tuk-tuks do this as well. And cows? Well! The cows seem to meander up and down the highways, keeping mostly to the central reservation, they say it's because there are fewer insects there and so their tails don't have to be constantly flicking the flies away!

Eventually, after traversing much of southern India, we make our way (or our train makes its way!) to Rajasthan and the Golden Triangle. Old Delhi takes a day by bicycle, new Delhi another day. Train to Jaipur and the brilliant amber fort there. Another train night and we're at Agra by dawn. Just the moment to see the Taj Mahal; which we do in all its wonder. We feast our eyes upon this spectacular edifice. We walk round its tour and back again.

It seems a fitting end to Lesley and my trip to India and to my Around the World in 80 Months – which has actually been about 40 months; but I didn't know this when I set out to South America in 2007. A very splendid set of trips with some wonderful friends...

Book Three
Fact and Fantasy

Chapter Twenty Eight: 2020

World-Wide Virus – Coronavirus

It all started in China. The fastest-moving, most highly contagious virus, Covid-19, or Coronavirus. Within days it had established itself on every continent except Antarctica – people flying home from holidays, flying back from business agendas, all of them – ALL OF THEM – seemed to bring back the virus with them – not yet knowing that they were ill – so that, within a very few weeks, with death tolls rising, all air travel was stopped, motorways fell quiet, and people across the world were in varying degrees of lockdown. After China, the worst hit country was the US, then the UK, Italy, Spain and France. America had a strange situation, being so remote from Europe and Asia, yet it was remarkably high in cases and deaths.

In the UK, there were upwards of half-million deaths, all told – when finally they included those from Care Homes and all deaths in homes and areas other than hospitals... It was the worst outbreak since the Spanish Flu following WW1. It saw such heroism as peacetime rarely brings. Hospitals were built in just 9 days – the several Nightingale Hospitals sprang up like nobody's business, in other organisations' pre-existing shells – the London Nightingale with 4,000 beds; all upon the 200th anniversary of the birth of Florence Nightingale on 20.05.1820.

The dreaded breathing assistance, ventilators, seemed to get a bad name, as so very many of their users died soon after they were applied, but I think that it was the extreme nature of this erratic disease that caused the deaths, not the ventilators themselves...

*　　*　　*

Lockdown

In the UK, partial restrictions to people moving and gathering were announced on March 16th; a total Lockdown on March 23rd; we sat at home and shivered and hoped for the future as daily death tolls ranged from 500 to almost 900. But it was on 22nd April, when we were all hoping for good news ahead, that the announcement was made that our lockdown was very likely to continue till the end of the year, even beyond, that so darkened our hearts; allowing us to speculate on all sorts of highly implausible outcomes...

Our economy: the world, the US, European and UK economies, all, all suffered losses, of some 40% over the period, a baffling situation we are even now seeking to recover from... Just so very bad...

Returning to work, either late in 2020, or in Spring 2021, we found a minor devastation all around us: People we knew only distantly had died, and even people we knew quite well had also died, but so completely had information of family, friends and local communities overtaken us we had forgotten about our work friends...

*　　*　　*

The Plight of Businesses

Businesses had gone bust, practices had ceased to practice, there was massive unemployment, and widespread depression. People who had been hairdressers and graphic designers and landscape gardeners, now all seemed to become counsellors and psychotherapists, with really quick courses being arranged by the Tavistock and other authorities; and new recruits found no lack of takers for their services... some using phone lines to reach their clients.

The economy was in such a bad way that there was an announcement of an extra election to occur in May 2022. Probably Boris was, as usual, absolutely certain to win again with flying colours – as indeed he had in 2019 – and no one was able to strong-arm him into considering alternatives.

*　　*　　*

Education

Lockdown meant that kids couldn't go to school – they were home-schooled by teachers and parents using the web; that all pubs, clubs and restaurants were closed; that most people couldn't go to work – they worked from home where possible; that shopping was reduced to just supermarkets, food shops and pharmacies – but always at a social distancing space of 2m or 6'6" from the next shopper.

People found that they had very long hair, being prohibited from visiting their hairdressers; that they went shopping just once each week (the elderly had special morning slots to shop in); that they had to bide their time WHOLY at home; except for a brief 30-minute "exercise" walk just once each day; that they couldn't move around by public transport, unless they were key workers (ie working in the NHS, chemist and food shops, public transport and development jobs, and a skeleton staff of teachers – to cover those kids who had still to go to school as their parents were key workers themselves).

Sport, exhibitions, festivals and events generally were all – _all_ – cancelled. Parliament met with 2m separation one from another; so they went in one day in three; biding their time by their computers on the other days. Oh yes! Webcams were everywhere and Zoom quite came into its own for this period – Zoom linked people in families, in government, for teachers and students, for church services, for business meetings, and for groups of friends getting together...

*　　*　　*

A Terse Chat

Lesley and I were walking through the woods in Essex one day in the midst of all this, alone and alone with our thoughts. How manifestly our country had fallen in a few short weeks – no less than other countries, no doubt, but nonetheless fallen... onto what appears to be hard times, with the Chancellor of the Exchequer handing out more moneys than it looks like he properly should... and yet, and yet, no, he should have handed to those who were prevented from working by the virus; the standard agreed upon of 80% of their pay or salary; yes, and even to the self-employed.

"But how – *how* – HOW - are we ever – *ever* – EVER – going to rise above all this and lead ordinary lives once more!" says Lesley in a near rage at society.

I'm pensive for a moment, then reply tersely "For once, I don't know the answers here, dearest. I'm now so very retired – much as they may like, occasionally, to drag me back in again – but I don't any longer have answers to situations as manifest as all this. So, so many people unable to get to work, so many kids off school, so many students unable to take exams, so many dying each day, each week, each month..."

"...and yet, and yet, even if we get to the hideously high figure of your supposed 50,000 dead, this is still less than 1% of the UK population."

"Actually just 0.075! This doesn't answer the awful loss in a single family where maybe the main breadwinner and spouse have both died – it's unheard of outside of war and plague."

"It's the plague we have then! I've got a better idea... Let's go home for crumpets and tea-laced-with-whiskey! Should cheer us up!"

*   *   *

Dying Alone

Perhaps the most terrible and quite hideous aspect was the fact of dying alone, without one's family around the bed... Such family presence had been denied by the government and the NHS, as it would have exacerbated the total illness and death toll. As the death toll for each day would scroll up on the 10pm news, the hard fact that the 547 – or whatever the number for the day – had all left this life with their hand held by an NHS nurse; so very sincerely held, but nevertheless not your nearest and dearest. It was like wartime deaths, with kindly nurses to see you out of this world, not your beloved... So very sad.

* * *

BBC News for Two Months

For TWO MONTHS, in its 10pm News Bulletin, the BBC carried, NOTHING BUT reports on the spread of the Coronavirus around the World, the UK, Europe, hopes for a vaccination, the scandal of the Care Homes (lack of Personal Protection Equipment, death tolls in Care Homes not being counted in with the national figures for the first two months after Lockdown); education during Lockdown.

The Economy and emerging reports that we were already in a recession while the virus was expanding; the aviation industry, now in free fall (reports from both BA and Virgin that they were very unlikely to restart their operations from Gatwick); the depression across all holiday companies following the news that no significant holidays were thought to be possible until the far end of 2021, if then.

For two months after Lockdown, the BBC News didn't waver from its commitment to keep the people informed, night by night; as if we were at war. Nothing else featured on their 10pm News Programmes.

* * *

Unintended Benefits to the Environment from Coronavirus

Hark! Traffic noise? No? Well – that's because there almost isn't any! Can you hear the birds? Yes? Because, although there aren't any *more* birds, without the traffic noise we can hear them brilliantly! Do you note the clear skies, the serene sunsets, the glorious dawns? The clear water, the ambrosian air, the wonderful walks, the exotic times we had WITHOUT all the traffic and life's usual hubbub going on all around us?

Yes. Well, I thought I'd take a glance at what Google has to say on matters of climate and environment. This is what I found:

Most people are only still just getting their brains around the reality that they're not going to be able to go to work, or their kids to school, for the foreseeable future. How many of us are ready for a 3-4 month forced lockdown? Or longer? Lockdowns are no fun and create a host of challenges and sacrifices. But they may be absolutely necessary.

Economies are crumbling, stock markets crashing, people are practicing social distancing.. There's a silver lining in benefits for the climate - in the short term at least. Canals in Venice have clearer water than they have had in 60 years. Due to everyone self-isolating, there has been less boat traffic - which in turn makes for less water churn. Emissions are down and credit can be given to Coronavirus.

There has been a 15–40% reduction in the output produced by key industrial sectors and has lead to a 25% depletion in the emission of Carbon dioxide gases over the past few weeks.

NASA released two images of China showing Nitrogen Dioxide levels recorded to be less than previously. The first image reveals pollution over the cities; the other shows it seems to have disappeared. NO2 is closely related to fossil fuel burning and the average levels were seen to be 36% less than usual.

Travelling has gone down significantly. according to researchers at Columbia university. Traffic levels in New York were estimated to be down by 35%. Their research also suggested that there was a drop in CO2 as well as Methane over New York. China has also shown signs of improved air quality, said a researcher from Stanford University.

Travelling and especially flying comes with certain costs to the environment. One of the biggest contributors to CO2 emissions, the aviation industry, globally, accounts for around 2.4%; with other gases and water vapour trails produced, it accounts for around 5% of global warming.

With the ongoing crisis and countries opting for shutting their borders, the aviation industry is in free-fall now. This turns out to be quite beneficial for the environment...

Will the government use the same old methods to boost start their economy or will they try to make these changes permanent and alter their strategies for bringing the economy back to normal. We as responsible citizens now have to be very cautious in the choices we make and the impact it has on the environment around us.

* * *

Will we ever see an end to Covid-19?

Doctors, scientists and sociologists all seem to be talking a common language: at the centre of all the talk lies the notion that we aren't going to rid ourselves of Coronavirus any time soon (depending of course upon the fluke finding of an effective vaccine) and that we might have the virus on our hands for many years to come. This is indeed a horrifying thought. Passing people at a distance of 2m – a smidgen over 6'6" – is all very well, but not for the long term future.

Coronavirus is the most manifest evil since Nazi concentration camps. It may appear otherwise, but there is no better comparison. Not so obviously the work of evil people, but as far-reaching and death-inducing as those simply dreadful camps. Perhaps Coronavirus is like being at war again, and, as with WW2, no end in sight in 1940.

Is 2020 a repeat of 1940?

Chapter Twenty Nine: 2021

Little Local Difficulties

Brexit seems to have delivered such a lot of calamities to our door. Going-it-alone seems to be such an arduous business. Much better to be wrapped up in a continental deal – of a sort – as we did have; at least then we could complain about the officialdom in Strasburg and Brussels, and bring about a slow change.

Cameron got his knickers firmly in a twist. And opposition from within his own party – chiefly Johnson and Gove – so widely missed their target, but were *believed* when they wrote on the side of their battle bus "Save £350 million weekly from our payment to the EU and pay it into the NHS." How can such ludicrous figures be dreamed up?

Anyway, that was all back in 2016–2019, and we can see the fiasco it created in the UK. Theresa May, left without a majority, standing down as PM and the unlikely Boris Johnson stepping into her shoes... Loss of the support of the DUP mostly because of Ireland Problems and Boris's bombastic ways...

There was a surprising about-turn between Northern Ireland and Eire, giving a new rapprochement and an agreement to become one united Ireland, to avoid the problems over the border between North and South. Maybe this was in part because Mary Lou McDonald had just taken over from Gerry Adams as Leader of Sinn Fein, and Michelle O'Neill had taken over from Martin McGuiness as leader of Sinn Fein in the North. It's surely nothing to do with Arlene Foster, leader of the DUP. We'd all wondered what WOULD happen at the Irish Border, but no one, not even the Irish Press, could conclude that the Irish would make such a plea for common sense! It was right that the two should be united – only a pity they hadn't seen it this way, decades beforehand...

Loss of support from Nicola Sturgeon – and her holding the next Referendum... No doubt, had there been no Brexit, Scotland would have had little foundation for subjecting all Scots to a second Referendum. But the sweet lady at the top – Nicola Sturgeon – always sucking at a toffee that turns out to be an acid drop in her words. We all knew that Ms Sturgeon wasn't going to, post Brexit, put up with membership of the UK, when she wished with all her heart that Scotland should be a member of the EU.

There's a possible answer to the question why they won. In late July, 2020, the oil giant BP's figures were worse than the previous quarter, owing to the world-wide Coronavirus, but there was much speculation as to why investors were hanging onto these shares. An investors' paper had been putting it about that BP was just on the point of discovering whole new under-water fields of gas and oil deposits, with potentially quite reasonably-priced mining costs and which was all in Scottish territory. Such a find was rumoured to keep Scotland fully supplied and yet exporting most of its haul for – well – some said *fifty years*...

This hyped information, and then, little by little, additional – maybe spurious – accounts from other petroleum, kerosene and gas explorers, somehow filled up the nest-egg of hope in the typical Scottish mind, and maybe it brought about the – of the actual voters – 57% to become independent. True, there were, of the total vote, 11% don't knows and spoilt papers; and that the total voters made up only 64% of Scotland's population – but never mind these niceties, it didn't stop Nicola Sturgeon, from declaring an absolute victory and thereafter getting a really enormous amount of congratulatory mail. Apparently all those dour faint-hearts had come home to love their country again... Thursday 11th September 2021 was going to go down in history as A New Beginning.

*   *   *

Just England and Wales

I suppose, looking back on it, our deep steep decline, after Corvid-19, started for real with the surprise result from the Irish and the Scottish decisions. Nicola Sturgeon had in every way been 'looking good' – including her bravura talk of it being a walkover – which, like the singing saint walking into the flames – she had kept up, with her bouncy, laugh-off-the-opposition, demeanour, till the end. The stats were against her right up until those last weeks, Nicola saying the while that the canny Scot only has to get it right once, on polling day, and the rest is all down to history, in a dour reply to incessant journos and market research analysts asking questions.

We all expected to keep the Union Flag the way it had been, and for BBC coverage to Scotland and Ireland to continue, and not to have to turn Hadrian's Wall into an international border crossing – all this now seemed an inevitable outcome. Even the strange bedfellows, Tim Farron – Lib Dems, Caroline Lucas – Green party, and Nigel Farage – Brexit Party, whose parties together put on a voluntary 'England Replies' and 'Wales Replies' quasi-referendum, asking the English and the Welsh if they wished for Scotland to leave the UK – *that* had been very poorly responded to, but, insofar as it was a reflection of how the Scot's partners felt over the issue, it was frighteningly strong on the "Stay in the UK" – 72%. Had these voters realised the sudden reversal that happened amongst the Scots, they might easily have voted in much higher numbers.

For England and Wales, an Immediate severe national depression set in; we were seen to have failed in some way. Indeed, we thought this of ourselves. The Bank of England announced that the now-smaller Britain did not at this time feel inclined to share its Pound with Scotland, Brussels confirmed that Scotland could not yet join the Euro, nor the EC; and Matthew Parris's suggestion that they name a new, intrinsically Scottish, currency the Kilt – of which smaller denominations might well be called Sporrans – went down very badly north of the new border. Someone asked in parliament whether we'd now have to pay to import the legions of TV and radio presenters that currently hail from Scotland. Even Samaritans bewailed that they could no longer administer Scotland across its new border, and showed its usual co-operative spirit by saying it would somehow hang on in there till Scotland had invented its own version of an anti-suicide line. Meanwhile, distressed calls to Samaritans in everywhere other than Scotland, increased immeasurably. The charity was struggling to keep afloat...

*   *   *

A Torpid Malaise

In England and Wales – we never nowadays use the term UK if we can help it; it's hard to remember – so much had happened since to distress us – it's hard to recall the feelings exactly then, between the Scotland thing and the run up to the General Election. Everyone was personally down, and this affected attendance and achievement at work, with a great deal more knocking off early than used to occur. Doctors' surgeries were full of unexplained aches, pains and tirednesses, ME was like a plague, (and Coronavirus had not completely gone away). Banks continued to not lend money where even slight risks existed. Inefficiencies occurred everywhere – in working life, in driving home, in cooking supper.

So – accidents on the road rose hugely, setting statisticians' jaws wide open. MPs, feeling really down themselves, were unclear in their now-muddled minds what panacea for the people would be best. One route was to empathise and say we all need to take time off, go more easily, take holidays, enjoy our marriages and families where we have these – go back to basics (as John Major used to say in another context). The other seemed to be to ask for a sort of friendly pep-talk, encouraging people to find that extra mile's worth of distance run to energise them to just complete their days.

Unemployment was very high, at 15%, following the main brunt of the Corvid-19 pandemic; people working on shorter hours – and scarcely making up a proper family income. Both women and men found serious problems with their Contracts of Employment. Yet their cries of protest were little heeded in this, the New Britain.

So – the mood of the country was no way anticipating nor looking forward to a General Election, now so shortly ahead. The Con-Lib Coalition had vanished on Cameron's gaining a majority in 2015. Give me that 'seen-it-all-it's-really-very-simple-stop-spending-so-much-money' Vince Cable any time. Actually, he ought to be PM...

Parliamentary Bills were abandoned, the Business of the house was cut down to manageable levels, and the old Minister for Scotland actually left politics to become England's ambassador in Scotland. Probably about 100-plus MPs weren't re-standing for their constituencies again. And this left the way in for some very wet-behind-the-ears would-be politicians. The House no longer sat way into the night, as those last mortals in the building were too often found to be asleep. Only on one occasion did the BBC's Parliament programme, running live, find no one left awake to talk; luckily the speaker, however drowsily, called the debate to a close for the day.

One tiny extra bit of uncertainty: the law has laid down, regarding the Scottish Referendum: If Scotland votes to leave the United Kingdom in the independence referendum on 18 September 2021, it is expected that a 2022 General Election would still take place in Scotland, but the status and role of MPs elected in Scotland would be unclear.

Muddled thinking? Or did no one apart from Nicola and Arlene think it was going Scotland's and Ireland's way?

As an outcome of the Brexit debates and decisions, we lost Theresa May as Prime Minister, to be succeeded by Boris Johnson – not a wholly loved figure, but at least a voice and a view and a direction in the uncharted post-Brexit waters ahead.

Vince Cable stood down before the 2019 general election, to retire; and first Jo Swinson (who lost her seat in the 2019 Elections) then Sir Ed Davey, who became leader of the Lib Dems for the 2022 General Election.

Jeremy Corbyn stuck to his leadership non-style through thick and thin, until the election in 2019 almost annihilated the Labour party; Sir Keir Starmer took over this leadership and did a great deal better at PMQs against at Boris Johnson than J Corbyn... Ah well...

Chapter Thirty: 2022

Armageddon in England

In a stroke of non-competitive honesty, David Cameron had opened his first parliament by establishing the date of its close. The last Cameron election was to be held on Thursday 7th May 2015, established under the terms of The Parliamentary Voting System and Constituencies Act 2011. The Theresa May election (fiasco) was held on June 8th 2017. The Boris Landslide was held in 2019 in December. The next election is now scheduled for 2022, early owing to the extreme unease in the country following Covid-19, the ensuing economic hand-outs, the recession and the unemployment stats.

Television debates started in late 2021, as anticipated by the PM, Boris Johnson, who chose the date in May, to achieve the maximum vote in times not traditionally for taking holidays. Arguments from Greens and UKIP – and the BNP – for inclusion in these debates were long, difficult and at times unpleasant, with the only tool available to the bigger parties being the power to simply opt out. So it was finally left to the BBC, ITV and Sky executives to decide, as they had in 2010, 2015, 2017 and 2019, how the debates were to be staged. Three debates would be shown simultaneously on all the main news channels – BBC1, BBC News, ITV1, C4, Sky and others. They would be difficult to avoid. Of course, none would run against a soap on another channel, thus upping the potential viewing figures into the 30 million level, it was hoped.

In each case there would be three Leaders Debates, all in Prime Time. But now the first would be in Manchester in late November 2021 – as it turned out, just twelve months after the Scottish debacle – one in Birmingham in

January 2022, and the final one in London at the end of March 2022, just before the four-week pre-election campaign. All would be with equal time for four parties, parties currently in government – after the main three, also the Greens, but not the UKIP, nor Brexit, nor the BNP. and the official opposition and any with seats in parliament – Conservative, Labour, Liberal Democrat and Greens. This was a hard-won victory, pressed for by B Johnson and K Starmer.

There would be other, less crucial debates, for the three principal governmental departments – the Foreign Office, the Home Office and the Treasury – in which the Minister and his Shadows would debate in prime time. These were seen as of lesser importance, the biggest viewing figures were expected from the Leaders Debates. The first two debates went off quite well, in Manchester, then in Birmingham, with the Greens being given an almost undeserved equal ranking; and at times it looked more like an edition of Question Time, except for no comedian. Huw Edwards (David Dimbleby having recently retired) was being saved up for this last debate, in London, just before the election.

The conference centre building booked months beforehand for this final debate was the so-dubbed fortress in Parliament Square: Congress Hall, where it's claimed that helicopters cannot land on its roof; it is so anti-terrorist it's almost unbelievable; brilliant for access from the House of Commons and for the BBC London Unit. Its format, being a modern multi-functional hall, supplies all the camera mounts and kit. The audience is, of course, restricted, and very well screened, and they always sit in perfect silence unless requested to respond. I always think – as with tennis and other mass-events – you're much better off at home watching your picture-window sized television, for the detail, the replay, the analysis, and the close-ups of glistening sweat and scarcely-coping psyches. And you can have a cool beer on hand, go and get another one, fondle your cat or your girl on the sofa, and let out expletives if things get just too much. Yet these Invited Audiences like to think they're very, very special! They dress to the nines, they flaunt themselves a touch; but they mustn't so much as sprawl out, they can't see the replay, nor the close-up, and even a single fart is definitely off-limits. I digress. Sorry. But I thought, before the next bit, you needed a diversion...

Look, I can tease you all the way up to which speaker was just saying what, who was doing better on the swingometer, or I can just tell you, cold. I think I'll do just that. Prepared?

The entire building was blown up, three political leaders, question master, cameramen, hostesses, staff, security men and everyone in the audience. The most horrifying single act outside of a war to – probably – have ever happened on these shores. The Gunpowder Plot was prevented, the several people who died in IRA atrocities never approached these numbers nor significance, Airey Neave was, bless him, just one man, individual acts of murder and treason line the history books. But nothing – nothing at all – comes even close to the cowardly killing of about 800 people, among them the leaders of the three largest political parties, journalists and TV and Radio people in great number, and scores of security and establishment staff, and a willing, pliant, intelligent, talented audience. Gone. All gone. Completely. Thin air and a whiff of smoke.

Police, ambulances and fire engines were on the spot within four minutes. Apart from some injuries outside the hall – from falling debris and blast – there was no one – absolutely no one – to pick up. The building's remains were kept under fire hoses from the engines for about six hours lest outbreaks of fire occur and adjacent buildings become a danger prospect. Police set up a cordon at some distance around the building, closed adjacent roads and kept a presence there all through that night. Unbelieving people came to stare at the pall of smoke and the nothing; as if to see with their own eyes what they could not have imagined from radio, telly, Google. That police presence was there for three months. For, as you will soon gather, they had reason to increase that cordon, quite drastically.

First reports went out on the Ten O'clock News. Sophie Rayworth was visibly and terribly moved. She didn't say as much, but a not-inconsiderable number of her colleagues would have died. There was a studio full of debaters to take this final debate far into the night. That forum was used to act as a comment space, and became a phone-in to hear a nation's stricken grief. David's brother, Jonathan Dimbleby came into the studio and was encouraged to step into his brother's old shoes; this place would have been taken by Huw Edwards, anchorman extraordinaire. Peculiar sentiments about politicians – 'they are

197

all good men', 'they all had the nation's very best interests at heart – and on their sleeve', 'why do we have to have these beastly elections, they bring out the worst in people – look at Robert Kennedy', 'What good does it ever do? Talk talk, not shoot, shoot', 'This wasn't even shooting, this was the most cowardly way'.

For days, people were weeping suddenly in doorways, in shops, supermarkets, and health and community centres, people hailed one another who hadn't spoken in years, people were friendly, and so wanting to comfort one another. Strangely, suddenly, people were more alert, less poorly, much kinder to neighbours and to unknowns. Lots of impromptu hospitality just happened – "bugger the cost" one said. Doctors reported that, significantly, everyone was very polite, would suddenly put up with their problems, would happily postpone their appointments so another could have the benefit...

As the political parties, less their leaders and some significant people, were gathering together for this most awful route ahead, to a General Election in a touch over a month, and no main party with a leader, an enormous feeling of consensus was just plain happening; not realised nor identified at first, but, gradually, as the days went by, it became a call first within each party and then between the parties.

However, there was sad work to be done to honour the dead. London was in a mess and people said please not Westminster Abbey, please also not St Pauls – so please not London. An invitation arrived at political HQs and family addresses, from the Mayor of Birmingham: "In our attempts to understand these futile murders, we realise that perhaps London may not be the best place for some things in the near future. As England's second city, Birmingham would like to welcome you; so please use our fine city as a headquarters, for a short or long period. Our Cathedral is a fine place in which to celebrate the lives of the fallen; or – and we have spoken to Coventry about this – you may like to consider our adjacent city's services as available as ours. We cannot find the words to adequately pass on to you our condolences. But they are deeply felt. Please make use of Birmingham and Coventry at any time."

Well, it was a good suggestion. It was also decided that to have enormous funerals at this moment was kind-of outrageous.

"We will do what we each have to, to commemorate our dead, now, and fairly privately, probably where we live or in our constituency, and then we will choose new party leaders, we will keep to our promise to the King, and hold the General Election; and then, when we can sort out what to do, we hope to have a combined service, somehow joining people throughout the land in this our act of worship and commemoration. We will make of something so very dreadful, a matter of light and hope."

This was spoken by a leading woman lawyer representing the wives – and husbands – of the dead, after long and careful consideration of the words each would best like to hear read out to the land. So England set Coventry cathedral aside for a moment to get on with their private grieving and the choosing of new party leaders.

Choosing the leaders might, for each party, have rules, but what happened – they may well have bent the rules to fit – is that a senior group from each party met and made their choices privately in discussion. It was long, deep and very thorough and feeling-provoking. Availability and willingness each had to go hand in hand with appropriateness at this very particular time.

The Conservatives would now be lead by their recent Home Secretary, Amber Rudd; the Labour Party by their outgoing Shadow Foreign Secretary, Emily Thornberry; and the Lib Dems – again – by the outgoing Business Secretary and sometime previous leader, Vince Cable, now back from retirement. They would do no more TV or radio debates, all MPs would represent their constituencies, and the General Election would go ahead in three weeks' time on Thursday 5th May as planned.

In a statement composed and read by the Speaker of the House, on TV and Radio, the nation learned that "We have soberly re-formed under new leaders. The General Election will take place. We ask for as many in the nation to vote as possible on this very unusual occasion. We call on your support, please, at this difficult time in our nation's history. The three leaders of the main parties have asked me to express that they will be running, in so far as is possible, a friendly election. No one wants any further problems. Soon there will be a new government and we can work forward together from that point. My best wishes to each and every one of you. And the three leaders also send their good wishes. Goodnight."

* * *

Why? Who? How?

It was always said to be about the ongoing difficulty of the two-party system in the UK, the unapproachable main parties who seem to have their own agendas, difficulties militant Muslims see in getting a toehold in Britain, and the impossibility of getting minor issues aired while the first past the post system continues.

Reviewing this manuscript in 2024, I can only say that, to date, however many so-called terrorists have been brought in for intense questioning, there is, as yet, no cogent notion as to: Who did this ghastly act? Why they did it? and – most intriguingly for security engineers the world over – How did they do it? Even the 9/11 Twin Towers had its culprits, though most died in the action. But the dreadful remains at Congress Hall issued of course much DNA from people in the hall, absolutely none of an outsider.

This building had 24/7 cover with a senior security team, none of whom had just joined, and all had long service records. Scans with dogs for explosives – also for drugs – are carried out every two hours for four days in the run-up to a sensitive booking, and for this booking, the final Leaders Debate in the run up to the election, incredible care had been taken. Maybe one day someone will proudly write their memoires and reveal how it was done...

I, of course, have had my training with the likes of MI5 and MI6, I know what to expect. The only bits I can put together by elimination are that nearly every terrorist cell is made up of two, three, four or more people and they have to have a command structure, and they have to communicate. There is only one instance where communication is unnecessary: where the terrorist is working absolutely alone, no boss, no commander, no need to communicate at all. He (or she, but I've never knows a woman involved in this kind of work, although they'd be very good at it) he would have to have appropriate knowledge about the building, about the event, and a sheer determination to do what he had set out to do. He may have had the building and the project in his sights for many years. He may also have struck lucky. But it won't be simple opportunism

In England we have an inordinate number of CCTV installations. We are filmed daily, most-wherever we go. As I'm not a criminal, I don't mind particularly. But from all the footage – mileage – examined by not just police but by hordes of quickly-trained ordinary men and women, all after evidence of a face that doesn't fit. Oh, the hundreds of tourists, and people out on-the-sly, and indeed real burglars! we followed up is a credit to assiduous police action – one by one they were all tracked down and all had a story – a true story, usually – about why they were where they were seen by a camera or three. Maybe a straight story, maybe a story of quite minor crime, maybe a seamy story you wouldn't want disclosed to your family...

Yes, you ask, I had had my moments in consultation with our defence and spy and surveillance organisations, and yes, even though I had some years back given up most of this kind of work, nevertheless, when the call came, I attended a meeting between the chiefs of MI5, MI6 and GCHQ. It won't have gone unnoticed that I value my ability to see from outside the box, to think laterally, to allow the very width of my mind to be open to problems. Indeed.

But either I was getting older, or no longer needed the money so much, or maybe – after offering my notion of a likely perpetrator – I was unable to solve this case. Taking my notional identity of a committed loner working under no one and able to finance simple things, a peerless digital electronics engineer, unrecognisable on CCTV as he's expected to be there – well he could be alive and well and living with a wife and children – or would they have left home by now? – in Bexley Heath, or Leamington Spa, or Ealing. But probably not Pakistan nor the Yemen. Oh, and I guess he has white, northern European, skin.

The number of potential culprits is hereby lowered from the UK's 66 million, by adding gender, likely age range, and potential opportunity, to about 13 million. Interview all those! So – the perpetrator has never, not for an instant, surfaced for questioning.

Chapter Thirty One: 2022

Armageddon Again!

On Saturday morning, breakfast time, 25th April 2022, the weather forecast had at its end an unusual announcement: Carol Kirkwood on the BBC Breakfast programme said at the 6.20 bulletin: "In addition, we ought to tell you that we are getting signs of a small asteroid belt that may break through into our atmosphere, and is likely to land in the sea, if it doesn't all burn up on entry. We'll have to keep an eye out for this and so – do keep tuning in to your weather forecast; and back to you, Dan and Naga!" And so, very light-heartedly, the morning news and magazine programme continued down its 6-9.15 a.m. run.

At 7.20, Carol said, after the weather, that the asteroid patch had shown up better on the radar, and was likely to burst through into our atmosphere, but its area of final landing was extremely wide, and hopefully it would hit the sea... By 8.20 she was saying that it might be the South of England, and a meteorologist had come onto the programme to answer questions. He'd so recently been hauled out of bed to attend to this on live TV, that he descended to a usual pack of truisms including "the chances of anyone actually being hit by an asteroid cluster is one in a ....(he stated a quite outrageously enormous number, he'll be likely to regret quite soon).

The One O'clock News made the asteroid cluster their third news item, but had little more on location. By the Six O'clock News, it was now-number one and an emergency for the Home Counties, but no one could say where exactly; when, however, was thought to be tomorrow, Sunday, about 3pm, but could be 1pm or 5pm. By the 10pm News, most-everyone in the country was aware of the danger. This was the most direct information yet. It would land in central London about 2.45 and an immediate process of evacuation was already in hand, priority being given to the elderly and to hospital patients.

By now the AA estimated that 1.5 million cars were streaming out of London, mostly North; and that the motorways were full, the roads were slow, but indeed people had sandwiches, chocolate, bananas, hot tea or coffee in flasks, blankets – and hopefully full petrol tanks. The Mayor of London had taken upon his neat self to appear on London TV on a special new Red Button channel for the crisis. His exit will be 12 noon tomorrow from the Battersea heliport, he reassures viewers.

Strategic drivers try for the 4am start, and they do do quite well, until they catch up with the tailback still straggling North of Luton. But where is everyone going? Take me – I have only so many people I can call on in times like this, and I know hundreds and hundreds of people. Hotels will shove their prices right up and people will pay. What a lottery! Then suppose these asteroids fizzle out in the atmosphere?

The next morning it's interesting to realise that the BBC have relocated to Manchester – well, Salford, whatever, just beside Manchester. Today sounds like this is the bad idea come good for once. So their team is quite cool, considering, but a bit down, and thank goodness there's Click (the computer show) and the Travel Show to take up time. Then 9.00 and Andrew Marr comes on, still a bit like a wounded soldier, nursing his left arm following his 2012 severe stroke. He seems to have transported himself to Salford for the day – the set is disarmingly different.

The programme's newspaper reviewers aren't those publicised, but a couple of MPs from the Manchester area who've clearly never done this before. An attempt at humour over people who live in the likes of Manchester, and are not exposed to the current problem, falls very flat. Slots in the programme are taken up with scientists talking from local-to-their-home studios about earthquakes, tsunamis, asteroids and the like. Police report that central London is mostly empty, but there are still old people holed up in houses around the back of Waterloo and in those Peabody Buildings, but they're working on it, and should be clear by 12 noon. They're clearly trying to strike a line between serious information-laden broadcasting and a duty to the viewer to help people to be calm.

Well-publicised throughout the morning shows, at 10.00, radio and many TV channels are presenting simple statements from all the political leaders, straight to camera, no artifice. Acting Prime Minister Amber Rudd: "As the election is still nearly two weeks away, I'm your stand-in Prime Minister for this short period. We're all speaking to you this Sunday morning before the asteroid cluster enters our atmosphere. I have to say that I have no good news. From all the accounts I've seen, London will receive a direct hit early this afternoon. I want to wish you all a good outcome from today, and my heart goes out to you, at home, and travelling those many miles to your place of safety, or receiving guests and acting as the country's open hotel – thank you, all of you."

For Labour and the country, Emily Thornberry said: "We leaders want you all to know that we are here and working and making quite sure that everything is being done as it should be, for the best for us all. I'm afraid to say that this afternoon will bring casualties, let's hope it's really a small number. Bless you all." For the Lib Dems, Vince Cable – back from his retirement and now in great form – said: "We all have to brace ourselves today. However well the police and army reserve are briefed, we simply don't have accurate information on the landing position, and we just need to be very grown up and look after one another." Caroline Lucas said: "From the Greens, and from the green spirit within all of us – I know it's there – I wish you the best possible outcome today." For UKIP, Richard Braine spoke: "It's serious work being a politician and no more serious day than today. The broadcasters will continue to bring you the up-to-date news as it happens. I wish you all well."

And then we were alone with our vigil. Our waiting. It was over at 2.37pm.

*　　*　　*

Very Old Testament

When the asteroid cluster fell at 14.37hrs – you might say with precision – *right onto* our Houses of Parliament, it produced the most monumental spume of debris, smoke, fire and water; which rose high above London and was seen, this otherwise clear April day, friends tell me, from Haywards Heath, Henley on Thames, and Bishops Stortford; so a good 50-mile range. The mini-tsunami on the Thames, responding to the asteroid cluster falling partly into the river, destroyed Westminster, Lambeth and Vauxhall Road Bridges, and also the Charing Cross Rail Bridge, was a tidal bore-like wave, that travelled up stream as far as the first locks at Sunbury, and down river beyond the Thames Barrage, and, unhappily, took riverside loners or couple walkers completely by surprise and sucked them into its path, where most of them – 11 people – died.

Three died in the Westminster area; none was merely injured. Apart from the three who died – all were loners who resisted all attempts by the authorities to inform them, to help them move on - those aside, there was absolutely no one there, even the two night watchmen at the Houses of Parliament had been allowed to leave their posts. The police – absent from 1.30pm till 4pm from the cordon around the flattened Congress House – on their return had to stretch that cordon very much further and, if they'd been silly, would have stretched it twice across the Thames. The story of the great plume into the sky sounds so like Elijah going up to heaven, and other Old Testament happenings I learnt at my first school. Perhaps the origin of those stories was also geophysical events such as we've just experienced...

It would take, the seismologists guessed, four-seven days for all that granite in the air to settle down; perhaps a fortnight. People wore gas masks during this period. The Seat of Government was completely written off; nothing remained that could be used, nothing at all. Amber Rudd, that evening, at home, holding her fourth stiff gin in one hand, called her parliamentary colleagues on her magic phone, using the Cabinet Conference Facility; viewing each person as they joined the cyber 'room', she noticed, for a Sunday evening, that there were rather more ties and jackets than you'd expect in off duty homes.

She spoke tersely: "Well, you all know about all of it. It's simple for us, we've lost our office and debating room; but for the country, it's lost an icon, a symbol of forever. People will start to be superstitious. We are going to have to try even harder to get ourselves across, and I say to you all, that the election goes ahead even after this. I will seek an audience with HM – who I'm glad to see was safe at Sandringham – to clarify this. The King, together with the new Queen Mother, returns to Buck House on Tuesday. So – we've all had a dreadful day – any faint-hearts amongst you? I don't want a yes, but I'd prefer them all now, and get them over with...." She finished her conversation on a strong note of all pulling together behind her, and no one even thought of mentioning that bad luck comes in threes...

"Hello, Emily? Answering your own phone on *this* evening of all evenings? Well, even if we only know each other this well for these two weeks, I guess, Emily, I can work with you.... Yes? You too? Good! Now let me say: I really believe this" – under her breath – "sodding" – back to normal – "general election should go ahead on 5th April as agreed. I really do hope you're going to agree this?"

"Yes, Amber, I do. I've thought about it a lot and can't see what we gain by postponement. It's just harder this way, but that doesn't matter. How about Vince? And you're not asking the others are you?"

"I'll speak to Vince shortly. No, Caroline doesn't have strong Westminster representation, so I think the three of us will decide and then I'll see the King on Tuesday, if that can be arranged." Talking to Vince gave similar responses, so thereafter, Amber, armed with a fifth gin, settled deep into her sofa and snapped on a DVD of Brief Encounter, possibly to give excuse for any tears she might then shed?

Tuesday evening, once again it's the Speaker of the house, 10pm before the news, a special slot: "Good evening, to everyone in England and Wales; and, for information, to those listening from abroad. Once again I represent a parliamentary decision arrived at by the three senior parties, regarding how England is today and how the General Election will proceed. First of all, this is the first opportunity I or any MP has had on an official programme to record the manifest complete and total loss of the Palace of Westminster by extra terrestrial asteroid cluster at 2.37 pm on Sunday 25th March 2022, just two days ago.

"My driver this evening brought me as near as we could go to the devastating scene of desolation and rubble that was, to over 600 MPs and many, many staff, the Head Office of the United Kingdom. But – to you and to our millions of tourists, it was indeed an icon, and it has utterly gone. The Palace of Westminster, Big Ben, Parliament Square and Westminster Bridge are no more. Indeed the Millennium Wheel has also gone.

"I regret to report that with the dying eddies of granite dust in the air, emerges a really filthy city, just as if you'd had the builders in and much of their work was demolition and then were was the construction in plasterboard and plastering. Now magnify that a hundred thousand times... Many of you will know what I mean? Following my broadcast will be an early and simple statement by the Mayor of London on what action London intends to take.

"Meanwhile, in just 9 days' time, we have a general election. It is the will of His Majesty the King, and of the leaders of the three main parties, that this election goes ahead, as it is so very important to know that we have a government elected by the people as soon as possible. We hope that all of you will vote – it's a real chance to express your individual selves. As I asked barely ten days ago in this same studio, we appeal to you to remain peaceful and calm in the coming days, so we may all have the communal strength to bear this triple burden, first of pandemic virus, next of terrorism; and the third, of geophysical calamity."

*   *   *

General Election – Votes

I suppose it was something to do. Rather than mope on about having lost some really good politicians and our national historic seat of government – and lost perhaps the most flamboyant of the countries that used to make up the UK – you could *get involved* in this election. Politicians going round the houses and community centres with chats and speeches; shaking hands, not-exactly-hugging, (Coronavirus avoidance) – and most of all, Touching Flesh – that activity, which used to be shunned at all costs, everyone needs right now. And young people *are* interested! Over the last forty years, politics has been seen as a nasty, dirty, dishonourable activity, sneered at by kids and teenagers and young people alike.

So. After such losses. A potentially enormous electorate, willing to do their bit in the polling booths come the day. Politicians looked like Cheshire cats! Where did the older and wiser that went before them go wrong? But we all knew, they hadn't gone wrong, there was just a phase when politics was passé...

Thursday 5th April 2022 was moderately fine, but colder than one could have hoped. Getting the Vote Out was what we all did. Remarkably friendly between parties! Stories of drivers bringing in people who they knew were going to vote against their party were all brought in anyway, why spoil a good *party*? Numbers on the door were prodigious. Interesting point – with all this swell of new voters, which party would they favour with their vote?

Out of retirement, both Jeremy Paxman and Jonathan Dimbleby fronted the all-night show on BBC tv. No polsters had got anything right at all. It was uncharted territory. All you could do was flannel about the MPs up there, and wait for the conclusion.

By the following evening, most everything had been counted and the seats and votes were huge and near one another. Against the turnout in the 2010 elections of 65%, in 2015 this was 89%, an unbelievable and, until the recent tragedies, unexpected outcome. And of course, to get up to this figure, it has to be contributions from every age group. The so-called disaffected young voted in their millions, the middle-age – the huge hump of the UK population – voted massively as never before; and the elderly – those who find it difficult to get out, and who have recently also been seen as the disaffected – voted very solidly.

Results of the 2022 General Election

	contested	*seats won*	*and votes won*
Conservative	568 seats	291 seats	12,683,261 votes
Labour	568 seats	276 seats	11,179,997 votes
Lib Dems	137 seats	69 seats	7,237,176 votes
Plaid Cymru	16 seats	5 seats	3,276,762 votes
Green	22 seats	6 seats	3,530,034 votes
UKIP	30 seats	2 seats	2,312,502 votes
Speaker	1 seat	1 seat	
TOTALS		**650 seats**	**40,219,732 votes – 89%** of those eligible to vote
TOTAL VOTE POTENTIALLY			**44,448,912** 100% of votes votes possible, total possible

So, again, from the votes cast, there was a hung parliament, to be solved either by one party running as a minority government – thought to be inherently unstable – or two or more parties could form an alliance as the 2010-15 coalition had done recently.

King Charles III, after taking advice, called Amber Rudd to the Palace and asked her if she thought she could form a stable government; and also asked her how she intended doing this. Amber, who hadn't decided, asked for one week to work this through with colleagues, which was granted, and a fresh appointment at the palace was made.

Mrs Rudd then approached her colleague leaders, and said to each, alone: much as her predecessor had in 2010 – "How can we best form an administration that continues to run the country, the economy and our social lives, with stability, dignity and also with kindness, bearing in mind our recent disasters – can you help me?" UKIP didn't feel they could respond, preferring to be a ginger group on the edges, Greens and Lib Dems were both interested in a coalition, Labour needed time to think and suggested a dinner out, just the two leaders.

Amber and Emily sat in the exclusive club in Pall Mall and talked first over tea and tiny sandwiches. Two hours later they called for aperitifs and later still took dinner together. Their conversation seemed to be finding a natural level together, and possibly went something like this:

"So, Emily, you think that, while the country is in the current state of depression and distress at our recent losses – and that includes Scotland and Northern Ireland as well as the Leaders and the Seat of Government – we should – err, actually *I* should" – smiles swapped here – "ask the King if it would be constitutionally acceptable to run the country for a limited period as a complete Coalition of all parties, as happened during World War Two, in order for the country to rebuild its self-respect and eagerness to re-enter the competitive world market place again.

"You would feel that the Foreign Office should be yours; with dear Vince at last as the Chancellor he has always been cut out to be. Caroline Lucas may be very surprised to – already – be offered the post of Climate Change and Environment Minister, but she'll soon get used to it. Meanwhile I have to think about what I can do with my right-and left-hands who've helped me so much just very recently – architects and colleagues through the last government. They don't feel ready to graze just yet.

"Immensely interesting, Emily, thank you for promulgating this notion with me. I'll talk to appropriate people and I suggest, before I go to the Palace next, that we have a pow-wow in my new office in the New Building – have they found one for you there too? Oh, good. Wednesday after lunch, when we've both got those PMQs off our backs? By the way, I propose getting that Mayor of Birmingham on the line to discuss the huge, huge international memorial service we'll need to hold, and could they kindly do it there? And, as it is our Second City and we need a debating chamber, offices, and so on, how about us seeking premises there while the ashes settle?"

"I do agree, Amber, but it will be hell for me and commuting. I think it will say something very special. I always think" – she chuckles – "of Birmingham being England's navel. Just the place? Can I help?" "Well, yes, thanks, that would be good...." And they left the club and taxied to their London homes.

*   *   *

Next

King Charles III, accompanied by his mother (the new Queen Mother, so recently the monarch reigning from 1953 till her 95th birthday in 2021), were both empathetic, approved the Government of National Coalition. And so a Government of Complete Coalition was formed, and ministers came from every party. How they'll get on with Nigel Farage as Home Secretary, the other leaders don't yet know, but they severally think that a powerful and difficult job may lessen his cocksure ways. And, as Amber said to her now very strong friend Emily, "I can always sack him!" and that was that. The most obvious fit was Caroline Lucas as Environment and Climate Change Minister, although in the interests of the New Coalition she has had to agree to drop some of her more extreme (some say absurd) tax reform ideas.

An unimpressive building in the very centre of Birmingham has been found to become the nation's debating chamber, much to the country's apparent delight; debates about what to do with Westminster, or whether to use this 'awful' opportunity to de-centralise, is all years away in terms of decisions.

In late September, when such an enormous international event could be gathered together – to get Kings and Queens and Emperors and Presidents and Prime Ministers and Ministers and Chairmen and CEOs together with a free date takes months – was when the National Grieving Weekend was fixed – for the fallen ministers, the question-master, the people who perished in the blown-up Westminster Congress Hall and the evident yet so very tragic Fall of Westminster.

One of the PPSs organising the event told the story from Yes, Prime Minister of a funeral of a PM – perhaps Thatcher was implied – and a junior saying: "Shall I just seat them in the cathedral in alphabetical order of countries?" and the senior barking back "Never – be more subtle! Else you'll get Iran, Iraq, Ireland and Israel sitting next to one other!" But, after the problems with security in London in March, all went well and England was for three days a hospitable place once more.

London fared very badly – crime up, businesses fleeing – always seemingly dirty and littered. Its theatre-land, loved across the world, had partly closed down, many theatres were dark. However, the City of London, with all its financial services, was a bright, clean adventurous place, now down in Canary Wharf, of course. London as a financial centre remained almost as it had been. Good!

I've told you these last three chapters to inform you about history and why we're all so depressed now. You know it all of course... No, I haven't said what I've been doing at these times, but working quite hard behind the scenes to help to hold society together. There are others who do my kind of consulting now.

Chapter Thirty Two: 2024

Relative Marbles

It's interesting to observe how we disintegrate. In a relative sense, that is. It's the words and the limbs that seem to malfunction first. Our hearts and brains come next on the list, and can be much more disruptive. Cancer is another subject! So, where we can remember all the verbs we (almost) ever knew, and the exclamations and adjectives, adverbs and prepositions, it's the nouns that take the fullest knock; both proper (in the sense of names of people and countries) and common nouns, flee from our immediate memory as we travel through our 60s, 70s and 80s – and no doubt 90s and 100s as well, but I haven't yet been able to observe this – yet!

Words can be identified as having, say, three syllables and beginning with, say, an M; and this is all the more tantalising... They can be brought back to mind, given 20 minutes or 12 hours, or 10 days, and they pop back into the consciousness remarkably unannounced. However, if we cannot complete our conversations because of a lack of a crucial word, life can get very difficult!

With our limbs, we celebrate the occasions of new hips and knees as if these were passing the time of day with a neighbour. Heart attacks are more problematic, leading to uncertainty about life expectancy; and strokes can lead to a loss of communication of a radical kind.

So, how are my friends and I doing in this battle with near-endings? No one of my close-friends' generation, has yet died; extraordinarily! Well, except for my wife; but that's another story... Sloane has the greatest difficulties in that her double hip replacements seem to be troublesome, and her speech may have been impaired by a slight stroke; she keeps laughing, though, and her relationship with her close friend Marge seems to persist. A real shame for such a great organiser and administrator to be so debilitated... They still live at Muswell... but there they have had to grieve through the death of John, their chief thinker. Josh lives on on his own there.

I'm so very pleased that the love of my life these days, Francesca, is sound of limb and mind, but she's in her early-60s – a mere nothing compared to the rest of us. She radiates such happiness! She'll typically leave her "native" Wales at night and drive over to my Essex haunt, arriving needing a sleep but having overcome traffic problems. She'll stay about four or five days and then set off home at about midnight. I really love seeing her...

How about Quad? My Friends' Foursome, set up at Bedales and lasting through Edinburgh Medical School and beyond throughout life until this very day...

My faithful friend – and twice my lover – Lesley is 'full of beans' and yet is very retired now, her twin daughters living nearby to their Thring cottage, helping them out a bit. Yes, they always used to live in Thring, but then the 'marriage' split way back in 2003 when her partner, Garth, went off with a male friend; and now they've moved back in together again, and secured a bungalow/cottage in Thring – again! They said they had friends there, and indeed they have. Not so long-lasting as Quad has been, but nevertheless good mates to play bridge with and go for the slow walks that octogenarians tend to take. She's turned a very graceful-looking steel grey from her old mouse topping.

I still find I love Lesley really warmly, a seat-of-my-pants kind of love... My more recent memories of sleeping with her on my round-the-world trip, in India, are just so heartening and warm – not then the energy of sexual union we'd known for so many years at Bedales and in Edinburgh, but a fantastic new kind of care for one another that I miss now...

Anyway, how is Lesley now? Slower at 83 of course – we all are; but substantially well if one leaves out her forgetfulness of names and things. She can never remember the name of her favourite fruit, mango, nor coconut (which she doesn't care for so much) – nor somersault, which is weird, it also being a verb! and she can't recall the names of Dustin Hoffman nor Meryl

Streep, and she's always trying to tell a story about the film Kramer vs Kramer which added so much kudos to both these stars, and faltering, and giving up, stranded without her key words...

Derek Widmer is all of one piece, all 6 ft of him, but sadly his blonde locks have recently given over to a very wise looking bald pate. His wife Sonya is with him still – and they still live at Taynton, their shared estate. They have managed to get their council to allow the building of some idiosyncratic elderly persons' chalet bungalows, in which they severally live, while (usually) their children occupy their old, spacious – *draughty!* - houses.

How did they get planning permission? Well, their land is quite massive – about 50 acres – and so, by claiming that they wouldn't be seen from the road at any point, by using a brown field site, and by building these chalet bungalows in such a manner that they would be unlikely to be useful to buyers on the general market. This was achieved by various measures of shared facilities – a staircase would serve four different houses, with a couple of loos and a washroom beneath these stairs, the upper area being for one's children or friends or carers to stay. Brilliant solution to old age care and companionship – if one of them dies, there are still several community members remaining who are already friends and have been so for about 55 years. It won't shield you from grief, but it will help.

Derek is hard of hearing, mostly. He walks with a limp, but that maybe a characteristic of tall people. Sonya is numb down one side – no one knows why. And she's had new complete knees on each side, which makes her walk a little wobbly without a stick. Perhaps this will improve, perhaps not. With both of them, their words flow ok, but remember that Derek has a very circuitous way of explaining things; and this and his deafness gets on the nerves of Adolf and Quentin, their sons. Adolf now lives in the old house with his family, and Quentin runs the business, now quite a slick affair.

Wonderful, colourful Shirley Carnt, originally Shirley Shawley, keeps her red hair, although it's a bit moth eaten these days; and she shares her time between her lover Josephine, and her husband Jerd, and their four children, Harebell, Sorrell, Delilah and Xavier. So she's kept pretty busy in her eighties. None of her kids has thought to take her in or live near to her, as has happened to Lesley. Josephine is a mite younger – about 77 I think – and so she has someone to care for her a little. Jerd remains useless! She still dresses in violently clashing clothes, always composing a rich and unjustified harmony... Boots and colourful stockings often accompany richly rural coarse skirts and tunic-like tops, with long scarves an essential.

And how is Shirley, how have the years and those mid-life stresses left her now? At a guess I'd say she's the best of all of us four Quad. She is sound in mind and limb, has still a speedy delivery of excitable speech, can still walk us all – except Derek – off the map. She's a bit farty, but probably the rest of us are too, but hold back in company. She says she has aches from sciatica in her thighs, but she doesn't go on about it. Above all, she's just great fun to be with, and never loses her wit and charm...

Before myself, I must include my sister, Camille. Her husband, Maurice, died three years back now, in 2021; and she has recently bought an old rectory in the UK, in Suffolk, with an eye to building a zero-costs-for-heating German house, and letting the rectory as workshops for local craftsmen, and as a small community centre. At 82, this is indeed a grand gesture, and I do admire it, especially as she will be running a small old age care centre in the rectory itself; allowing perhaps for her long-term old age; and allowing for mine too, methinks. Her three daughters, Hermione, Rosanna and Clarissa, are now 43, 41 and 39; two live in the UK and one in Canada. Rosanna is the one Camille is closest to and she lives in Bury St Edmunds, close by the Rectory.

How is Camille, health-wise? She's still exceedingly beautiful, with iron-grey hair, and has a figure most women would die for, and looks about 65 instead of her real 82. She doesn't seem to have the slowing-up kinds of debilities most of us are prey to. Her spoken words, still in her silvery voice, with just a touch of Canadian after so very many years of living there, are a refreshing and relaxing joy to listen to – and that's not just me with this notion. She is a bit private about her health, since she had a bowel cancer scare and a light operation to remove a small part of her gut two years back. She is still capable, even with rather arthritic-y hands, of the most beautiful handwriting.

As for myself, in my recluse near to Aldeburgh, I'm slower of wit and of limb these days; but – so others say – not that an outsider could tell! I potter towards my nineties with a certain style, can I suggest? No longer travelling, no longer on retainerships to government departments, the arts council and so forth, I've been put out to grass to slowly end my days here. Thank goodness I've – for my age – so many friends to keep me company and youthful…

*   *   *

01.07.24 – my 84th Birthday

I now live near Aldeburgh on the Essex coast. I live in a wee place called Bothy Cottage, quite near the sea. It's lovely of a morning to hear the dawn chorus, chattering away…

All these brave people are coming to share my birthday today, this very afternoon. First will be my current lover, Francesca, who's coming soon after lunch. The rest will be here at about 5pm. Wild sleepovers are anticipated, just like university life…

Francesca prefers to come at night, but this time we've persuaded her to travel during the day; she'll stay on for a few days. A purr and her ancient Saab is with me, and we hug, very affectionately.

"Elliott, my darling, hi, my love, how are you? Filthy A13 and M25 – I could so easily have done a night trip – could have stayed with your sister if you didn't want me here till now? The mists – even in July – are really something here, aren't they?"

We go for a walk along the jetty by the sea. Not a long walk, but enough for us to get a blow of fresh air and some simple exercise. "Funny, this afternoon air, it's so misty and yet… and yet… one can see the sun through it… Mysterious… Calls for my watercolour palate – no one will ever believe it! Too weird a sky to paint…"

"Weird indeed!" I say, lost in thought. "Will the mist be a hazard to friends arriving soon?"

"No, I don't think so. I buzzed along with just the faintest of mists around me. Think they'll be OK. Now, where's this washed-up old boat you want me to sketch?"

"I didn't so much want you to sketch it as I thought you'd like the subject and be drawn to it! Just over here, down on the beach."

"Mmmm – I like it! I'll save it for the days ahead I spend with you. Now, shall we be getting back to your Bothy Cottage to prepare foods and drinks for everyone?"

"Yes, I suppose so. Thought I'd done it, really. But a lady's touch is always such a help."

Back at the Bothy, I notice a big Ford with "CONVERSION" written on its rear. And I know that Sloane has turned up an hour early! She's asleep in the driving seat… We go in quietly to arrange a kind of supper meal for seven, my closest friends on earth.

Camille is next to arrive, in a Range Rover Discovery. Hugs and kisses all round and Sloane's now woken up and joins in. At twenty past five, with a roar, come the remainder of Quad. Driven by Derek, with passengers Lesley and Shirley, the oldish Volvo arrives with a clatter and ribald good cheer. We all come outside to have a great communal greeting.

∗   ∗   ∗

Our Supper Together

Now I sit with Francesca on one side and Lesley on the other; my sister Camille opposite me. Supper is a composite event. Lesley has prepared a delicious salad of smoked salmon and samphire – the stuff of the Essex Coast she knows I love. Francesca and I have prepared a carbonnade de boeuf, accompanied by a rich beetroot, cabbage and onion side dish and a wonderful, zesty potato mash with mustard and cheese by Sloane. Camille has prepared the most toothsome – and extravagant in terms of booze – Tiramisu; with an alternative of Mangoes in their own juice enriched by port.

And Derek has taken on the entire supply of wines for this repast – a delicate Lacryma Christi del Vesuvio, an Italian white, for the salmon dish, a full-blooded Hungarian Bulls Blood for the Carbonnade, and a sweet Frascati for the pud – served with verve by my tall, now so bald, friend.

"'Tears of Christ' this time, I fear to say" says Derek, as he pours the Lacryma Christi into fresh glasses.

"It's not the Last Supper! – is it Derek?" Camille asks.

"No. J. Christ never let a tear drop in the Last Supper" Derek, using remarkable conciseness, knowing his ways of talking round things

"Anyway, who's for puds?" says Camille

"I think I'll just have the Mopeds, dear Camille, thanks" Lesley tries to order her pud.

"So sorry – what was that?" says Camille, serving out the dessert.

"The Mopeds..? Oh no, horrible mistake, so sorry, no, it's the Dogmas. I'll just have the Dogmas, please, Camille." Lesley is distraught.

I burst in: "My love it's the _Mangoes_ you're wanting, not Mopeds nor Dogmas – nor Dingbats nor Sambos nor Dumplings nor Dustins!

Laughter with Lesley and her difficulty of remembering Mangoes is kind but heightens our sense of weirdness and the impossibility of coping with word loss. It's sad but we're all together and we sing together too.

*   *   *

Happy Birthday to you, Elliott

"Happy Birthday to you, happy birthday to you, happy birthday, dear Elliott, happy birthday to you." All of them singing to me. To me. To me. Hard to take, really. But this is no time for remorse – they are all so excited and happy. My cake – made by the lively Shirley – as you'd expect from such an inventive soul, is a fruit cake with just so much fruit and nuts and spices and booze aboard, that it's both really heavy and also as light as a feather as it goes down.

Afterwards I'm allowed a cigar; the fragrance of this beautiful baccy wafting around the low-ceilinged room amidst the partakers of port or cognac or drambuie... I catch several people enjoying the baccy fragrance... What a thing to lose from the world...

Bedrooms are a spot of bother, but only a spot. It's when I see that Sloane would really be much better off asleep in her own converted car, much suited to this practice, that things work out. With Lesley and Shirley asleep in the Spare Bedroom, and Camille at home in her eerie at the top of the house – the Bungahigh bit of the Bothy – that Derek can bed down in the sitting room (with a window open to reduce the tobacco fragrance!) and Francesca and I can make our way slowly to bed where we normally sleep...

*   *   *

The Next Day

It's 10.30 or so in the morning when I stagger down, to find Derek and Camille – strange to see them together – wielding frying pans and coffee pots in an aim to get us all bacon butties and rich dark coffee to get everyone going.

Which we duly do, in one way or another: Sloane's feeling her arthritis after the shenanigans of last night, and walks today with two sticks. Derek has a real smile on his otherwise lantern-jawed countenance. Camille is keeping herself to herself until we find ourselves alone together on the outside steps. Then it's:

"Elliott, my old darling, what about this half-sibling bit? I'm having some people over from Canada to repay some of the hospitality they showed us and our family. Do you want to be involved or no?"

"Yes, sure, and if I can help with the hospitality, please let me know. I'm happy to still regard Peggy as my quasi-mother. If Monica had died before mother I'd have not one clue as to my real parentage."

Lesley joins us: "You two still getting on so well after – was it? – Monica's outburst? You have strong souls, you really do!"

Camille says: "We were just talking this over. Facts are facts, and I wouldn't want to consider a life without my half-brother. He's terrific!"

"He certainly is" says Lesley "I wouldn't have spent so much of my life as his partner had he not been very special."

Francesca joins us: "YOU had his prime years, Lesley. No regrets, but I can see the charisma stretching right back over the decades."

It's as if I wasn't there! All this praise for an 84-year-old, going a wee bit downhill these days. However, there's a move on to move out, to go home. I suggest a walk along the still-misty seafront and then a brisk 1pm lunch at the pub and then to go.

Which we do, although Sloane decides to drive away before this, so we say our farewells "Till we meet again" –

"Till we meet again" and off she drives...

* * *

Francesca and I alone together

Walk and lunch over, we hang on just a few seconds before it's Off Time for the rest of them – save Francesca, who's staying on for a few days with me. It's a real trill of thanks, of love you, of keep well, of blessings, of so many good things I cannot in my head accept that all these are my – mostly – lifelong friends, that I take to bed with me each night and hold them close.

Francesca and I wave them off. She turns to me and there are tears in her eyes, and smiles on her face. "I'm just _so_ enchanted by them all, I feel I've known them a lifetime but it's been scarcely two years since Barcelona... And she hugs me then, warm and close.

Chapter Thirty Three: 2025

By Any Other Name – July 1 2025
(Originally named: 1.7.25 My 85th Birthday)

Birthday again, 85, so what? The past four years have not really allowed me to forget finding my ex-wife hung up by the yard arm on that Burgh Island hotel's so-called quarter-deck, for us all to see after that oh-so-memorable evening and dinner and – for the younger ones – dance. By the time Magnus and Dot and I had settled our final account with that hotel, we felt as though we had brought this bad luck upon the place *intentionally!* How good service can turn sour on you. So, when we drove away from that Devon car park, we made a point of stopping an hour later, at a not-posh, not-important pub with OK food somewhere along the way – I don't suppose I could remember exactly where. Lillibet and Wolfgang joined us there a touch later. The purpose was simple: to begin a long and difficult process within ourselves to both accept Charlotte as the mother of Magnus and Lillibet and my sometime wife, and also to try to live with her death and not turn Charlotte's memory into a sort-of living horror. Nothing at that time seemed freed by her death – had the death been more natural and normal, well, perhaps... We each (well Magnus, Lillibet and me, anyway; Dot and Wolfgang were trying to understand, but it was foreign territory) wanted this moment to be a start towards a – well probably – a *spiritual* healing of Charlotte's memory. So we stayed some hours together and quietly promised what they call in parliament 'cross-party support' for each of us, lots of phone calls, skypes (so popular now), e-mails and visits. It was the best we could do.

And the next week, with Robert and Minx and Dirk – and of course their twins, Georgia & Joanna – our bridesmaids at Charlotte and my wedding – these girls – women – are now 53! – to arrange Charlotte's simple funeral. And so we did, all four years ago now, and the whole matter is as satisfactory as it fucking well can be; which is that it is NOT ok at all; it's grim.

Dear Francesca comes to see me often, but she really knows there's been a deep change in me and at 85 I doubt it will much improve. And my lifelong friends – Quad – spend their ageing days caring for me, now. No one was ever counting the cost, but if there's a God above doing the sums, I might be the one found to have done more for my friends up until recent times. But no longer...

I have a Russian man-and-maid servant who live in with me now. It's helpful, with all those little bits of life where my forgetfulness is foremost, where my bladder lets me down, where my mental arithmetic leaves me a bit wanting, where my shopping list would make for a fridge full of smoked salmon and no potatoes and veg, where my diary would leave me apparently stupid!

I'm not feeling too well today – don't know what it is exactly – a feeling of faintness and not being quite with it, a queasiness in my stomach. Olga and Alex are out today, damn it. I'm looking forward to a little celebration this evening with all four of us Quad and with Francesca – and possibly Sloane who just might shuffle over... I'd like to be feeling better for them all.

Oh, I make a fair show of it. Either Lillibet or Magnus come to spend a day with me and we go out drawing together. Lovely! Well – OK anyway... And I do this with Francesca too, and she's *very* good, very proficient, very loving... And with Camille, now my neighbour... Oh, Sloane pops in – no, she doesn't pop these days, but she shuffles determinedly. We have a good natter, but she can see the zest has gone away.. Perhaps I need a dog. Why? I dunno, just occurs to me. Wind me up someone will you? We do try to think about Charlotte positively. I do love my son and my daught......

At this point, working on his laptop, Elliott Self died, seemingly peacefully. His heart was in order, he didn't have a stroke, he was generally in good health. But, at the post mortem, they discovered he had been poisoned by a scarcely-detectable substance: a nerve agent, probably. Whether or not this was administered by Olga and Alex is unknown, but these two did not return that evening as expected; and eventually Interpol discovered that they had made their way across the channel at Dover, there to become lost in the miasma of railway lines and roads that all come to a head in Calais.

Elliott Self was thought to have been in fairly bouncy good health, and people hadn't realised how these last five years had taken their toll on him. 1,500 people came to his funeral, which at his request, was held in a large community centre before cremation.

Magnus Self, son

Elliott Self's life-partner since 2023, wrote this:

Since my first meeting with Elliott just two short years ago in Barcelona, we were inseparable friends, although I live in Wales and he in Essex. He was just so fine a man, such a joy to be with, and indeed his friends, signing below, are all such treasures to know; I hope we will keep up our friendships, I really do! But for Elliott himself, I cry myself to sleep over his memory, his kindness, his humour, his companionship. Long may his soul rest in peace...

Francesca Morley

Elliott's sister left these words

Maybe Elliott lived a little on the edge... However, for a distinguished man of Elliott's stature to be hastened to a sudden death by a foreign power is utterly contemptible. He was worth so very much more than this sad epitaph. A truly wonderful brother, a man (along with all his friends here) I truly loved.

Camille Self (Salter)

Lesley Grant, of Quad, left a note for people to read:

Of all the things that Elliott did in his wonderful life, three of us – the undersigned – feel that his greatest human work was in friendship. In 1956 he proposed to the three of us that we should form a friendship to last throughout our lives, to enjoy and love one another, and to help where we could. He always did this, always, always — and I shall — with Derek and Shirley — all of us will miss him immensely

Lesley Grant – Derek Widmer – Shirley Carnt.

....and Sloane left a note also:

I feel latterly that I've got to be an honorary member of Quad; and indeed Lesley did ask if I'd like to be enfolded in their remarks... But I felt a little like an intruder! My role in Elliott's life was so very professional as he and I ran the Elliott Consultancy — together. I shall miss my friend very deeply.

Sloane

...and his doctor wrote:

I would so like to have written: cause of death: old age; but, unfortunately, the hand of spies was involved in Elliott's death, which rather lets down his terrific life as a citizen.

Dr Alan Robinson, family doctor.

Epilogue
2025

by Magnus Self, son of Elliott Self: 1940-2025

My father's later years still were hale and hearty and full of the joys of living; he was also remarkably without those debilitating problems besetting older people — not much arthritis, heart good, brain good, no stroke. He had lived a life — yes, everyone knows this — of outrageous bluff in his consultancy work, advising governments on so many aspects, national security issues, the law, finance — and also the arts and cultural life in England. He was above all a great England nationalist, such as we really need at these times, especially since the triple disasters of 2020-23: virus; terrorism; and asteroids.

But above all, I believe his strength came from his friends and his friendships, and this gave him the power to continue. It's unfortunately a public matter, so I can refer to my mother's death four years ago. It is since that moment that I believe Elliott started to lose his grip on the good things of life.

In 2021 he celebrated his four score years (plus one, owing to Coronavirus putting paid to big parties in 2020...) with a party. Friends and colleagues representing a long and interesting and mostly successful life came and enjoyed again the man of wisdom, wit and action. We all thought he would live forever. A century? He would-walk it! He and a new companion of recent years, Francesca, would travel and enjoy the world. He had so much ahead of him. No thoughts of taking out Power of Attorney — indeed why should he? His death was in fact a killing, an infamous way to end a brilliant life.

Euphemistically, perhaps he died of compulsive over-doing of everything, trying to solve World Peace, Climate Change, the Population Explosion. He died on his birthday, on his own, at 4pm, unexpectedly, without apparent symptoms, except a nerve agent poison. His heart was OK, he didn't have a stroke.

He died from attack by a nerve agent. His death remains An Enigma. File: UNRESOLVED; In sorrow...

Magnus Self

THE END

Biography of Breo Gorst

Breo Gorst was born on 7th June 1942.
The Polymath is his first novel. He has written
three plays, published privately. Also he's penned
many tracts of English for Reports, Estimates
and Specifications for his business –
which was in Design and Shop Fitting; and
included Interior, Furniture Design and Inventions.

He has been involved with Counselling;
and Telephone Advice Work with the Samaritans.
He has acted in plays and stage managed productions.
He's made films for fun and for profit. He was
Chairman of the SBFVM – Surrey Borders
Film and Video Makers 2003-06;
and of Braziers Park School of
Sensory Research 2006-09.

He lives in a community of co-housing
in Hampshire with his wife; they
have two grown-up children
and three grandchildren.

Breo Gorst

Breogorst.com
BreoGorst@gmail.com
07815 885861

Thedden Grange,
Beech, Alton, Hants,
UK, GU34 4AU

20-84
the Novel

Printed in Great Britain
by Amazon